SNOW WARRIOR WHITE

A Glass Slipper Adventure Book 5

Allie Burton

Allie Burton

Snow Warrior White

A Glass Slipper Adventure

CONTENTS

INTRODUCTION

Join my newsletter and receive a free book!
Details at: www.allieburton.com

Stay in touch with Allie:

allie@allieburton.com

www.twitter.com/@allie_burton

www.facebook.com/AllieBurtonAuthor

www.instagram.com/allieburtonauthor

"I'm sure I'll get along somehow. Everything's going to be alright."
- Snow White

CHAPTER ONE

I'd been kidnapped.

Everything inside me stilled, realizing the truth. Heated breaths rushed in and out of my lungs like an overplayed accordion. My stomach churned and my mushy brain couldn't figure out how I'd been taken captive.

I'd had an argument with Stone about fighting in Prince Zacharye's battle against the regent's evil forces. I'd huffed to a distant stall in the royal stables to get some sleep before continuing the argument. A hooded majik had approached and given me an apple. I'd taken a large, angry bite.

Not any majik. A banshee.

My rushed wheezing stopped and air leaked from between frozen lips.

Everything had gone black.

It no longer smelled of the stale straw in the stables. The steady hum of an engine hurt my head. The ground beneath me moved—or I was moving. Whatever I traveled in provided a smooth ride. I forced my eyes open a slit.

Currently, I laid on the ground of a transport similar to the ones I'd traveled in with the royal guards when I'd been forced to track for the sinister regent. Fast and sleek. A pilot wearing a dark uniform flew the transport and hooded majiks lounged in the comfortable seats. Their hoods were off so they weren't afraid of disclosing what they were to me or the human pilot.

Banshees.

A half-excited, half-fearful shudder rocked my body. Grandfather had mentioned a secret banshee clan on my very first transport ride to Reximus Palace. I'd always believed we were the last two banshees in the kingdom. My chest contracted. After being captured, Grandfather and I had been separated. I didn't know where he'd gone or if he was alive.

Pushing the worried thought aside, I jiggled my arms. I tried to pull them apart and couldn't. Not because I was paralyzed, but because I was restrained. I fisted my hands and dug my nails into my palms. What was going on?

A male loomed above me. The distinct banshee mark on his forehead confirmed the truth. Hope and apprehension stumbled over each other. There really were more banshees. Why was I tied up and he wasn't?

Something about this guy seemed familiar. "You're awake, Destiny."

I tried to hide my sharp intake. He knew my name. "Where am I? Where's Stone?"

My heart thumped. Stone would believe I'd run off on my own like the night of the ball. That night he'd wanted to whisk me out of the palace to safety and I'd wanted to help my friends. Instead of waiting patiently for him, I'd snuck back into the dungeon to help majiks escape. So this time he'd believe I'd left on my own out of anger. Stone didn't believe I could fight.

"I'm Charmig and my father is the Grand Lord Justicar of the Skjult Banshee Clan." The way the banshee spoke suggested I should be impressed.

I wasn't. Grandfather had only mentioned the secret banshee group the one time when we'd both been in jeopardy. Otherwise, he'd kept us hidden and claimed we were the last banshees. The regent believed that too when he'd sent the guards for us.

Acid swirled in my gut. "Where am I? Where are we going? Why did you kidnap me?"

And the most important question: What did they want with me?

Charmig smiled, expecting everyone to fall for his white-toothed grin. His dark eyes appeared bottomless. His long, black bangs covered part of the banshee mark on his broad forehead, while the longer strands in the back of his head were tied in an elaborate leather strip with beading and colorful feathers. "I didn't kidnap you. I'm bringing you to your kind."

Struggling, I held up my shackled wrists. "Why the handcuffs and anti-magic bracelets then?"

"A precaution." He winked, bringing out a dimple in his cheek.

He was handsome and flirtatious but since I was taken against my will and handcuffed, I wasn't buying any of his charm.

My body tensed and I tried to shift my legs again, twist my body, raise my head. I couldn't move which meant I couldn't escape. Of course, I couldn't jump from the transport and fly anyway. Plus, heights weren't my thing. Controlling my fear and frustration, I decided to ask as many questions as this guy would answer. "How long was I asleep?"

I noted the transport vehicle's windows had a blackened tint and I couldn't see out, which was okay since the thought of peering down made my stomach queasy. Blue sky shown through the windshield.

"The rest of last night and late into the morning." His indulgent smirk made me squirm. He thought I regularly slept away my days.

Stone would notice me missing. We might've fought, but he'd try to find me even if just to confirm I'd been sent away before the final battle. After what I'd been through in the past few weeks, I didn't understand why he didn't trust me to fight. I'd been kidnapped by the regent, forced to live in a squalid cell in a dungeon—where I'd met my friends—stayed in the human palace to learn my banshee powers, and then I'd returned to the dungeon to lead the rescue of the imprisoned majiks.

My lungs shredded. We'd been mostly successful.

I noted the six banshees relaxing in the transport vehicle. If they were human, I could've taken them. Of course, there was the matter of the handcuffs and something binding my legs. Since I didn't know or completely understand banshee powers, I didn't know what to expect from them. Straining to lift my head, I wanted to get a better view of the pilot.

Charmig shifted and blocked my view. "The grand tradition of the Skjult Banshee Clan is to bond and teach banshees, keeping them safe and whole."

Sounded noble, unless by bond he meant handcuffed. What had Grandfather been afraid of? Learning about my magic and how to use it would be an advantage. The piecemeal teaching I'd received from Professor Nilsen and Stone curled in my veins. To know my banshee history and be able to use my powers would be great.

Except I had something more important to do first.

"I need to get back to fight with the majiks against Regent Theobald." Even if Stone didn't want me there, I wanted to be alongside my friends. To prove to other majiks that a banshee wasn't about death, that I could be part of a team and be loyal to my friends.

As long as I could shake off this lethargy. More panic rose. Why was I lethargic? How did they get me out of the palace stables with so many others nearby? What did Stone think of my disappearance? Each question whirled in my head causing more panic.

Charmig turned his nose up. "Leave the fighting to the warriors, not the ruling elders."

"I am a warrior." I firmed my lips. I'd helped rescue my friends. I'd fought against the guards. I wanted to fight again for the right cause, for justice.

At first, I didn't want to fight. I'd refused to take the majik side against humans. Majiks despised banshees so why should I get involved? That was Grandfather's belief. But I'd learned and changed and showed others my worth. I'd convinced my friends to stay and fight for the prince and I wanted to fight too. Twisting in my handcuffs, I struggled to get free. I couldn't let Charmig keep me contained.

"If you struggle, the restraints on your wrists and ankles will get tighter and bruise your lovely skin." He slid a finger down my cheek.

Controlling my grossed-out quiver, I didn't want his flirtations. I only wanted Stone. Desperation sizzled in my blood. I needed to get back to him. Twisting again, I tried to get loose. The bindings tightened, cutting into my skin. Charmig was right. I couldn't fight now, and I hadn't been able to fight when they'd taken me.

He raised his hand to my neck. A needle flicked between his fingers and before I could stop him, the injection pierced my skin.

I licked my lips and tried to shape the words with my mouth. "What're you doing to me..."

My body floated.

Someone strong carried me.

Stone? My hazy mind hoped he'd found me. I'd dreamed about him searching a forest.

I flickered my eyes open, and disappointment swamped me. It wasn't Stone who carried me in his arms. Two bulky strangers from the group of banshees lifted me. Their shadowed faces had a similar structure to Charmig, and even my grandfather.

Broad shouldered and strong, the two men carried me with ease. They didn't wear the dark cloaks with hoods any longer. They wore bright red fabric wrapped around their waists with sewn patterns. Draped across their bare chests was another bright fabric. Each of the males had their hair tied back in long dark braids with plain leather strips.

"Where are you taking me?" Wiggling, I tried to get them to drop me. I was still bound and hated this helplessness. "How long did I sleep *this* time?"

Neither answered or even grunted.

Lifting my head, I tried to figure out where we were. The transport lifted into the blue sky, leaving us behind and flying past the mountains surrounding us. The chillier temperature shivered against my bare skin. I must be in the mountains of the small Kingdom of Alandaska.

"Roarrrrrkch. Roarrrrrkch." A deep rumbling noise reached my ears.

I lifted my head again and found a small herd of gray animals blending with the cliffs surrounding us. Resembling elephants but with long spiky tails and sharp teeth, the animals had intricate saddles and a couple of the other banshees rode on their backs. The animals wore some type of shoe with a hard sole, making it difficult to walk.

One of the animals had a decorated canvas tent strapped to its back. The flat bottom was strapped to poles and the animal's spiky tail curled through the ring at the tent's peak, holding the contraption in place.

The males carrying me stopped in front of this animal.

Charmig sat inside the tent on a pile of warm blankets. His clothes were similar to the two banshees carrying me except his wrap and shawl were orange. He grabbed my arms. "Be careful with our precious package."

"I'm not precious or a package." I firmed my lips not able to protest in any other way.

I struggled as the men lifted me into the tent on top of the animal. They set me down on the blankets next to Charmig.

My body flopped and tensed at the intimacy of the tent. I had to get away. I couldn't fight tied up and didn't know where we were. But I'd escaped from tight places before. I could do it again.

He supported my back and helped me into a sitting position. "Comfortable?"

"No," I spat and went to cross my arms. My wrists clashed. I clenched my fists and kicked, anything to make this more difficult for the banshee. "What is this animal?"

"An eleram." Smiling, he lifted a dark blanket. "Cold?"

"No." I shook my head even though the air chilled and I held back a shiver. I didn't want to answer in the affirmative. I'd freeze to death before being nice or helpful.

Freeze to death like Violet. Except she wasn't dead. Not yet.

My chest clutched. My friend Violet had been the one casualty in the great escape from the dungeon. She'd sacrificed herself, flying toward the guards to access her magic, and frozen all of them. Including herself. She'd taken several bullets, but her frozen body hibernated, stalling the bleeding. I hoped she wasn't dead.

Dying wouldn't help my situation.

He set a blanket near my feet. "You will be. I wouldn't want you getting sick."

"Why do you even care?" No matter what he said or what his reasons, he and his buddies had taken me against my will. I'd never forgive them.

One of the banshees handed Charmig a steaming bowl and towel.

Now that I was awake and feeling more myself, I continued to argue. "I need to go back and fight alongside my friends. I committed to helping Prince Zacharye and Princess Ellery."

I added on the majik princess name to prove I believed in the young prince and the fairy princess. It might take days, but together they'd defeat the evil regent. Surely, a banshee could understand the importance of the upcoming battle. The prince and princess were a couple and would provide equal rights for all.

"It's your duty to learn the banshee ways." Charmig dipped the rag into the water and reached toward my face.

I ducked away. "I've been learning."

And right now, I needed to learn as much as possible so I could escape. Glancing around, I estimated a half dozen male banshees in our group.

"From a human." It sounded like a scoff, but something was off. Whatever he felt about humans, he tried to hide.

How did he know about my lessons at the palace?

He grabbed my chin in a rigid hold and gently wiped my face with the wet cloth. The different touches threw my mind in a tizzy. Was he nice or rough? Did he care about me or was he obeying orders? Could I convince him to let me go?

The last thought had me smiling in my own attempt at flirting. "Why are you doing this?"

"Your grandfather didn't teach you about your past or your powers." Charmig held contempt for the man who raised me.

My eyes pricked. My grandfather was missing and might be dead.

Charmig wiped the other side of my face. "Your grandfather didn't keep his promise to bring you back to us."

My mind flashed back to a dream that was a memory. Right after my parents died, Grandfather had brought me to a group of banshees where I was tied above a boiling pot and my memories and magic had been locked away. He'd promised them that he'd bring me back to have the lock on both removed. In the years since, my grandfather had never mentioned the incident and refused to talk about the past.

Since my memories were suppressed, I hadn't remembered until recently. Glimmers of my past came to me in dreams.

Was Charmig part of the same banshee group? He looked to be a couple of years older than me. If he'd been present at the strange ceremony, he'd been a child.

He took hold of my hands and washed them with the same cloth. His strong and calloused hands proved he'd done physical labor in his life, and yet on this trip he appeared to be spoiled. The others seemed to be serving him. "Hungry?"

The single word exploded in my head. Now I remembered him. He was the leader of the kidnapping crew. Hungry had been the first word he'd spoken when he'd given me the poisoned apple. Frowning, I bunched my eyebrows and glared.

His constantly suave smile stumbled. "I mean, you've missed several meals while you slept."

Panic shot through me. "Several?"

How long had it been since I was kidnapped? When I'd first awoken it had been at least a day. My heart fluttered wildly, imprisoned by my ribs, just like I was imprisoned. What did Stone think had happened to me?

And what about my friends? Were they still fighting? Was it over? Were they, I swallowed, dead? I didn't even know the outcome.

I peeked outside the tent. The sun set behind one of the gray cliffs. It was night and I'd skipped at least an entire day. The battle against the regent had probably ended and I'd missed it. I didn't know who'd won, who'd been injured, or who'd died.

My stomach grumbled. If I wanted to stay strong enough to escape, I needed to eat and stay warm. "I'm hungry. Is dinner poisoned, too?"

He laughed. A light, tinkling melody. As if his life had been full of fun.

Maybe the banshee group wouldn't be so bad. But as soon as I could, I'd get away.

Charmig signaled and the same banshee brought a tray. "He is a banshee warrior."

The male had some sort of tattoo on his inner wrist. Charmig had one too.

If I couldn't escape, I'd learn all I could about this group until I did. Trying to play nice, I forced a stiff smile. "Are you also a banshee warrior?"

Charmig certainly had the body for it. Broad shoulders, carved abs visible above the material wrapped around his waist. He dressed similar to the other banshees, except his clothes were more refined. More patterns and beading and a different color. The leather band holding his ponytail had more beads and feathers. A long scar trailed from his neck to his chest.

"I'm an Elder."

I held back a chuckle. "You're not much older than me."

"True." His gaze narrowed and roved over my face and my body.

Creepiness crawled across my skin. The stretchy pants and top had been for my yoga sessions with Stone. I'd put them under the nice dress so after I snuck out of the palace I'd be wearing something comfortable. Comfortable and revealing the way the dark fabric clung to my body. I should've accepted the blanket.

"Here." He held a spoon full of what appeared to be oats mixed with a paste.

I closed my lips. "What is it?"

"High protein pudding." He held the spoon closer to my mouth. "It's healthy."

I arched a brow and sniffed. It didn't have a smell. I opened my mouth and he fed me a spoonful of the pudding. The oatmeal texture sat on my tongue while I waited a moment to see if it went numb or I got sleepy or some other foul effect. When it didn't, I took another spoonful and another.

"How does someone so young become an Elder?" I questioned between chewing. He'd mentioned his father was the leader of the clan. "Is it because of who your father is?"

His cheeks reddened and heat flashed in his eyes. "I fought for the position. Fought my way to the top."

My questioning must've scraped a raw nerve.

I lifted my cuffed hands and pretended to caress the scar at his neck. Stone had a similar scar. I knew how he'd gotten his. "Is that how you got this scar?"

"No." The monosyllabic answer meant Charmig wasn't going to say more.

He shoveled another spoonful into my mouth, and another. He wasn't so chatty anymore. My shoulders slumped. Getting information would not be easy.

"If you uncuff me, I could eat by myself." And have a chance to escape.

"I enjoy feeding you." His lips lifted slowly in a charming, flirtatious grin.

I could tell the smile wasn't real because his dark eyes were flat. Either way, his efforts at flirtation didn't affect me. His words did though. He'd said something about my grandfather promising to bring me back to the clan. Grandfather had blamed grief for my suppressed memories and magic. It was not until my stay at Reximus Palace that I learned and started remembering.

Since I hadn't known where Grandfather was or how to find him after we'd been separated at the palace, I'd stayed focused on rescuing my friends and fighting for the majik cause. The fight might be over and while I needed to find out the result, I also needed to find Grandfather. I didn't have a clue where to search and had been told he was no longer being kept at the palace. I refused to give up on him as he'd given up on me.

"My grandfather was taken by the palace guards. Like me." If the banshees felt any loyalty, maybe they'd help. "Will your banshee clan help me find him?"

"*Your* banshee clan." Charmig angled his head in expectation. He wanted me to acknowledge the clan was mine as well.

Silence ticked past. Until I agreed I'd get no more information.

"*My* banshee clan." But I knew I'd never stay. "Are there other clans?"

Now that I'd experienced the kingdom and other majiks, I couldn't stick to one group. My friends were different kinds of majiks. Stone wouldn't fit in here.

"No. And we won't help you find your grandfather."

Disappointment and sadness wove through me and squeezed in my midsection. "If banshees stick together, why wouldn't you help find one of your own?"

Charmig's smug expression annoyed. "Because we've already found him."

Chapter Two

Anticipation tingled on my skin, and I leaned forward hoping to catch a glimpse of my grandfather as we rode into camp. Charmig had removed the restraints around my wrists and ankles when he realized I wouldn't run away because I wanted to see Grandfather. He hadn't removed the anti-magic bracelets. We'd traveled through the night, and I'd asked question after question.

"When did Grandfather get here? How did he arrive? How did he escape his imprisonment at the palace?"

Charmig shook his head every time and responded in the same way. "All will be answered in time."

Annoyance dulled my anticipation. I wanted answers now. "What did my grandfather tell you? I'm worried about him. You have to understand." I shifted again, trying to put space between us.

The poles forming the tent shape didn't help the canvas hold form and throughout the ride I'd jostled against him. He seemed to enjoy it. Putting his arm around me or patting my leg. I'd tried to keep my distance.

"Roarrrrrkch. Roarrrrrkch." The animals had been quiet most of the journey, now they announced themselves like trumpets.

Steam spurted from in between dark rocks covering the ground. The smell of rotten eggs tickled my nose. The ground was made up of shiny black rocks that glistened in the light. I'd never seen anything so dramatic.

The animals circled around while their riders jumped off and patted them down, careful to avoid their jagged teeth. The beasts had worked hard climbing up steep pathways leading to the camp and were probably too tired to bite. Plus, some type of halter had been fitted in their mouths and around the long trunks.

Banshee warriors, male and dressed in similar colors to the riders, marched across boarded platforms to help with the animals and the loaded bags they carried. I could only guess their contents.

The rising steam blocked my view of the entire camp. I saw patches of tents dotting the area. Many appeared quite small. A few were as big as the fine houses I'd seen in the city of Linden-hamn. Banners flew from the tops of those tents.

"Where's my grandfather?" I was ready to hop out and go straight to him. We'd say our thanks and make plans to leave right away. I needed to find Stone, and I'm sure Grandfather would want to go home.

"Wait." Charmig's command rubbed the wrong way. He pulled wooden sandals from a bag. The sandals had hard platforms with leather straps and decorative beading. "These should fit you."

I didn't want a gift from him. "No, thanks."

He chuckled and his lips twitched in a way that said I amused him. "They're special coverings to protect your feet."

My brows gathered. "Why do my feet need protection?"

"The rocky ground is as sharp as glass." He held out his hand. "Give me your foot."

I held out one foot and then the other as he tied the shoes on. I felt like Cinderella trying on the glass slipper, but he was not my Prince Charming even though his name was similar. And even though Stone wasn't a prince, he was mine. We hadn't had the chance to declare our feelings yet because I was kidnapped. I frowned and furrowed my brows. He must feel the same way.

Charmig quickly slipped on his special sandals then scooted to the edge of the small tent and jumped down. Turning back to me, he held out his hand. "I'll help you."

Ignoring his condescension, I scooted to the edge. He put his arms around my waist and lifted me. He let my body slide down his and I held in a shudder. I tensed as he set my feet on the slippery rocks. "Thanks."

A girl around my age stood frozen a few yards away. Her prominent banshee mark stood out and her long, straight black hair shined. She beamed before dropping her gaze. Did she hate me on sight? I wasn't part of the banshee clan and maybe they didn't trust outsiders.

The female wore clothes similar to the male warriors. The purple skirt lay low on her hips displaying a pierced belly button. The top was a bikini with a colorful shawl draped around her shoulders. She swiveled around in less sturdy booties than the ones I'd been given. Her hips swayed, strutting in the opposite direction.

"Take me to my grandfather." I had no time to worry about the girl when I'd been worried about my grandfather for so long.

Charmig's nose angled upwards. He was offended by my demand. I didn't care. "First, you must speak to the Grand Lord Justicar." He held out his arm to escort me.

Since I didn't want to slip and fall in front of the other banshees, I took his arm. He strolled around the large campfire and paraded me past the planked area near the middle of the camp. The planked area was shaped in a circle and surrounded by large black rocks, sharp to a point.

A dozen or so male banshees stopped what they were doing and watched our progress.

My shoulders stiffened and I observed them with a sideways glance. I was used to people staring at me because I was a banshee. When I searched for food while living with Grandfather, when I first arrived at the dungeon, and when I'd stayed in the human palace. But why would they stare when they were banshees too?

The group wore a mix of the colorful, patterned clothes, some fancier than others. They ranged in age from around ten to twenty, and they had muscular legs and carved arms.

"Who are they?" I waved my hand, half to point and half in greeting. I wanted to get along with the banshees, once Charmig apologized for kidnapping me. Hopefully, they'd be allies in time. After all, Grandfather had once come here for help, and you could never have too many friends.

I reeled back. My opinion had changed greatly since being abducted from my small home and imprisoned in the palace dungeon. I'd changed. Had Grandfather changed too?

"They're not for you." Charmig's stern tone had me tucking in my waving hand.

"I'm not shopping for a boyfriend." I chortled because Stone had always accused me of the same thing before we'd gotten together. I couldn't imagine having a relationship with any of them. I had Stone. Or at least I hoped I did.

Charmig didn't laugh.

His lack of humor bothered me. He could be friendly and flirtatious, but I couldn't? Shaking my head, I didn't speak my mind. I didn't want an argument. I wanted to meet the leader of the banshees and see Grandfather. "Where is your father's tent?"

The camp wasn't very big. If I walked too far in one direction, I'd fall off a cliff. With several dozen tents circling around the center campfire, there must be less than a hundred members of the clan. Besides the one girl, I didn't see any women or small children. They must be inside the tents.

"Why don't you have any permanent structures?" Between the rich fabrics, beads, and other jewelry, the clan must have money. Plus, they had several of the large beasts and a modern transport vehicle.

Something small and fast sprinted from the back of one tent to another.

I shook my head, not even sure if I saw anything.

"We're nomadic." Charmig tugged me closer. "This encampment is surrounded by our fiercest banshee guards. We're perched high on a mountain near a volcano. There's no way to leave on your own."

My brow furrowed wondering if it was a warning. "I'm here because I want to see my grandfather. I'm here because I want to be," I said, taking his subtle hint.

For now.

"As I said, you must meet the Grand Lord Justicar."

"I know." A silly demand that I'd go along with. But I was done dilly-dallying around. We'd already passed the campfire twice. "Take me to him now."

"First, you must be prepared."

"Prepared?" Was he going to instill me with facts about banshees or was there a certain way to greet the Grand Lord Justicar? I knew nothing about banshee protocol. "That will take too much time."

"It's been a long journey. You need to bathe and dress properly." He ogled my body and sniffed.

Maybe I smelled. I'd been in the dungeon fighting and spent the night in an enclosed tent.

I jerked my arm out of his remembering how he'd washed my face and hands. "You're not bathing me."

Charmig raised his hand and signaled to the girl who'd seemed shocked when we'd first arrived. "Come."

She bowed her head and hurried to his side.

I shifted my feet. I hated how she acted subservient to him. I glanced around, confirming that I saw no other women. "Where are the women and children?"

"Working as they're supposed to be." Charmig's voice hardened. He didn't appreciate my questions. "Lykke will take you to your tent."

"Hi. I'm Destiny." I wanted to make friends with the only female I'd seen so far. Maybe she'd answer my questions.

He waved a hand in a dismissive gesture. "She will help you bathe and dress."

"I don't need help. Just point me in the right direction." I wiggled my shoulders. I might want friends, but I could take care of myself.

Lykke's gaze darted between both of us, lingering on Charmig. She still hadn't spoken.

"She will help you. It's her position." His expression was stiff and undebatable.

I smashed my lips together, afraid to speak up. It was similar to how the servant robots were treated at the palace. Except the robots weren't alive.

"I'll see you shortly to take you to my father." He started to turn away.

"And then I'll get to see my grandfather?" I held my breath. That's the only reason I hadn't fought on the journey.

"That's up to the Grand Lord Justicar to decide." Charmig spun away again and I grabbed his arm, stopping him.

Anger throbbed through my veins. He couldn't lure me to come willingly and snatch the prize away. "You promised I'd see my grandfather."

"I don't think I used those exact words." He leered at my hand gripping him. "I'm sure my father will agree to the reunion as long as you behave."

As if I were a dog.

I took a deep inhalation. All I needed to do was go along with this silly dressing and meet the leader, then I'd see Grandfather and convince him to leave. I gave Charmig a tight-lipped smile. "Fine."

"This way, um, Destiny." Lykke could speak. She indicated a large tent nearby while watching Charmig strut away.

I shivered, hating how he touched me in a way suggesting he owned me. I hoped I wouldn't see much of him while I was here.

Two banshee guards stood outside the door to the tent. The ancient halberds they held had black rock as the tip. For show or was the rock able to slice? It looked sharp. They wore the same type of sandals and the wrapping around their torso was a faded green.

"Hello." I nodded at the two guards.

They stared straight ahead and didn't respond or even smile. Were they to be my jailors?

I wheeled toward Lykke. Now that I knew she could talk I planned to ask her questions. "The clothing you wear is very beautiful. Do the colors mean something?"

"The bottom is called a shula and is a banshee tradition." When I quirked my head, she continued, "It's like a skirt or a kilt. The colors indicate rank in the camp."

"So those guys are...?"

"They wear green which denotes their guard status." Her tone denigrated the men right in front of them. "Warriors wear black."

"Charmig wore orange."

"He's an Elder." She spoke dreamily with a hint of respect.

He'd told me that much himself.

She opened the tent door and I stepped inside.

This must be one of the larger tents. The single room was twice the size of the small home I shared with my grandfather and slightly smaller than the suite of rooms appointed to Lord Vitor at the palace. I shook my head, remembering when he'd snuck me into the suite and I'd discovered he was really Stone.

Brightly woven carpets hung from the walls providing extra protection from the cold outdoors. A large bed with a canopy and netting was centered in the room. A row of wooden trunks lined up against one wall. Multiple chandeliers hung from the ceiling, the largest above a round table big enough to seat six.

Behind an open privacy screen sat a basin and a huge, clawed bathtub with steaming water. How had they gotten a tub to this location?

"Go!" Lykke yelled and a blur ran from behind the steaming bathtub.

"Was that a brownie?" I recognized it by the short stature and ears. "Why are brownies in a banshee encampment?"

Frowning, I thought of my friend Pith. I missed him. I missed all my friends.

"I'm sorry you saw *that*." Lykke's frown deepened and her nose crinkled. "I'll arrange to have a different brownie assigned to you."

"Assigned to do what?"

"To serve you."

Without thinking, I said, "I thought you were a servant."

Her mouth dropped open. "I'm a ladies' maid." She huffed toward the tub and put her elbow in the water. She acted haughty and offended.

My brow furrowed, trying to remember what I'd learned while staying at the palace. The robots were servants. There'd been no human female royalty to know how a ladies' maid compared. Either way, I didn't need a servant or a ladies' maid. I wouldn't be here very long.

"Give me your hideous outfit." She held out her hand.

I grabbed the stretchy fabric between my fingers and rubbed. Stone had given me this particular yoga outfit. "I'm not getting undressed in front of you."

"Get used to it. I'm charged to see to your every need," she snipped, obviously angry at her assigned task.

"What about the brownie?" I'd rather have the brownie stay.

She tapped her foot and kept her hand out. "Brownies are not to be seen or heard. At least by banshees of your stature."

Guests must be treated well by the banshees. Still, a different kind of dirt clung to my skin. A dirty scum where some majiks were treated better than others. But I did need to clean up. And arguing with her would delay seeing Grandfather.

I stood beside the large tub and took off my shirt. "What're you going to do with my clothes?"

"I'll take care of them right away."

Good. She'd get them washed so they'd be clean when I left. Even though I was uncomfortable with her watching me, I stripped off the rest of my clothes and tossed them to her. "What about these anti-magic bracelets? Can you take them off?"

"Not without Grand Lord Justicar's approval." She left with my clothes.

They might treat guests well, but they didn't trust them.

I slipped into the large tub and sunk low, covering myself with bubbles. With no cloth, I used my hands to wipe at my legs. What did I expect from a group living in tents? A soft cloth grazed my back. I jumped, splashing water over the sides of the tub.

"Don't move." Lykke had a wet cloth and soap in her hand. She sudsed up the cloth and reached low on my back.

I stiffened. It reminded me of Charmig washing my face and hands, except his touch had been gentle while hers was rough and hard. I snatched at the cloth and missed. "I can wash myself."

"It is my pleasure to serve." She seemed to be gritting her teeth as she spoke.

Arguing with her would waste time. I wanted to get the meeting with the Grand Whatever finished, see Grandfather, and pack his things so we could be on our way. I'd take him home and journey to find my friends. To find Stone.

When I was done, Lykke handed me a fluffy towel and I quickly dried myself while she rummaged through a large trunk. She carried back a pile of purple and light orange silk fabric. This wasn't the bright cloth the guards or warriors wore or even what Lykke herself wore. The fabric was luxurious with fancy beading sewn in difficult patterns.

"Those aren't my clothes and seem too nice." I thought she'd find similar clothes to the ones I'd given her.

"These are the clothes for you." Her reasonableness rubbed against my nerves.

I didn't want clothes from Charmig or the Grand Poobah or anyone else here. "No. I don't want to wear those." I clutched the towel around my body. The water had been warm and there were heaters inside the tent, but the walls were made of canvas and we were high in the mountains. It was chilly. "Bring back my clothes."

"I burned them."

My mouth gaped and a sudden prickle seared in my eyes. The clothes were my last connection to Stone. "What?"

"They were ripped and dirty." She set the new clothes on the edge of the large bed and held up one of the items. A purple silk skirt that would ride low on my hips. "Someone of your station shouldn't wear ruined clothes."

"A guest banshee has a station?" I didn't understand why they treated visitors like royalty, and yet were cruel too. I brushed off the sentimental emotions. Clothes didn't matter. Seeing Grandfather and getting out of here mattered. Finding Stone mattered. "Fine. Whatever."

Lykke gave a short smile and dressed me while I stood in front of a long mirror. Another unexpected piece of furniture.

The light orange top hung around my neck, crossed my breasts, and tied in the back imitating a sexy halter. It was similar to Lykke's top with extra beading hanging down and wrapped around my waist. The intricate beading made it heavy, pulling down my body. She placed an orange and purple cloak around my shoulders.

"Thanks." I tugged it forward to cover my bare midsection.

"It goes this way." She tugged the cape back revealing the bikini top and my stomach and let out a satisfied sigh.

She took out bottles, small pots, and brushes. Choosing several items, she brushed out my hair and applied makeup to my face. The entire time I held in snarky comments. I didn't care how I was presented for the leader, and my grandfather wouldn't care how I appeared. Just that I did.

Studying myself, I noted how my face shined from her attention but my eyes were dull. I'd changed since my time at the palace. My face looked more mature and strong. My gaze filled with knowledge about the kingdom and myself. My lips puckered with disdain.

The outfit emphasized my hips and tiny waist. The bikini top pushed up my breasts. What would Stone say if he saw me wearing this? He'd only seen me in prison garb, yoga pants, and dresses. I pulled the shawl over my front, not willing to display so much skin.

"Too bad your hair isn't longer. I can't believe you were allowed to cut it." Lykke yanked at a strand of my dark hair, piling it on top of my head.

There wasn't much to pile. While my hair had grown from the short bob I'd always worn, I didn't have enough length to make a simple bun.

"Allowed?" I decided how much Grandfather sheared off.

She pinned back my bangs to reveal the banshee mark on my forehead. Using more beads, she wove them through my hair. "It's a traditional banshee style."

That took way too much time for the life I lived. "Your hair isn't done this way."

Lykke's hair was long and straight. "I'm not important like you."

"Everyone's important." It's a lesson I'd recently learned. "Do you know where they're keeping my grandfather, Anvers Snow?"

Her fingers stopped moving. "He's been kept very comfortable."

Wariness twirled and tightened in my stomach. I wasn't sure what that meant. "That's very nice of you. I haven't seen him in a long time and would love to see him right away. Could we go there first?"

Her lips curled in a pout. "I'm afraid only the Grand Lord Justicar approves visitors to see your grandfather."

I jerked back and glared. "Is he a prisoner? Why don't you see him roaming around camp?"

Her eyelashes fluttered and she closed her expression. "Of course, I've seen him."

My shoulders relaxed. "I don't understand why I have to meet the Grand Big Cheese before seeing my grandfather."

She sucked in a loud, sharp breath. "He's the Grand Lord Justicar." Her tone suggested my joke was blasphemy.

Banshees had no sense of humor. Which was kind of how I used to be.

"There are rules in the banshee clan. If you don't follow, you'll be punished." She wasn't happy about the rules.

I wouldn't be happy about following strict rules and protocols either. Good thing I wasn't staying. I'd be nice to her and this Grand Lord Bigwig so I could see my grandfather.

Watching her finish my hair, I noted the heavy makeup she wore and didn't need. "You're very talented and very beautiful."

Her expression soured and her dark eyes filled with shadows. "Beauty means enslavement. Power is what's important."

Chapter Three

The tent that Lykke and I stood before was the tallest and the widest. The peak rose high in the sky with an opening where smoke poured out. The canvas walls widened and angled, holding several other rooms.

If the Skjult Banshee Clan was nomadic, why would they use such extravagant housing?

Two guards stood outside the tent's flap door. They held the halberds with the ax blades and topped with spikes. Jeweled daggers stuck out from their belts.

Lykke bowed to the two guards. "Destiny is here to see the Grand Lord Justicar. She's expected."

One guard leered, his gaze traveling across her chest and bare belly. "It is my pleasure to serve."

My shoulders curled. Something about his expression and tone demeaned Lykke. She kept her head downcast. If he'd talked to me that way, I'd tell him off. Or slug him.

The guard used the halberd to tap on the canvas door.

A man with shiny black hair stepped out and bowed. He appeared to be several years older than me. His pointy chin and thin face reminded me of a scarecrow. His slick hair was cut similar to Charmig's and he wore the same orange colored shula.

"I'm Svante." The man's thin lips twisted into a grimace barely passing for a smile. "I hope you had a pleasant journey, Lys Destiny."

The title caught me off guard and I wondered if it was similar to miss. His comment didn't sound sincere. I flashed him a fake smile. "If you count being poisoned and kidnapped pleasant."

Lykke gasped and her expression exhibited fear before bowing her head lower.

I refused to be cowed by this man. He was too young to be Charmig's father.

"You're here and that is what's important." Svante's dour expression didn't change. Did he practice his reactions?

"By your demeanor, I'm guessing Charmig's actions to bring me here are not a surprise."

As if saying his name caused him to appear, Charmig leaned out of the tent. "Destiny, I love how you say my name." He grasped Lykke's chin forcing her to stare at him. "You were supposed to wait for me to come get her."

I didn't want her getting in trouble because of my impatience. "My fault. I convinced her to head over as soon as I was dressed."

He dropped hold of her chin and took hold of my hand. "And you look amazing, Destiny."

Lykke frowned and a cloud of hurt passed on her face. She didn't say anything.

"Lykke chose the outfit and did my hair." I flicked the strange style on my head wanting to give her credit and soothe the insult.

She eased her gaze up from the ground to regard me.

"You look stunning." Svante took my other hand.

They treated me like a wishbone.

"Isn't beauty skin deep? Kindness and friendship are important." Which neither of these men had shown to me or Lykke. Only flattery and fake smiles. Besides, Lykke had told me beauty wasn't important.

Both men chuckled apparently in on a private joke.

My muscles stiffened. They treated me differently than her.

"You have so much more than beauty." Svante's compliment didn't make a dent in my skepticism.

We'd just met. He couldn't make a judgement on my personality. I hoped he referred to my intelligence or being a good person, but my instincts said that's not what he meant. My hackles rose.

"Come in and meet my father." Charmig tugged me forward, forcing Svante to drop my other hand. He held the canvas door open.

My pulse raced. For some reason, I knew this was a big step. An important step to seeing Grandfather. I had to hold my tongue and not be impatient. I had to be cooperative.

I stepped across the threshold.

The place could barely be described as a tent. Artwork hung in frames on the decorated canvas walls with lights to showcase the pictures. Thick and expensive carpet lined the floor. This room was larger than the tent I'd bathed in and canvas doors led to other rooms.

A large, carved wooden desk with a plush chair sat in the corner facing outward. Marble statues and gold dishes decorated the top of the desk. A seating area with a comfy couch and overstuffed chairs took up another corner of the room.

Smoke drifted through a hole in the ceiling from a firepit in the middle of the room, leaving behind a woodsy scent. A man sat in a fur-lined chair on the other side of the fire. Two smaller chairs, not as elegant, sat on either side of him, empty at the moment.

The man must be the Grand Lord Justicar.

His bulk took up the entire chair. Rolls of fat formed above the top of his bright red shula. He wore no shirt, displaying an unusual number of scars on his chest, shoulders, and arms. The tons of beading and jewels hanging around his neck couldn't hide the old wounds. His dark hair tufted up, trying to hide the bald spots. His weathered and scarred face made him appear older. In his hand he gripped a halberd with a blade and a black tip. It must be ceremonial because the blade was too dull to cut a piece of paper.

The silent room became noticeable after my visual gawking. The three men watched me with expectancy.

Was I supposed to bow or something? I glanced back to see what Lykke would do. She wasn't there. My breath stalled. For some reason, she hadn't come inside the tent. Prince Zacharye hadn't made us bow. I lifted my hand and waved. "Hi."

Charmig and Svante's eyes rounded. Their mouths dropped open.

The leader slowly lifted the ends of his mouth. "Welcome, Destiny."

The other two visibly relaxed and grinned.

"I'm Gorig, the Grand Lord Justicar." He patted the chair beside him. "Sit. We'll get to know each other."

Twisting my hands together, I took the seat. I didn't know what to expect. This man might've ordered my kidnapping, but I needed to make nice to achieve my goal. And I needed to remember to call him Grand Lord Justicar.

Charmig and Svante both rushed forward. Charmig grabbed the other empty chair, swung it around, and placed his butt down as Svante tried to sit—similar to a game of musical chairs.

Svante took a step back, gathered a blanket, and placed it on the ground next to my chair. Too close to my chair. He smirked at Charmig while sitting down, suggesting this had been his plan.

I had enough of these games. "Where's my grandfather?"

So much for being cooperative and patient. Internally, I shrugged.

"He's here and he's safe." The Grand Lord Justicar clasped his hands together on his lap. The nonaggressive action was meant to put me at ease. It didn't. "Tell me about yourself. Your likes and dislikes."

"I'd *like* to see my grandfather."

"Be respectful." Svante's reprimand had me jerking my head to consider him. His eyebrows thundered together, confirming he pretended to be nice.

"Now, Svante." The leader's glare shot through the guy sitting on the floor. "Destiny doesn't know our ways."

Did they not speak their minds or say how they felt? I'd learned a lot since being put in the palace dungeon. I'd learned to be confident about myself and my opinions. I'd learned others appreciated me for me and weren't afraid of my banshee status. And I wasn't afraid of him.

"Your grandfather realized it was a mistake keeping you from us for so long and you needed to learn the banshee ways which is why we've invited you here." The leader glossed over the fact that I'd been drugged and taken against my will. I fisted my hands at my sides. He must know. "To learn the banshee ways. Our history and heritage."

"And about your powers." Charmig leaned forward in his chair.

His father glared. Except in attitude, the clear resemblance gave me a chill. Charmig used charm and persuasion, while his father demanded acquiescence.

"Our powers are an important part of our journey as a clan member." Grand Lord Justicar spoke in a calm and soothing tone. I sensed tension beneath. He patted my thigh reminding me of my grandfather's sympathetic touch. "We have much we can teach you."

I'd always been curious about other banshees. I'd believed Grandfather and I were the last of our kind until recently. And while I needed to get back to Stone, this might be my opportunity to get to know other banshees and learn more about myself, my heritage, and my powers. As long as it was on my terms. I was sick of humans and other majiks blaming me for death, and while I'd tried to explain that banshees only predicted death, it would be great to have real knowledge and proof.

The push and pull tugged at me, drawing me in two directions. Grandfather came here for help. The banshees were extended family. With their magic, I could get a message to Stone to let him know where I was, and when his duties with the prince were complete he could come to me.

"I'd like to learn, Grand Lord Justicar." I warmed toward him. "I never knew there were more banshees."

"I knew about you." He patted my thigh again. "Please, call me Gorig."

"Gorig," I nodded. He'd brought me here because my grandfather was here and he wanted to teach me. "May I see my grandfather now?"

"Your grandfather planned to bring you back to us when you turned fifteen. But because of the treatment of majiks in the kingdom, the fear of being arrested, he was not able to realize his promise." His fingers gripped my thigh. "You belong here."

I shifted my legs and he released his grip. My brow furrowed, wondering how much of his statement was true. "My grandfather mentioned other banshees only once."

Svante gripped the edge of my chair. His pale cheeks reddened. "Your grandfather was defunct—"

"Svante." Gorig's harsh expression softened when he caught me staring. He seemed to be around the age my parents would've been if they'd lived. He waved a hand, dismissing his initial reaction. "Your grandfather was an advisor to me. He taught me many things and now I will teach you."

Grandfather hadn't taught me anything. He'd always put me off and I'd wondered if he'd been embarrassed by my lack of magic. If he'd known about the strange powers I'd discovered, maybe he would've been thrilled to instruct me. Since he'd come to the banshee group for help, he'd be okay with me learning as much as I could while I was here, and continuing my education with him after we left. "Why can't my grandfather teach me?"

Gorig tilted his head and studied me. "Your grandfather is not quite himself these days."

"What do you mean?" He'd been perfectly fine when I'd last seen him.

Charmig laughed. "He's out of his mind."

Grandfather lay on a cot with blankets piled on top of him. The sallow skin on his face had bruises and heavy dark spots under his eyes. He mumbled and shifted his body away from the door.

My heart dropped to my stomach and churned it apart. Grandfather might be old, and apparently injured, but I refused to accept he was out of his mind. He was intelligent and wise.

The simple tent held the cot, a table with bowls and bottles, and a chair next to the bed where a women sat sewing beads on an elaborate cloak. The smell of disinfectant burned my nose.

She stood when she noticed us at the entrance and bowed. "Charmig."

I jerked from his hold and rushed toward the bed. I'd never seen my grandfather so sick. He'd always been strong while facing much adversity.

"Grandfather." I found his hand under the blankets. His cold and clammy palm sent a shiver through me. "Grandfather, it's me. Destiny."

His cracked lips opened. "No!" Terror threaded through his scream.

Helplessness weakened my knees. He'd always been there for me. "Yes. I'm here. Everything is going to be okay. You're going to be okay."

I hoped it was true.

He sobbed. "I love you, Destiny. You must stand tall and brave."

"Of course, I will." I squeezed his hand and locked my knees straight. I'd do whatever he asked, whatever he needed, no matter what. "I'm here for you."

"No! No! Go! Run! Don't listen..." His mumbling trailed off and his grip grew weaker. What he said didn't make sense. Stand tall and brave was the opposite of running.

Leaning closer, I whispered to him, wanting to be alone and not have an audience. "Grandfather. Don't listen to what?"

"It's them..." His chest rose and fell. "They're lying. I'm not..."

Agony lobbed through my lungs. "You're not what?"

Charmig yanked me away and pulled me into his arms protecting me from my own grandfather. He held my head against his chest. "It's okay."

The woman's chair scraped behind me.

Suffocating from his unneeded and unwanted comfort, I struggled and wrenched out of his arms. "Let me go. I need to talk to him."

The woman or nurse tucked Grandfather's arm back under the blanket.

"What're you doing?" I didn't want anyone else touching him. "Who are you?"

She peered at Charmig, expecting him to answer for her even though she was the one taking care of my grandfather. "I'm the healer, Ursee."

"Your grandfather is delirious." Charmig's uncaringness cut through me. "He kept saying the same thing to me when I found him in the forest."

"What do you mean you found him?" I needed more answers. "What does he mean? Don't listen to who?"

"I don't know." Charmig shook his head in a slow, sad motion. "I wonder if it has something to do with when he was imprisoned at the palace."

Had my grandfather's imprisonment been worse than my treatment in the dungeon? I thought he'd been ensconced in a nice room at the palace similar to the one I'd stayed in when I'd been training with Professor Nilsen.

"I wonder if he was tortured." Dread surged through my veins, weighing me down with terrible images.

"Possibly. Who knows what happened to him after you were separated." Charmig tugged me in close again. His actions were proprietary.

I broke his hold. "How did you know we were separated? How did you know where to find me?"

"When I found your grandfather, I managed to piece together some of what he meant. I think he was in shock. He told us you both had been taken to the palace." Charmig's expression didn't change as he told the story. He didn't exactly show sympathy, though there was a touch of concern. "Your grandfather said you'd been taken from him and I," he cleared his throat, "I found a way to get information from the palace and forged a plan to rescue you."

My brow furrowed. "I was in the dungeon most of the time. There were hundreds of majiks down there."

"It was easy enough to pay a human to get the location of a banshee being held. You're quite unique." He waved a hand in front of his face and gave a flirtatious smile.

I ignored the compliment. "You found my grandfather?"

"Yes." He took my hand between his two and rubbed. "Once at our encampment, I'd sit and talk to him so he'd feel less lonely."

I softened toward Charmig. He'd been nice to my grandfather so I could put up with a little flirtation. I was still angry about the kidnapping, but maybe it wasn't his idea. He'd called it a rescue plan. If I'd known my grandfather was here, I would've come willingly. Of course, I would've told Stone and waited until after the battle against the regent.

"He's gone downhill." Charmig stepped closer and I took a step back. "He refuses to eat and he goes into these tantrums."

That didn't sound like my grandfather. A strong shudder wracked my body. I watched his feverish mutterings, unable to make sense of any of the words. He'd changed so much in a few weeks.

Charmig's father and Svante strolled into the tent. The two finished whispering about something. Svante gave me a dirty glower and I stepped closer to my Grandfather.

Gorig nodded at the woman. "How is our patient?"

"No! Please don't!" Grandfather thrashed and yanked his arms from beneath the blanket as if pushing imaginary demons away.

He must be having life-like dreams similar to mine. But I'd never heard him scream before. My gut knotted and I glanced between Ursee and Charmig. "What's wrong with him?"

Charmig bit his bottom lip. Svante's gaze darkened.

Gorig rolled his shoulders. A shadow crossed his face. "Your grandfather escaped the palace on his own and made his way to us. He knew we'd help you." Gorig shook his head sympathetically. "Your grandfather hiked miles up the mountain. He had no gear. No food. No water."

I remembered the perilous trip on the back of the strange animal. For an old man to hike alone without any supplies must've been daunting.

"One of our perimeter patrols—"

"Led by me." Charmig's grin brightened.

Svante scowled.

"Found him on the side of a mountain. Hurt, dehydrated, starving." Gorig frowned. "Your grandfather must've fallen down a steep ravine because he had severe bruises and gashes. He mentioned something about torture at human hands."

My heart, and the rest of my body, ached for him. I imagined his pain.

"He looks much better now than he did a few weeks ago. He almost died."

"Charmig said he talked to my grandfather at first."

His father waved his hand in front of his face. "Your grandfather had more lucid moments in the beginning. Our healer brought him back from near death, but he's in decline again."

My forehead crinkled and I moved closer to his side. Bruises from weeks ago should've healed. I kissed his brow. "Why isn't he healing?"

"Prigmrmgrmmmm," he muttered.

"Our healer is doing everything possible to help him."

I glanced at the woman who avoided my gaze. Her white cloak had a hood shadowing her face. She and the other banshees were doing their best to help my grandfather. Charmig even visited with him.

"Thank you. I appreciate it." The banshees only had a simple healer. They didn't have advanced scientific information or medical technology like humans. They didn't even have the powers of a fairy or a witch. "I want to transport him to Lindenhamn for the latest treatments."

"Majiks aren't welcome in human hospitals." Svante's dark tone challenged, indicating he knew more than me about the human world.

"Prince Zacharye believes in equality for majiks." My shoulders relaxed. There'd be professional help for my grandfather.

Charmig's lips twisted in a cruel line and the ends of Svante's mouth tipped up.

"The coup failed," Gorig announced.

"Coup?" I stood on trembling legs. "Prince Zacharye was taking back what was rightfully his."

"Unfortunately, the rebels failed." The banshee leader peered straight at me. "Regent Theobald won."

My gaze widened as what he said sunk in. No, I couldn't believe it. Stone and my friends fought at the prince's side. A sharp twinge went straight through my center, an arrow of despair. What had happened to them? If I'd stayed, I might've been able to help.

I swallowed the dread in my throat. "What happened to the prince?"

"He was executed." Charmig didn't contain his glee. Did he enjoy the pain of others?

The prince had been the rightful ruler and now he was gone. My soul deadened. There'd be no other rebellions to fight. The prince had been the only hope for majiks. "But...but..."

Were my friends gone too? And Stone?

My eyes prickled and I tried to control the range of emotions slipping through my psyche. So many what ifs... I sank onto the edge of my grandfather's cot. I didn't want them to know how much this terrible news affected me, but it was hard to hide.

"It was a horrible battle inside the ballroom. So many died." Gorig frowned. "The rest were taken prisoner and will have a trial."

An imaginary noose constricted around my neck. If Stone and the others hadn't died in battle, they'd be tortured by the auraguillotine machine—a terrible machine that sucked the powers and souls of majiks. The misery from the imaginary arrow spread, tightening across my skin with agony. I wanted to run down the mountain to fight for what was right. Without the prince, the regent was next in line and there was no one left to lead the rebellion.

My heart cracked thinking of Stone. He could lead if he wasn't dead. I sniffled, trying to hold in my dark thoughts. If he'd been captured, he'd be tortured while believing I'd run away.

Charmig knelt beside me and wrapped his arms around me in comfort. I tilted toward him, needing someone to lean on because I didn't know Stone's fate. A single tear fell, and I lifted my head to swipe at the drop.

Charmig's father beamed while Svante glared.

I didn't care what they thought. Too many feelings swamped my body making me want to sink and drown. Hope for a good future was lost. No prince who believed in equality. No Stone who cared about me. No Grandfather...

Straightening up, I couldn't lose him too. I'd do whatever it took to get him healthy. I'd sit with him and talk to him. I'd use whatever magic I had. I'd give him my blood to make him stronger. I didn't know what my future held, but I couldn't leave my grandfather.

"You understand why we can't take your grandfather to the city for treatment. Especially since he is a banshee who has escaped from the ruling regent."

What Gorig said was true. I tried to peek around the woman standing in front of the counter to see what type of medical supplies the banshee clan possessed. Maybe their magic could heal him.

"Banshees have magic to heal, right?" Though why they hadn't healed my grandfather yet, I didn't understand.

"We have limited healing." Gorig shrugged. "Our healer is doing her best."

His declaration slapped me. I'd probably lost Stone and my friends. I couldn't lose my grandfather. Panic shredded through my lungs and I heaved a breath. "What if your best isn't good enough?"

The three men exchanged glances. They knew something more.

"What?" My pulse charged and I perched on the edge of the bed. Tension threaded through me. "Tell me what you're thinking! What can you do to help Grandfather?"

"We can do nothing." Gorig swiped his hand and pointed at me. "But you...you have the magic to heal him."

Chapter Four

"*She'll be miraculous,*" *a familiar female trilled.*

I opened my eyes. The woman peered at me. A single streak of green ran through her dark hair. Prominent on her forehead was the banshee mark.

"Incredible." A male stared down at me. He also sported the banshee mark. He resembled a much younger version of my grandfather.

Turning my head, I took in the environment. Bars went around the soft cushion I lay on. A brightly colored padded cloth ran around the lower half of the bars. I lifted my feet and realized they were covered in tiny pink booties. I was a baby.

Startled, I couldn't believe I could remember a time so long ago. A time no one should be able to remember.

"Exploited." A third face leaned over the top of the bars. "You think adding a mark will help?"

Grandfather. Warmth stole around my heart. He was okay. Healthy and alive.

And younger.

I stiffened. If this was the younger version of my grandfather...my hope soared...and the other man looked similar to him only younger...I held my breath...and the woman's voice was familiar...

These were my parents with Grandfather.

Love rushed through me. I'd lost the images and memories of time spent with them. All I had was a tiny photo of my parents, and Grandfather's biased recollections.

I screamed with joy. Joy to be with them. Joy to finally be remembering.

"She's upset." Mom cradled me. Holding me close, she cooed.

I stopped crying and nestled closer, glancing at her with love and tear-filled eyes.

Her white skin had no wrinkles or scars. Just the banshee mark on her forehead. Her hair held a strange green tint. Her grayish-purple, almost lavender, eyes seared into my mind. Mine were the same color.

"Are you sure about this?" Father took me into his arms and rocked me up and down.

His smell of citrus filled me with a sense of wellbeing and protectiveness. He'd take care of me.

"I'm sure." Grandfather's grimness cooled my optimism. He was always grim.

Were they talking about me? They were staring at me with concern in their expressions. Was something wrong?

Mom used a delicate finger to stroke my cheek. "That's why my grandmother named her Destiny. She knew. It's why she prophesized..." Mom started crying.

"Now, now Keene." With the name, Dad confirmed these were my parents.

My heart swelled and I wanted to yell out how much I loved and missed them. I opened my mouth and a squeal came out. I was too young to talk.

Dad's darker complexion contrasted with Mom's. His dark hair was cut short. His dark eyes showed concern and fear.

He pulled Mom into a hug with his free arm and the three of us cherished this close family bond. Grandfather joined in. Their love surrounded me and I never wanted this hug to end. This time I'd remember them and this moment, no matter what spell was cast upon me.

Love.

Unconditional love.

Tragic love.

Because even though they'd born me, taken care of me, raised me until the age of seven, my parents had died tragically.

A tear slipped onto my cheek. I missed them so much. Even more now that the memories were returning.

Dad used a finger to swipe the tear. "You don't know for sure why your grandmother wrote the prophecy and named her Destiny."

My name.

"My grandmother said our daughter would be special." Mom's voice quivered with love and also worry. "She said Destiny would control everyone's destiny except her own."

The words drilled into me. A prediction or a prophecy?

"And you brought her to Reximus Palace." Grandfather's tone held a bite. He wasn't pleased with my parents' decision.

I didn't understand because he'd worked at the palace too.

"It's where we live and work. Where you live and work." Dad's defense of their choice had me pulling back my tiny shoulders. I was proud of him. "Where else could we have gone? Certainly, you're not saying we should have brought our baby to the banshees?"

"King Jostein is a good man." Mom's expression was gentle and she smiled. She stroked my nearly-bald head and I pressed into her palm. "The king would never take advantage of a child or abuse her powers."

"He might not but others would." Grandfather was his usual grumpy and contradicting self.

As a baby and a child, I never realized that about his personality.

"King Jostein is the ruler of the Kingdom of Alandaska. What he says goes."

"He's a man. Human." Grandfather scoffed. "Mortal."

My mom's hand stopped rubbing my head and a chill went down my spine.

"Keene, what's your read on the king?" Dad seemed the most reasonable.

Her expression dimmed. "There's a shadow over his heart."

"Is the king ill?"

Mom shook her head. "The king will not die of illness. He will die much earlier than expected."

My mind buzzed. My mom knew things even though her name wasn't Destiny.

By both my father's and grandfather's expressions, they believed her.

"What about the new baby prince? He'll be as upstanding as his father." Dad's deep timbre had a sense of desperation.

"If he learns from his father." Mom didn't sound so sure.

Knowing what I knew now, Prince Zacharye was mostly raised by his evil uncle.

Dad's hand clutched me tighter. "We'll protect our child with our lives."

Grandfather dropped his head. "You might have to."

⇢⇢⇢ ⇠⇠⇠

Sadness and sleep clouded my vision. I swiped the tears streaming down my face. The dream or memory was disorientating.

I lay on a thick mattress with a canopy above my head. Steam poured through the strategically cut holes in the wood-planked floor. The smell of rotten eggs filled the air.

Burying my head in the pillow, I tried to recall details of the dream. I'd been a baby and they'd been worried about me. Exploitation of my powers hadn't happened because my powers were weak and uncontrolled. A shattered breath escaped my lungs. I missed them so much. And Stone and my other friends too. I'd dealt with my parents' deaths. Sort of. But I didn't even know if Stone and the others were alive or dead. If they'd been imprisoned and tortured in the auraguillotine.

"Good morning." Lykke carried a steaming bowl. "How did you sleep?"

My brow furrowed. I'd just woken up. How had she known?

A brown blur scurried from under the bed and ran through a small black slit in the canvas walls. The brownies must spy on me.

"Morning." Grouchy and sad, I yanked the covers up to my chin. I'd had difficulty falling asleep because the Grand Lord Justicar refused to tell me anything more about healing my grandfather. He'd said he'd have to release my memories and my magic. And to do that I had to become part of the clan.

A process that might take too long to heal Grandfather. I'd visited him a second time and he'd been completely unconscious.

"I've brought fresh clothes." She set the basin down on the table and pointed to a pile at the edge of the bed.

I tilted back warily. Had she been in the tent earlier or had one of the brownies brought the clothes in while I slept? I'd have to talk to Gorig about not needing servants or help getting dressed.

"We need to have you cleansed and purified for the Warrior Initiation Ceremony. The bath has been heated for you." Lykke picked up a washcloth and stepped over to the steaming tub. "Grand Lord Justicar will be informed you're awake. We need to hurry and get dressed. He does not like to be kept waiting."

She spoke from experience. Why did she put up with this kind of treatment?

Why did I?

Because of Grandfather. I couldn't take him and leave. He was unhealthy and they believed I could help. I'd do whatever I could for him.

I threw the covers off and yanked them back up. The nightgown I'd been given barely covered my thighs and breasts. Tonight, I'd insist on sleeping in something else.

"You'll get used to the clothes." She smirked.

Had she gotten used to the low skirt and bikini top? Especially in the coldness of the mountains? Granted, the steam vents kept the area warm but outside there was a definite chill.

I threw back the covers again and stood up. "Isn't there something more you'd like to do other than bring my clothes and run baths for me?"

"Of course." Her voice edged with hurt.

I didn't want to upset her or make enemies. I wanted to do what I needed to heal Grandfather and possibly learn about my powers. Then, we'd be on our way.

"I'm sorry. I didn't mean to insult you." I stepped toward the bath. "I meant I'm not an invalid. I can take care of myself."

She took hold of the edges of the nightgown and pulled it over my head. "It is my pleasure to serve."

The rehearsed line tied my belly in knots. "How is my grandfather this morning?"

The silence grew tense. Had something happened last night?

"I want to see him." I grabbed the nightgown.

She snatched the clothes back. "I'll have a brownie check on him right now."

A brownie, who'd been standing behind one of the hanging rugs, stepped out, nodded, and ran from the tent.

"Please get in the tub." She used the word please even though there was no request.

I couldn't find my grandfather if I wanted to. They'd forced me to leave him, telling me he needed rest and so did I. Charmig had done a good job of walking me around the encampment in circles trying to get me confused. Only a few tents were different. All the others were the same. "Will you take off these bracelets?"

"No."

I sunk into the tub and let the water sluice across my skin. Lykke used a cloth to rub at my back and I tried to relax. How could I relax when I didn't know what was wrong with my grandfather?

The brownie scurried back.

I sat straight up, sloshing water over the sides of the tub. "How is my grandfather?"

The female brownie trembled to a stop and rounded her eyes wider, her large pointy nose in between. The hem of her brown tunic dress was ragged and uneven. The color blended with her skin. She bowed her head, darted forward, and whispered to Lykke.

"Your grandfather's condition hasn't changed." She had no sympathy.

It was difficult to like someone who exhibited no care for someone you loved.

Shifting in the tub, I controlled my urgency to get to him. The sooner I got bathed and dressed, the sooner I could see him. "Let's hurry so I have time to see Grandfather before meeting up with Charmig and his father."

After a good scrubbing, Lykke let me get out of the tub and dry myself. She helped me get dressed in a low-riding skirt and bikini top similar to yesterday. The outfits were too revealing and didn't keep me warm. Glaring at my reflection in the mirror, I didn't want to take the time to argue. Besides, I didn't think she was the one to argue with. She was just doing what she was told.

Rushing out of the tent, I found Charmig waiting. His orange shula had more beading and a cloak was held back with a large diamond brooch. He tapped his foot on the ground.

I knew I was early so how did he know to show up at this second? I quirked my head at Lykke. Maybe she was the one spying.

She kept her head down and her posture straight displaying her physical attributes. She said nothing.

"Heard you wanted to see your grandfather before the Warrior Initiation Ceremony." Charmig presented his charming smile.

His white teeth were in a straight line, while the other banshee warriors I'd seen had yellow teeth with jagged tops. Why did he have perfect teeth?

And perfect skin, except for the scars? Again, most of the other warriors had acne or other marks. Which was fine. It was just that he appeared so different. As did his father. Did their status in the banshee society enable them to get modern medical treatments? Or maybe it was their magic?

"Yes." I gritted my teeth. I'd wanted to go alone and he wasn't going to stop me.

Charmig held out his arm. "I'll escort you."

Inside, I sighed. He acted like a gentleman, but I could walk on my own. "Thank you."

Lykke hurried in front of us, and I noticed how his and some of the other male warriors' gazes followed the sway of her hips in an obvious way. I frowned. The girl was not an object.

"You look beautiful this morning." He meandered toward the main campfire.

My frown deepened. Beauty wasn't important, something I'd learned in the dungeon, and he didn't even look at me as he spoke. He must have lines he'd practiced. Besides, compliments wouldn't work on me. I loved Stone. Once I helped Grandfather heal, we'd leave this place and find out who had survived the battle against the regent. I'd search for Stone and my friends.

It seemed I was always searching for someone.

We strolled past two other large tents. Two guards stood outside the front doors. These tents were identical to each other and as large as the one I stayed in. The rest of the tents in the camp, besides Grand Lord Justicar's, were small, simple dwellings. Gray canvas with sagging roofs and fraying ropes tying them down to the hard earth.

The leader's tent stood taller than the rest. A metal pole held up the high point and a flag blew in the breeze. Guards surrounded it on all sides.

In front of the leader's tent was a large fire pit stacked with wood ready to be lit. Brownies scurried behind and between the tents while guards in brown shulas marched around the outside ring of the camp. Were the guards for protection or to keep the brownies inside?

"How is the Warrior Initiation Ceremony going to help my grandfather?" My nerves tangled. Gorig hadn't explained anything last night. Just said I'd need to commit to the banshee way through a ceremony in order to heal Grandfather.

"Committing to be a banshee is the first step." Charmig strutted around the large central campfire. He apparently had all the time in the world.

He might, but my grandfather didn't.

"I am a full banshee." I'd dealt with majik reactions to the mark on my forehead my entire life. "How could I not be committed?"

"You need to commit to the warrior way." And yet, he'd told me I wasn't a warrior and shouldn't worry about fighting for the prince. The seesaw of explanations made me dizzy.

"What is the process? How do I do it?" I used a pretty-please-tell-me tone and squeezed his arm.

His lips twisted in a confident grin. "You'll see."

My gaze narrowed. "Don't you know?"

"I do." He took a turn and we ended up in front of another tent similar to the others. "My father will explain everything. Here we are."

The word commit ruffled my skin. I'd commit as far as I could to get my banshee powers and heal Grandfather.

The encampment wasn't very large but it had taken forever to walk here with Charmig. I didn't know if he wanted to spend more time together or if he was trying to confuse me about the camp layout. But this time I'd paid attention. You never knew when you would need to run.

Passing the two guards at the door, I pushed open the canvas tent and went straight to the small cot holding Grandfather. He hadn't changed. Still pale and sallow. His chest still moved too fast up and down beneath the blanket.

"Good morning, Grandfather." I picked up his hand and pressed two fingers against the pulse in his wrist.

The slow tick didn't surprise me. The red circles around his wrist below his watch blared a warning. "What are these marks?"

The same healer stood in front of the table. Did Ursee stay with him all the time? She cleared her throat. "When he gets, um, restless we've had to restrain him."

Her nervousness scratched against my senses. Had they used similar handcuffs to the ones they'd put on me?

"He's attacked several warriors and the healer." Charmig tutted. "He's a danger in his current state."

Shaking the negative thoughts off, I had to focus on Grandfather getting well. I hoped he could hear me. "It's me, Destiny. I came to bring you home."

"Go home!" He screamed and thrashed.

I jerked back. His harsh words hit me in the solar plexus so hard that I lost my breath. I knew he didn't mean that he didn't want me here. He couldn't mean it. He'd taken care of me forever. Now, I'd take care of him.

Moaning, his body continued to thrash and wiggle. He swung out at an imaginary foe. His fist connected with Ursee's stomach and she screamed. "Help!"

The guards outside rushed in and held him down. With efficient motions, the healer filled a syringe and plunged it into his arm.

Watching with wide eyes, I couldn't believe it. Grandfather acted crazy. Now, I understood why he might've been restrained. I hated seeing him this way. "Is that normal? What did you give him?"

Ursee put the empty syringe on the table. "He comes in and out of consciousness. Most of the time he fights against us."

"Why?" Besides a few bruises, I saw nothing wrong with him. "His body looks fine."

"Whatever injury befell him must've put him into shock." She spoke soothingly.

"How?"

"The mind is a mysterious thing."

With modern medicine, the human doctors had learned so much about the mind. Ursee had a modern syringe. She must have more advanced technology somewhere. "What is your training?"

"How is our important patient today?" Charmig's father strolled in with Svante by his side.

Ursee would never answer me now.

Their shulas were finer and more beaded than yesterday. Both men stood tall and pompous. Svante's dark hair was groomed.

"The same, Grand Lord Justicar." The healer kept her head down.

Why was everyone afraid of the man? He had major control issues. But he cared about my grandfather and brought me to him. And he was going to help me heal him.

"Now that his granddaughter is here we expect him to improve immensely. Don't we, Destiny?" He patted my arm.

"I'm not sure how I can help." The weight of his hand depressed me. He expected a miracle. "My powers are unusual but they're not the magic of a healer or a doctor."

He angled his head. "Your powers? Have you used powers even though they were locked down when you were a child?"

"How do you know about that?" The returned memory of me sitting above boiling water gleamed in my head.

"Your grandfather brought you to us right after your parents died." Gorig's lips pursed together.

Had he been in charge?

"Your grandfather was concerned about you. Between your grief and the possibility of your powers emerging prematurely, he wasn't sure how you would handle things." He spoke fast and then slow, as if he wanted to hurry this along and get answers from me but wasn't sure how much to divulge.

I wanted to know everything. Glancing at my grandfather, I wished he could tell me.

"Your grandfather planned to bring you back to us to have your magic and memories unlocked. Then with this human versus majik conflict..."

"What powers do you presently have?" Svante's question slashed.

Wariness rippled through me. I didn't want to share everything. Some of the facts were intimate and I didn't trust the banshees gathered round. Plus, if they believed my powers were locked down, why use the anti-magic bracelets and handcuffs when they'd kidnapped me?

They certainly hadn't been forthcoming. "I can read human minds."

The particular skill wouldn't appear a threat to banshees. I didn't add that I could change human minds and force them to do things. I didn't mention the heks scream or the fact that I could blast items to pieces. A vision of Lord Vitor's chess pieces exploding into fragments came to mind. The professor had taught me how to internalize the power with what he called a heks scream. I could be silent but deadly.

If my banshee powers were locked down, what was that magic?

The three men dissected me with their gaze.

I wiggled my shoulders. "So the ceremony," I changed the subject, "will unlock my memories and my banshee powers?"

Gorig nodded. "What do you mean by reading minds?"

Shrugging, I decided to act casual like it was no big deal. "I focus and I can hear what humans are thinking. What they're having for dinner, how they feel about their spouse." I forced a smile, trying not to act too magical. I wanted to know what was in store for me. "And this initiation will bring my memories and powers back?"

The three men glanced at each other and the leader spoke. "It's a process. First, you must accept the banshee warrior way."

Not super specific.

"Today." Svante scrutinized my expression trying to read my mind.

"Okay." I swallowed my anxiety and decided to go along. "If it helps my grandfather, I'll do anything."

"There are steps," Charmig repeated.

"That's correct." Gorig patted his son's head as if he was a child. "First the initiation to commit to the banshee clan and warrior way. Then, another ceremony which will unlock the memories and the power."

Poooowwwweerrrrr.

The way he spoke the last word echoed in my head suggesting a siren's call. Was my power what was most important to him?

Chapter Five

Hours later, I left the healer's tent in a daze. The cold air was interrupted by the steam vents causing the clouds in the sky to get darker. Grandfather had mumbled things like *home* and *trick* and *stop* and fallen into another restless sleep. I'd watched him until my stomach growled so loud I'm sure the healer heard. Svante, Charmig, and his father had left right after our conversation about power, but not before Gorig had acted concerned and fatherly toward me, asking if I'd be okay through the long ceremony.

His concern made the hairs on the back of my neck stand at attention. Was he concerned about me or my powers? He hadn't realized some of my banshee powers had broken through the lock.

Stepping outside the healer's tent, I was surprised no one waited. It's not that I was a prisoner—believe me, I understood real imprisonment—but someone always escorted me where I needed to go. When it was Charmig, he took me the long way trying to confuse me or show me off.

A short brown blur ran around the edges. Another brownie? Why not take a shorter route through the center of camp?

"Challenge accepted." A deep, intense voice caught my attention near the main firepit and I headed in that direction.

Curious, I wanted to know what regular life was like for a banshee.

Male banshees stood on the outside of an area lined with wooden planks. The planks had been cut at the ends to form a circle and the black rocks rose higher around the edges. Steam poured through the cracks of the planks.

A male banshee, bare chested and wearing a black shula skirt, faced a child. A boy who couldn't be much older than ten wearing a gray shula. The boy stomped one bare foot and then the other trying to menace the older male.

Comical, the child trying to intimidate the muscular man.

The older banshee, who seemed about my age, returned the strange greeting adding a grunt. They both held long wooden poles sharpened to a point at both ends. Not deadly but honed enough to hurt.

The male flexed his muscular arms and the crowd cheered.

The boy pursed his small lips in a determined frown. He bent low and growled.

They charged each other.

My pulse raced. The hard smack of the poles clanged in my ears. My eyes rounded watching the fight. This wouldn't go well for the boy.

The older one took a step back and laughed. "That's all you got?"

The boy's cheeks flamed. He swung his pole from above his head toward the other. The older guy spun and easily blocked the attack. The boy thrust forward with the pointy end.

I sucked in a breath. The boy was going to get injured.

The man blocked the thrust and pressed the middle of his pole against the boy's neck. One of the boy's hands lost his grip on his pole and it clattered to the ground. He reached up to snag his opponent's pole and yanked. The man's pole didn't budge. He and his over-buffed muscles held firm.

Air screeched out of my lungs. The man would kill the boy.

The crowd of banshees didn't move.

They watched the fight passively, suggesting killing a child was no big deal. My blood pressure skyrocketed, roasting me inside. It was a big deal. I'd been picked on by other majiks in the forest where Grandfather and I lived because I was a banshee. To see banshees picking on each other roiled in my veins.

The boy's other hand chopped at his opponent. His eyes bulged out of their sockets. His mouth gaped as he struggled to breathe.

With my blood now boiling, I darted into the circle. If no one else would halt this insanity, I would.

"Stop!" The command rushed out of me with my angst. I wouldn't watch one banshee kill another. Especially a child.

The large male loosened the pressure on the boy's neck. He turned his head and leered. The boy's body flopped to the ground. He gripped his neck and curled into a ball.

The bare-chested males surrounding the ring swiveled to glare. They zeroed in on me. I was their target now.

I gulped. I didn't want their attention or their displeasure. At least I'd stopped the fight.

A banshee with a strip of beaded, wrapped leather tied around his bicep pushed the others aside as he made his way toward me. He was around twenty, but his gaze held a decade more of knowledge as if he'd already experienced all life had to offer. Odd there weren't any older warriors in the group.

I refused to back down, the heat of anger shifted to char my skin. "Are you in charge?"

He pounded his muscular chest. Scars zigzagged his abdomen. "I am." He gave a mocking bow. "Teinn."

"Well, Teinn. This is an unfair fight. The boy is a child and could be injured badly." I acted calm while my skin blistered with anger.

Grinning, he showed broken and yellow teeth. He grabbed my arm and led me to the edge of the circle. "It's how a boy becomes a man."

"The boy," I emphasized the term as my skin crackled and flared, "hasn't filled out. He doesn't have muscles like the other guy. I'm sure he hasn't been trained in hand-to-hand combat." I remembered how useless I felt going on tracking missions without having a clue how to track. This was more dangerous.

When the boy stood, the warrior punched him back down. The boy stumbled onto the ground.

A chuckle erupted out of Teinn and the other warriors joined his laughter. They thought the situation was funny.

The fever of anger combined with my racing pulse. My fingers itched and I clenched them into fists. The boy was going to be killed. How would they feel if someone more powerful picked on them? "If you're not going to stop the fight, I will."

"The child is training to be a warrior. To earn his position, he must fight."

Sparks ignited from my fingertips and I fisted my hands higher. Worry for the child fueled my fight. I pulled back my shoulders refusing to be intimidated. "I understand training and this isn't it."

Stone had trained others. He didn't abuse his position. He trained with dignity and respect.

The warrior smirked a smug, I-know-something-you-don't grin. "Good."

His superior smugness set off something inside me. The heat—my heat—erupted and I flung my hands forward, aiming at Teinn's bare chest. A wave of power emanated from me. A heks scream without my usual concentration.

Teinn flew backward and screamed. His body flopped against a rock on the far side of the circle.

Shaking out my arms, I took a wheezy breath. I hadn't meant to hurt the man. Just stop the fight.

Which I did.

My mouth dropped open. What if I'd made him explode like the chess pieces?

The two opponents stopped to stare. The crowd froze and their fearful expressions peaked. They were afraid.

Afraid of me.

I shook my head back and forth. That's not what I wanted.

A woman broke the silence, rushing to Teinn's side. He waved her away. So the jerk was alive.

Murmurings broke out from the crowd. They whispered about me. My mind whirled. I couldn't hear what they were saying. I understood it was bad. I hadn't killed him or anyone else. Not yet. I studied my hands.

"What's going on?" Svante hurried toward us. "Destiny, what did you...how did you..."

He trailed off and I jumped in not wanting to explain more about my released powers. He was a banshee. He could do the same thing. The question was why didn't he?

"Why are banshees fighting against each other? Against children?" There was enough violence in the world.

Ignoring me, Svante yelled at the men, "Why aren't you training?"

He wasn't much older than Teinn, and yet he held more authority, especially wearing the Elder orange.

"Lys Destiny had an issue with our training methods." Teinn struggled to stand and gripped his ribs.

I'd thought Lys was similar to miss. Coming from the guy, it sounded like an insult. I lifted my chin and glared, challenging him to say more.

"Get back to work. We need to be in top shape to prove our abilities to re—" Svante clamped his lips shut. He pivoted toward me. "What're you doing roaming the encampment?"

I lifted my chin higher. "Am I not allowed to freely walk around?"

"Of course. I thought you'd be preparing for the ceremony." He tugged me toward the main campfire where a few women worked on piling wood in the middle where the fire would be lit.

I waved his concern off. "What are they doing?"

"Building a fire."

"No." Annoyance made my tone sharp. He'd purposely misunderstood my question to make the obvious statement. "Why would the male banshees hurt each other?"

He kept a grip on my hand and kept leading me further away. "It is the Proving Sphere where Grand Lord Justicar demands we prove our worth."

"What are they proving? That they can beat up a small boy?" I couldn't hold back my indignation. I'd been teased mercilessly as a child. I'd seen abuse in the palace dungeon. I didn't expect to see it between my own kind.

"It's part of the banshee warrior training." He dismissed me.

"I'm going to be a warrior." My stomach flipped. Grand Lord Justicar wanted me to commit to the warrior way. Did that mean fighting huge males? There were no women standing around the ring. Maybe the female warriors trained separately. "Is this how I will be trained?"

Laughing, Svante patted my arm. His chortle squashed any respect I'd gained. "You are special."

"Special how?"

"Your warrior status is a figurehead." He sounded like Stone, not believing I could fight. My spine hardened. "So warriors can use your powers."

I could fight. Once I figured out how to use my powers, I'd be a great fighter. "What if I want to be a real warrior?"

"Ridiculous." Svante gave a short chuckle and glanced around to see who listened. He lifted his chin and spoke louder. "Women aren't warriors."

$$\text{\textbf{----}}$$

"What does the initiation ceremony mean?" And why did I need to do it if women weren't warriors?

Trying not to inhale the strange incense in the tent, I stood in front of the mirror as Lykke tightened the bright red shula around my waist.

I understood first initiation into the clan, then the warrior bonding, then the ceremony to unlock my memories and magic. In between, I hoped to talk to Grandfather to get his advice.

My lungs filled and I slowly exhaled. I wasn't sure if I was thrilled or scared about receiving my magic. Once I got my memories and my powers, I'd prove to Svante that I could be a warrior, not just used for my magic. I'd prove it to the banshees. My magic was as good as theirs.

He'd stopped talking and refused to answer questions as he'd escorted me back to the tent I stayed in. My brow furrowed. Svante, Charmig, and his father had been surprised that I'd already used powers. I thought it was a good strategy to tell them only about the mind reading. Now Svante had witnessed another strength. Would he tell? Though everyone would discover everything I could do after the final ceremony.

One step at a time.

Lykke tugged a brush through my short hair. "The first ceremony bonds you to the Skjult Banshee Clan."

"Is there another clan?" I cringed at her forceful use of the brush.

"No." She tugged again. "Of course not."

"So I'm a member of the family." I enjoyed being part of a group. I'd learned that when I'd made friends in the palace dungeon.

My heart contorted thinking about Stone and the others. If they were alive, I would find them. I squeezed my eyelids closed. They had to be alive. Stone had to be alive. First, I needed to get my memories and magic back so I could save Grandfather. Then, I'd take him home and find my friends.

One step at a time. It had become my mantra.

Worry for Violet seared in my chest. She'd been taken to a witch coven for treatment and hadn't fought in the battle against the regent. If there still was a witch coven. The regent would destroy all majiks and the banshees would need every warrior to fight, including me.

"We're more than family." Lykke divided my shoulder-length strands with decorative clips. "You must act for the good of the clan and take the appropriate place for you."

Healing Grandfather would be for the good of the clan. He had knowledge of banshees and the kingdom. He knew the regent and could help us strategize.

"Most banshees do one of the initiations as children." Her hands faltered. The bright smile she gave me didn't connect with the sheen in her eyes. "You're lucky your position is secured."

My midsection clenched thinking of the fighting warriors. Did she mean I wouldn't have to fight for my position? Svante had laughed at the notion. He'd said I was special. Because of my age at being bonded or my magic?

I shook off the mismatching thoughts. I loved my grandfather. He was my immediate family, flesh and blood. I'd risk everything to save him. I'd help the clan in any way I could, even fight against the regent. But eventually, I'd have to leave. I hated the isolation at the encampment. The banshee clan must've faced discrimination which is why they kept themselves apart. Except I knew there were humans and majiks in the kingdom who didn't hate us.

A brownie scurried low carrying a tray of dried apricots.

I reached out to grab one and Lykke slapped my hand.

"No eating before the initiation."

"Who is the food for?" Normally, the food brought into my tent was for me and I'd eat alone. I rubbed my empty stomach.

"For me." Lykke snatched an apricot.

The brownie served her too.

"What's your name?" I asked the brownie.

Her entire body stiffened. "Iban," she squeaked between pale lips.

Lykke gasped. "You're in no position to talk to it." She'd called the brownie an *it*. She must hate brownies.

I glared at her. "What do you mean?"

She waved at the brownie. "Please take the tray and stand by the back door."

Clamping my mouth shut I wanted to defend the brownie, but Lykke used the brush like a lethal weapon and I wanted to keep my hair. I'd approach her later about her treatment of the brownies.

"As I was saying, it's a spiritual ceremony." She picked up several beaded necklaces and wound them through my hair. "Your body becomes a vessel, and the vessel needs to be empty to receive the spirits."

Mumbo jumbo to me. Grandfather had never been a religious man. My brow furrowed. He had been healthy. When we'd been taken by the palace guards, he'd been extremely fit for his age. Unless his imprisonment at the palace had weakened him, he should've made the difficult hike to the banshee encampment.

"Turn." She pushed on my shoulder to help me rotate. Then, she draped necklace after necklace over my head.

Between the heavy beads strewn through my hair and hanging around my neck, I wouldn't be able to stand much longer.

"The final touch." She put something on my head.

The heavy weight of the hat pressed down. It was more than the physical weight though. It was the weight of doing well, the weight of healing my grandfather, and the weight of the banshees' expectations.

"What actually takes place in the ceremony?" A shiver slowly shimmied up my spine remembering the last banshee ceremony I participated in as a child.

"What happens to you will be different." Lykke gritted her teeth. Was her experience bad and she didn't want to say? "It's different for everyone depending on your place in our society."

Confusion rang through my brain, and I let the weight of the beads lower my head. "What is my place?"

She gripped my arms and rotated me toward the mirror.

Bracelets laced around my ankles clinking when I moved. The shula skirt seemed to hang lower on my hips than normal. It must be the weight of the beads sewn into the material in wavy patterns. The bikini top blended colors of purple and red. Beads had been threaded throughout the minimal neckline and wove around my waist. Those beads also jangled. Between the styled hair and makeup, I barely recognized myself.

Lifting my gaze, I spotted the final touch.

A flower-filled headpiece sporting curved goat horns covered in gold.

It resembled a crown.

Chapter Six

The big orange ball of the sun fell behind the mountain peak. The purplish-pinkish-orange glow gave the banshee encampment an otherworldly atmosphere. A perfect setting for a mystical ceremony.

My legs trembled. A mystical ceremony where I was the main attraction.

The fire rose as high as the mountain peak. The flames kept me warm even in the skimpy outfit. I tugged the cloak to cover my body.

Deep drums beat a fast tune. A horn wailed. Women and children danced around the bonfire, chanting and raising their hands. More women than I'd seen the entire time I'd been here. The women wore strips of leather around their ankles and the beads clanged together making music of their own as they moved. Their feet were mostly bare and many had scrapes or old injuries. The shulas and small bikini tops they wore were in various colors. Dozens of beaded necklaces draped around their necks and seemed to be a symbol for something.

Similar to the heavy headpiece—I refused to think of it as a crown—that I wore on my head.

The children ran around, chatting and giggling. They had dirty faces and kept sneaking food from a table.

I wished I could sneak food. According to Lykke, I couldn't eat until after the ceremony.

The table bent with the weight of the plates and bowls. Roasted meats, root vegetables, and bowls of pasty mush.

The bare-chested warriors stood behind Gorig with their expressions blank and their bare arms crossed. Cold must not bother them. The leader sat in an ornate chair, the ceremonial halberd at his side. The chair was covered in blankets and the beads hanging from the bottom blew with the slight wind.

The entire banshee clan had turned out for the event.

Sitting in a less-decorated chair on the opposite side of the fire, I turned toward Svante who sat on one side of me. He'd explained a little about the warrior training so maybe he'd answer more questions. "Did these banshees travel from far away?"

His brows rose and he angled his head. "We live here, together."

My jaw dropped. I used to believe Grandfather and I were the last banshees but there were actually hundreds.

I scanned the small encampment of several dozen tents and then the number of banshees standing or dancing around the bonfire. How did they fit? There must be more tents I hadn't seen. The smaller boys danced with the women and girls. Anyone who seemed to be older than ten stood with the warriors.

I fingered the horns sticking out the side of my headpiece. The smooth cold of real gold chilled my skin. The valuable headwear must be passed from one initiate to the next. How would a child hold this heavy thing on their head for any length of time? My neck had a crick in it. I'd asked about the crown. Lykke had rushed me out and told me most of my questions would be answered during the ceremony.

I leaned to my right side where Charmig was seated. "Where are the brownies?"

Surely, they'd be part of camp events even if they weren't banshees.

"Brownies are not to be seen or heard." His distaste was similar to Lykke's. The two would make a perfect pair.

Shifting, I sealed my lips. I had a brownie friend. Once I was officially part of the clan, I'd take on the responsibility of getting them fair treatment.

Grand Lord Justicar stood and blew a horn. The drums and other horns stopped. The women and children stopped dancing. Even the roar of the fire quieted. The only noise was the whistling of the wind against the nearby cliffs.

He handed the horn to one of the warriors and flung his fur lined cape back. His scarred chest shone in the firelight. Tons of beaded necklaces decorated his body, wrapped around his neck, his wrists, and his ankles. The crown he wore featured tall gold antlers, jewels, and feathers.

The banshee clan didn't appear wealthy with their small tents and nomadic lifestyle. If they sold a few jewels from the crown their leader wore, they could build permanent homes in a more hospitable location.

He raised his hand as if protesting my thought. The wrap around his hips slipped and a warrior rushed to his side to tie the wrap tighter without a word or signal from the leader.

Why couldn't he fix the shula himself?

Charmig and Svante stood. They were both dressed similarly, but in different colors. Charmig wore orange. The many rows of beading on the shula must've tugged on his hips. He had almost as many lines of beads as his father. His cape flowed behind him calling attention to his bare-muscled chest. The feathered headdress on his head didn't have gold or jewels. It wasn't a crown.

Svante's outfit sported more beads on a purple shula and more feathers in his headdress. He wore the cape forward.

The two of them held out their hands.

Nerves twisted inside me. I put my hands in each of theirs and stood between them. This was the first step to healing Grandfather.

The women and children gaped as we paraded around the campfire. Their rapt expressions showed curiosity and envy. Trying to ignore everyone watching, I couldn't help but notice the sharp prick of their stares.

I shouldn't think of them as strangers. We were about to become family.

Spotting Lykke's face in the crowd, I relaxed. Her familiar face gave me encouragement while Svante's serious expression gave me pause. My pulse raced. I jerked my gaze to Charmig. He winked.

Even though the wink meant nothing, it gave me a burst of confidence. I could do this without falling on my face. He could become a good friend, once he understood there could be nothing more between us.

"Hoo! Ha! Hoo! Ha!" the crowd of women and children chanted. They bent their knees in a jerky action.

My steps faltered. I remembered the chant. They'd screamed those same nonsensical syllables in the dream memory when my powers and memories were locked away. I'd had no clue what was happening. This time I didn't know much more. I dragged my feet. I needed to fully understand what was happening before committing to the banshee warrior way.

Svante and Charmig continued moving forward and tugged me with them.

The warriors stayed standing behind the leader. Their lips curled. I refused to be intimidated by them. I'd faced more fierce opponents.

"Hoo! Ha! Hoo! Ha!"

The pace was agonizingly slow, and yet too fast at the same time. If I refused to go through with this, what would happen to Grandfather?

"Hoo! Ha! Hoo! Ha!"

Each step took me closer to the ceremony.

With Stone and my friends there'd been no formal ceremony. We'd bonded over time and forced closeness. We'd accepted each other by getting to know each other. They hadn't even trusted me at first because I was a banshee and they'd believed I'd betrayed them.

Why would the banshees accept me immediately? What if I was a terrible member of the clan? Maybe I was. I did plan to leave as soon as Grandfather was able.

"Hoo! Ha! Hoo! Ha!"

We reached the spot right in front of the Grand Lord Justicar.

Clap.

The warriors' unified, single clap thundered in my ears.

They raised their hands and spread their fingers, their palms facing toward me. Each of them did the exact same movement at the exact same time. Each had the exact same mark on their left wrist.

"Greetings in celebration, family." Gorig raised his hands. Gold twinkled on his finger. The ring had a symbol stamped into the gold and reminded me of one Grandfather used to wear. "Prospectives bestow your favors."

A small boy ran up with two pots in his hands.

Svante dipped his finger into one of the pots, covering it with the purple color of his clothing. He reeled toward me and swiped his wet finger across my left cheek. His stroke left a trail of icy shivers.

I stiffened, and lifted my right hand to wipe off the mark he'd left.

Charmig slapped his fingers around my arm, stopping me. He gave a slight shake of his head.

Charmig dipped his finger in the second pot. With his finger dripping in orange, he placed his wet finger high on my cheek. His finger caressed as he slid over my skin. He grinned, his lips lifting on one side suggesting intimacy.

A creepy jitter slid down my spine. I saw the smarminess, but I wasn't attracted to him. I held in a retort and a slap.

Svante frowned and his bushy eyebrows furrowed together.

"Lys Destiny." Charmig's father clapped.

Jerking back, I recognized the word that a few had called me. What did it mean? I peered at Charmig. He stared straight ahead at his father.

The man gripped my chin. "These two bands represent the feelings and hopes of their givers. Their spirits will guide you in your journey and bring you safely back home."

I'd already been on a journey, several actually. And while this wasn't my home, it was a temporary reprieve while Grandfather healed and I figured out where to search for Stone. And to figure out how to help the majiks against the regent. Nothing too big.

I peered at Charmig and Svante. Was helping the new initiate part of their roles as Elders? I imagined being a young child and participating in the ceremony. They'd be scared. Anxiety curled in my gut.

"Purple represents power and leadership."

My brow rose. Does Svante want power and leadership from me or with me?

"And orange represents leadership and a healthy relationship." Charmig winked.

I wasn't sure what he meant by a healthy relationship. Certainly not what he had with Lykke considering the way he treated her as less. I didn't understand what the banshees truly meant, or why they expected such things from me. I'd been clear about my reasons for staying and when I was leaving. Hadn't I?

The lonely wail of the horn pierced the air and wallowed in a stark place in my soul.

Boom. Boom. Boom. The drum pounded deep in my chest.

The women began dancing. The jangling of their anklets mixed with the drum and the horn. They wove their way around the bonfire and created two rows with a narrow channel between them.

Gorig raised his hands and stepped toward the women. They bowed and pawed his naked chest. A flirtation or a signal of availability? It sure wasn't respect.

My cheeks warmed and I squirmed internally while trying to make myself comfortable with the touchiness of the clan.

"Hoo! Ha! Hoo! Ha!" the women chanted.

I took a step, wondering if the women would paw me as I passed. Bringing my arms closer to my body, I took another step.

Charmig and Svante walked behind.

"Hoo! Ha! Hoo! Ha!"

Continuing forward, I wondered what would happen next. Was the ceremony done and I was now part of the clan?

Charmig's father stood in front of a small, plain tent. Vapor steamed through the canvas walls and the distinct scent of sulfur and incense burned my nose. "My new daughter, Destiny."

My back stiffened. Not from the smell, from the use of the term daughter. I wasn't his daughter and never would be.

The leader opened the tent flap and steam poured out. "You may take one or both of your Prospectives into the tent to comfort you in your journey."

Say what? Prospectives is what he'd called Charmig and Svante. Prospective what? And why would I want them in a tiny tent with me? I surveyed them both again. I didn't know what this journey entailed, either way I didn't trust them. "I'll go alone."

The crowd *oohed* and *ahhed* and I couldn't tell if that was good or bad.

Charmig huffed and Svante grumbled beneath his breath.

I stumbled. "What am I supposed to do?"

"Lie inside and relax."

I choked. He'd wanted me to lie with Charmig or Svante or both. Shock rooted me to the spot. "For how long? What is this place? What journey?" I asked a dozen questions and not even half were answered.

"Everyone has their own journey." Gorig signaled for me to crawl inside.

Hesitating, I wasn't sure what to do or who to trust. Fear rumbled in my core. "How long do I have to stay inside?"

"You will know when it's over." He pressed against my lower back and I stepped forward, away from him.

Bending, I moved inside.

The doorway flapped closed and held.

The intense smell seared through my nostrils and into my brain. My head pounded. The steam rose through holes in the tent floor from the ground beneath. Bowls of water dotted around the small space to increase the haziness. I found it difficult to breathe. Lightheadedness swirled in my mind and clouded my vision.

Bumbling toward the exit, I knocked off the heavy headpiece. "I can't believe they make little kids do this." With quivering fingers, I ripped at the flap.

The opening was sewn shut. Sealed.

There was no way out. Sweat formed on my upper lip.

Great. Locked in here without knowing what to do or how to begin the journey. They should've left instructions or a map. And also told me how to breathe. I sucked in another pungent smelling breath.

The drumming and whooping and jingling of anklets went silent. It was as if the banshees had disappeared.

Dizziness from the stuffiness, the incense, and the hunger spun in my head. I staggered to my knees. Crawling to the pile of blankets, I gasped for breath. My entire body weakened. Were they trying to kill me? My head swam and I closed my eyes, trying to stop the spinning. I fell back onto the makeshift bed.

Was this a test? What did staying in a hot and smelly tent prove? That I could survive. What if I went crazy or lost consciousness? I banged my head against the ground. Had Grandfather been injured by this same process? Except he'd become part of the banshee clan when he'd been younger. My brow furrowed. I didn't remember him having a mark on his wrist. Maybe he'd been too smart to become a warrior.

My pulse doubled with doubt. Would he be proud or disappointed when I took the next step and became a warrior?

An image of him hiding behind the boulders near this camp flashed in my head. Why did he need to hide if he'd wanted to find the banshees to help rescue me? Banshee perimeter guards surrounded him. They raised their weapons and attacked.

"No!" Why would they hurt Grandfather when he'd come to them for assistance?

The image kaleidoscoped and the perimeter guards searched the boulders, bushes, and caves.

My mind fuzzed. Who were they searching for? They'd already found Grandfather. Or had they?

My world tilted again, and I gripped my stomach to stop from being sick.

Stone hiked up a path on the side of a mountain. My heart ached. He appeared tired and disheveled. Dirt caked his handsome face and he wore the same clothes I'd last seen him in. "We'll find a place to hide and sleep for the night."

He must be hiding from the regent and his army. At least they were alive after losing the battle.

He crossed his arms and surveyed the area.

The path looked similar to the one I'd taken with Charmig to the banshee encampment. I'd been traveling in a tent on the back of the animal, but scanned around wanting to memorize where he'd taken me.

"I'll scout for water." Lukas wiped at his matted hair.

"Oh my stars." Cassia tugged her black and green hair. "I'll come with you."

"I'll dig around for a crevice or cave we can hide in." Pith took off toward the boulders.

All my other friends came into view except Violet, Helartha, and Gnit who'd ventured to a coven for help.

The vision changed and with it came blistering pain on my left wrist. "No! I want to see them."

"No!" Grandfather screamed before the healer gave him a shot.

He punched out and hit the healer on the chin. His wrist must've hurt when he punched because my own wrist burned like it was on fire.

"Let me go!" Grandfather's shout pierced through my lungs like a bullet.

Banshee warriors chanted in a deep, constant thrum. Were they inside the tent with me? Was Grandfather? The chant sounded dark and powerful.

Evil.

A dark chill drifted through my skin and into my bones.

Grandfather disappeared, but my wrist still scalded. I struggled to break free from whatever held me down. Opening my eyes, I realized the torment was real.

Svante and Charmig held my shoulders. His father clutched my left wrist in a harsh grip. With his other hand he held a fiery, molten, glowing steel tip. The tip dug into my skin and branded me.

"Ahhhhhhhh!" My scream morphed into dozens of screams.

Not screams.

Wailing. Banshees wailing.

An indication that someone was going to die.

Considering the intense gleam in Gorig's gaze as he carved me with a searing branding stick onto my inner wrist, I had to wonder if it was me.

Was I going to die?

CHAPTER SEVEN

The wailing continued, and I continued screaming. My throat hurt and my heart was sore. Sore from this painful assault.

Charmig grimaced and Svante's grim face exhibited strain as they held me down.

I thrashed. "Grandfatherrrrrrrr!"

If I wasn't dying, was he?

"Shut her up." Gorig's harshness sliced but did not cause as much pain as the blazing metal point scarring my skin. I thought he'd cared about me a little. "I'm almost done."

Done with what? Killing me? "Ahhhhhhhh!"

Svante's hand covered my mouth.

The wailing outside the tent continued.

If I wasn't dying and Grandfather wasn't dying, who could it be? Snippets from my dreams haunted me. I'd seen Stone, Lukas, Cassia, Pith, and my other friends. Was one of them dying?

Breathing through my nose, I tried to calm myself. If they were going to kill me, they would've done it already. I wished I could read their minds. If I wasn't being held down, I'd show them my powers and blast them to pieces.

Focusing, I narrowed my gaze and glowered at the leader torturing me. I bore deep into his eyes. I actually didn't care what he was thinking. I only wanted him to stop.

Stop using the hot metal stick. Stop using the hot metal stick. Stop using the hot metal stick.

The pain on my wrist ceased.

"Is it complete?" Svante asked.

"I think so." Gorig sounded confused.

Not as confused as me. What was he doing to me and did I make him stop? Puffing out in relief, I blinked a few times to clear my head. My wrist sizzled.

The hand slipped from my mouth and Charmig brushed a finger across my sweaty brow. "Destiny? Are you alright?"

My raw throat scratched. My body trembled and I was too weak to struggle against those holding me. "What...what...did you do to me?"

"You're a warrior of our clan." Grand Lord Justicar's voice rang loud. He stood at the tent opening. "Lys Destiny has joined the Skjult Banshee Clan and become a warrior!"

Cheers erupted outside.

"I thought..." I tried to clear my head. "I thought this was the initiation ceremony." That's what Lykke had said, that's what Charmig had said, that's what the leader had said.

Svante leered and grabbed my shoulder to help me sit. "Because of your age, we sped up the process and combined the ceremonies, Lys Destiny."

Something about the way he spoke made me not believe him. And what was this Lys nonsense? My mind was too hazed to comprehend. I wanted to lay down again.

Charmig grabbed my other shoulder, and the two of them lifted me to my feet. They half-dragged and half-carried me outside the tent. Gorig clutched my arm and raised it high.

A mark—no, a tattoo—burned on my wrist.

Shock stopped my heart for a second. Then it rushed forward competing in a running race. I blinked a couple of times trying to make out the tattoo held up high for everyone to see.

The crowd of banshees cheered again. This wasn't the banshee wail of death. It was a cheer of celebration or respect.

Except I'd done nothing to earn their respect.

I jerked my arm free and glared. The coarse black lines displayed a dark circle with interwoven points and curlicues. It looked similar to the tattoos I'd seen on Charmig, Svante, and the other warriors. Something about it was different. Maybe it was the fact that I was a woman or the red skin surrounding the branded area or that I might've stopped the leader from finishing the tattoo.

The fiery sensation returned, this time to my chest. "What the heks is this?"

The name of the special scream came out in my question. The searing raged into an inferno of anger. I wanted to explode. One brand was enough. Majiks already avoided me because of the banshee mark on my forehead. They had no right to mar my skin without permission. I'd been unconscious. There'd been no consent.

"What. The. Heks. Is. This?" I repeated, louder this time.

"Skjult Banshee Clan warrior rune." Charmig nodded at Svante and the two of them cut through the crowd, half-carrying and half-dragging me between them.

"I got mine when I was twelve." Svante boasted and flaunted his rune.

"I didn't give anyone permission to give me a tattoo." It was hard to sound furious when I couldn't even walk.

"You did when you agreed to be part of the clan and become a warrior." Svante dismissed me as if I was a child. "The hunt will complete the bond."

The two of them entered the largest tent and set me on a pile of blankets. A brownie scurried away from a banquet table filled with the same food from outside.

Charmig grabbed a plate and filled it. "Tonight, we celebrate."

"Indeed, we do." Svante filled two gold glasses with a sparkling red liquid.

No joy popped in me. I felt flat.

The two sat on either side of me on the blankets.

I crossed my legs and rocked back and forth. My dry mouth and fuzzy head were hungover. There'd been something in the steam to make me pass out.

"Drink?" Svante held out one of the glasses.

Shaking my head, I gaped at the tattoo. The black mark edged with red. It blazed like the devil himself.

Charmig held his plate in front of me. "Eat something. You must be starving."

Even though I should be hungry, I was queasy. I shook my head. Just as the tattoo scorched, so did my anger—an inferno banked to slow burn. I wanted to scream at the leader. Tell him he'd violated me and my trust.

"I'm going to talk to your father." I went to stand and tumbled back onto the blankets. My weak body wasn't ready to move on my own, causing the anger to turn inward and boil. I should be strong, not weak. I needed to tell him what I thought about them marking me without my permission and probably drugging me. I wanted to stand up for what I believed in, but I couldn't stand.

"Eat." Charmig tucked a blanket around me. "What's done is done. The mark is permanent. Nothing you can do about it now."

Smashing my mouth together, I fisted my hands. I remembered his father telling them to make me shut up. I'd thought the man cared about me, even with his brusque attitude. "Where is your father?"

We were in his tent. It was set up for a feast. But only the three of us had come inside. Charmig and Svante must be protecting me. Or watching me. Were they my guards? They'd been called Prospectives. What was that? The only ones I wanted watching over me were my grandfather and Stone. One was sick and the other missing.

My chest throbbed with pain.

"I'm sure Charmig's father is busy." Svante's sly smile raised my hackles.

My exhausted body trembled. My head hurt and I couldn't keep my eyes open. I wanted to collapse. I refused to fall asleep in a strange tent, especially with Charmig and Svante watching me.

"I'm tired." I yawned, emphasizing my point.

"May I escort you to your bed, Lys Destiny?" Charmig jumped at my statement.

Svante tensed beside me.

I couldn't stand, let alone walk. I needed help. "Yes."

Svante gasped and tossed back the rest of his drink acting the sore loser.

Loser at what I didn't understand. I didn't care.

Charmig reached beneath my arms and pulled me to my feet. He held his body a little too close and I leaned backward. Throwing a wicked smile at the other man, Charmig gripped my arm and helped me to my tent.

Stepping inside, he led me to the bed. "Iban, tell Lykke that Destiny and I have arrived."

My brow furrowed. I was too tired and achy to care about how he ordered the brownie. Collapsing onto the mattress, I closed my eyes and willed the haziness and pain away.

The bed bounced and a heavy weight settled beside me. Was Lykke going to force me to undress before sleep? I rolled over and a strong hand gripped the back of my head. A rich musky scent wove around me.

Not Lykke's flowery perfume or incense.

My body stiffened and my eyes flew open.

Charmig lay on the bed wearing absolutely nothing. His face was inches away. His lips came toward mine.

Shock shriveled my insides. I raised my free hand and slapped him across the cheek. I wished I wasn't so weak or I'd hit him harder. "What do you think you're doing? Get out of my bed!"

"Kissing you." He rolled onto his back, exposing his bare parts. "Unless you'd rather get right to the good stuff."

Adrenaline had me jumping out of bed. My knees failed and I grabbed the mattress to hold myself up. "You have no right to touch me."

His father had no right to brand my skin either. I rubbed the sore spot.

"I have every right." He pushed up onto his elbows. "You invited me."

"I did not." How could he believe that? Because I let him escort me to my tent? "I love someone else."

"Not Svante." Charmig sneered and his expression changed to disgust. "It must be the giant oaf."

Pinching my lips, I refused to acknowledge anything. I hadn't even told Stone how I felt, and the last time I saw him we'd argued. How did Charmig know about Stone?

"Charmig." Lykke stood in the doorway. The horror on her face would've been comical except she wasn't horrified for me. She wasn't upset by his nudity. She was upset at seeing us together. "Lys Destiny is tired after the ceremony. Now is not the time."

It would never be the time. He might act charming, but he was pompous and had kidnapped me.

All allure fled from his features. Red flagged his cheeks, and his eyes turned a furious shade of black. His anger directed at Lykke, even though she'd never raised her voice above a whisper. Leaping off the bed, he fisted his hands and I thought he might punch her.

Holding my breath, I got ready to leap to her defense. No man had the right to hit a woman or take advantage of her.

He bent down to snatch his clothes from the ground and my body sagged in relief. He shoved his legs in the shula and strutted past her toward the tent door. "When you're finished here, come to me."

Lykke nodded and watched him flee the tent.

My stomach clenched as I approached her slowly. "Are you okay?"

She fake-smiled and pulled the covers down on the bed. "Would you like me to help you undress?"

Even though she asked, by her fast speech I could tell she'd rather be somewhere else. With Charmig to hopefully get an apology? Although I really didn't believe he'd give her one. He wasn't a nice guy.

"No. I'm going right to sleep."

"Are you sure? Is there anything you need?" She hurried toward the tent door.

"No." I plopped onto the bed and shivered. I didn't want to think about the night's events.

Hunting below the treeline on Drage mountain, I checked my new halberd for the millionth time. The black rock had been shaped to a fine point and was sharp enough to cut skin and kill. Leather strips wound around the handle while colored and carved etchings decorated the long stem.

Charmig and Svante trekked next to me, never leaving my side. Again, I had to wonder if they were my protectors or guards.

My sandaled feet clomped on the hard ground. The shula and bikini top had been replaced by a long, black tunic to blend into the mountainside. A long cape tied around my neck dragged on the ground. My body ached from hiking and climbing and the cold. Every chill hit my bones.

I scowled at my warrior rune. "Why aren't there other female warriors?"

The initiation and forced tattooing of my skin had taken place days ago. My mind fuzzed. Or had it been last night?

"You know you're the only female warrior." Svante actually sounded considerate as if he wanted to tell me more.

"Why am I out here?" With the male warriors? If females weren't warriors, why had they initiated me? Why had they tattooed me?

Charmig patted my arm through the thick cape. "For the rune to bond you to my father, you must make your first kill."

Bile rose in my throat. "Of an animal?"

Svante whistled a short tune. "Sure."

"Of course." Charmig's more forceful answer satisfied.

Trudging on, I tried to organize my thoughts and emotions. I'd never killed an animal before. When I started gathering food for Grandfather, we'd become vegetarians. He was the only reason I stayed with the banshee clan now.

"This way." An advanced scout signaled our threesome and we followed on silent feet.

My feet might be silent, but my heart pounded.

I didn't want to kill. They should've warned me about this part, and the tattoo. My mind fuzzed again. I needed to complete the process of becoming a warrior.

We rounded a corner where the rest of the warriors awaited. In front of us was an entrance to a cave, an extremely dark cave.

Wooziness surrounded my head, and I blinked a few times. For some reason, the opening looked familiar.

Svante and Charmig conferred in whispers with the scout warrior. They came back to me standing at the edge of the pack.

Charmig smiled and winked. "There's a bear inside."

This was no time for him to be flirting. "Don't smile. A cute, cuddly bear is about to meet its demise."

"Bears kill." Svante growled.

"I don't want to kill a bear." I didn't want to kill anything, not in cold blood. Fighting the guards in the palace dungeon had been different. A battle for life and death. "Why don't you do it for me?"

Svante seemed to be the killing type. He frowned and exasperation flashed in his dark eyes. "This trip is for you. It's about you. We've found the appropriate target for you."

He made me sound spoiled. I didn't want my new family to believe I was selfish.

"You can do this, Lys Destiny." Charmig's cheering stiffened my resolve. "Remember this is for your grandfather."

He was right. Hunters, human and majik, killed animals all the time. For safety and food and clothing. This bear's meat would feed the clan. Its pelt would keep banshees warm. I could do this. I had to do this. For the warriors who'd trekked with me. For my new clan. For my grandfather.

I gripped my halberd tight, turning my knuckles white. Blowing out, I tiptoed forward. I edged around the rock to the front of the dark cave. The bear lay deeper inside. I crept forward. Its fur went up and down with its breathing. Moving closer, I smelled an evergreen scent.

At this point, if the bear woke up and discovered me, killing it would be self-defense. That could be risky. The bear could attack. I had to make the first move.

I raised my weapon high above my head. I'd need my strength to kill with one shot. The tip of the halberd would slice through the pelt and into the heart.

My body trembled. Adrenaline and fear pumped through me causing my pulse to race.

I started to thrust in a downward motion. A glimpse of blond strands bulleted panic through my bloodstream. I couldn't stop. Forward momentum carried the weapon down.

Everything inside me screeched. This was wrong.

The halberd pierced through its chest.

An agonized scream rose from the body. The scream didn't resemble a bear's.

It sounded human.

Horrified disbelief scraped through my lungs.

The bear flopped, and the fur fell away.

My brow furrowed and confusion swirled in my brain. How could a bear's pelt fall off?

The fur fell further revealing a man. A dead man.

Not just any man either.

Stone.

I swallowed the scream echoing in my heart.

I'd killed Stone.

CHAPTER EIGHT

"**I** apologize for my behavior last night." Lykke bowed to me the second I woke up.

I squeezed my eyes tight, uncomfortable with her observing me while I slept. Especially after my nightmare. I shivered. The banshees had tricked me into killing Stone. Was it a dream or a premonition? It certainly wasn't a blocked memory.

Staring at her I tried to remember what she had to apologize for. My mind was still hazy. She'd interrupted Charmig and I last night. A good thing. She had nothing to be sorry for. Fisting my hands, I wanted to punch someone. And it wasn't her.

"The one who should apologize is Charmig." I tossed back the covers. "What was he thinking trying to kiss me?"

"It is his right." She pivoted and gathered a bowl of steaming hot water and a towel.

"How is it his right?" I swung my legs over the edge of the bed and stomped my bare feet on the floor. "I just met him. I was tired, almost incoherent after the initiation ceremony. I appreciated that he wanted to walk me back to my tent. It was not an invitation for anything else."

"Our ways say otherwise." She kept her back to me, her cloak blocking her stance and body language. Her tone was loud and clear. Sadness and defeat.

She had feelings for Charmig. I didn't understand why. He acted nice. But I saw beneath the thin veneer of charm.

"Your ways are wrong." I wasn't going to go into a speech about rights.

"*Our* ways." Her emphasis punched me in the gut.

The red edges of the new tattoo burned and itched. I was one of them now. The tattoo proved that. But I wasn't brought up with their ways and I wouldn't succumb to everything Grand Lord Justicar decreed. I wouldn't jump into action at his request like the warriors. The thought of having an extended family and other banshees to teach me about my magic had lured me. The knowledge I'd be able to heal Grandfather incentivized me. But I wouldn't do whatever the male banshees wanted.

"*Our* ways need to change." When Lykke didn't respond, I rushed to get dressed. "I want to see my grandfather."

I wanted to show him the tattoo and tell him I'd be able to help him soon.

Entering the healer's tent, I surveyed Grandfather and any changes—good or bad. His eyes were open and he appeared more alert. Glee flourished inside of me. I could talk to him and find out what happened. He'd answer my questions truthfully.

Ursee used a spoon to feed him a thin liquid.

"How is my grandfather today?" I wrung my hands. Worry and anxiety tied a knot in my belly. I had so many things to tell him and to ask. The initiation ceremony was fine. I was a banshee after all. But the tattoo...

"You're alone today?" She spoke quietly. Her cloak covered most of her body.

Did she not want to startle my grandfather or was there a more nefarious reason?

A male brownie scurried out of the tent. So unlike Iban who I'd spoken to a couple of times.

Nodding at the healer, I stepped closer to the bed. "Can I help feed him?"

"Of course." She stood and handed me the bowl. "Go slowly. He hasn't eaten in a while."

My hopes rose. It was good that he was doing better, maybe then I could get him transferred to a real hospital. There he could get nutrition through feeding tubes, diagnostic tests and brain scans, and any other number of medical techniques. "Why don't you have any real hospital equipment?"

"We relocate a lot and rely on the ancient ways." She stirred something in a bowl with a stone pestle.

Some traditions were fine. But if there were modern ways to do it, why not at least combine the two?

"Hello, Grandfather." I slid a full spoon of broth into his mouth. "It's Destiny. You need to eat to get your strength."

His head turned toward me and his eyes flashed. He licked his dry lips and opened his mouth. "Dest—"

He coughed.

Squeezing his hand, I shifted closer. He was going to get better. "Yes, Grandfather. It's me."

"Destiny." His expression firmed and pain flashed in his gaze. "You shouldn't—" He coughed more.

"The broth will soothe your throat." I put the spoon to his lips.

"No!" He whacked the spoon out of my hand and it clattered to the floor. He grabbed my arm in an iron fist and gaped at the tattoo on my wrist. Horror etched on his face. "Noooo!"

I tried to loosen his hold as fear for him and from him ratcheted up inside. "Grandfather, you're hurting me." I glanced at the healer.

She paused her grinding. Her wide dark eyes showed surprise. Her mouth dropped open, and she flailed her hands in panic.

"Grandfather?" I used a pacifying voice even while my pulse charged. "You're hurting me. Please let me go."

His strong grip wasn't one of a man at the gates of death.

"You didn't..." He panted heavily and a tear slid down his cheek. "Tell me you didn't..."

"Didn't what?" Using my free hand, I rubbed his fingers trying to comfort him and loosen his hold. Now, I understood why they'd had to keep him restrained sometimes. He was strong.

He coughed and loosened his grip. "No, Destiny. Not you. I tried to keep you away..." he coughed more.

"Keep me away from the palace?" I'd been there. He'd tried to hide me in the other room at our home and didn't tell the guards that had come for him that I was a banshee too.

His chest rose and fell erratically. He was upset and I didn't know how to help. My mind whirled trying to find something to placate him. "I kept you hidden...you weren't safe..."

"What's going on here?" Gorig marched into the healer's tent with Svante at his side. The two wore shulas and warm cloaks. "Why aren't you keeping him comfortable, healer?"

"I'm sorry." Ursee bowed and picked up a needle.

So it wasn't only the warriors who jumped at his command.

"He's dangerous when he's out of control." Svante pulled me away from my grandfather but didn't hold too tight.

"No!" Grandfather yelled and thrashed on the small cot. "Please, don't. I need to tell..."

Jerking out of Svante's grip, I blocked the healer from getting closer, desperation giving me strength. "No. Give him a minute. Let him talk."

"Do it now," the leader ordered.

Svante grabbed my arms tighter and held me back. His expression was blank. "It's to keep him and others safe."

The shot went into Grandfather's arm, and he settled down. He stopped yelling and his eyes closed.

Svante let me go and I lunged to Grandfather's side. My lower lip trembled. "Tell me what, Grandfather? Tell me what?"

His breath evened out and he slept.

I didn't understand what was going on. He'd been so upset and stronger than expected. He'd been lucid. "Why did you do that? I wanted to know what he was going to say."

Ursee twisted her hands together and regarded Gorig. "Um...well...we need to...to keep him calm. It's best for his condition."

The brownie who'd hurried out of the tent and come back with the leader and Svante, picked up the discarded shot from the table and left again. Gorig nodded at Svante and left the tent knowing everything and everyone was under control.

"It's for the good of the clan." Svante spoke with stilted authority. His hand reached out toward me. "He's a risk to everyone here, including you."

"If Ursee was doing her job, my grandfather would be better." I swiped his hand off, not wanting his or anyone's touch. Anyone except Grandfather's. "What is his condition? Why isn't anyone telling me what's wrong with him?"

Ursee avoided my gaze. "You'll have to ask Grand Lord Justicar."

I hated how everything was up to him. When I could see my grandfather, the combining of the ceremonies, even the fact that I wasn't allowed to bathe or dress myself. I firmed my lips and straightened my back.

"Why can't you tell me?" I advanced toward her wondering how she'd react if I stuck a needle in her. "You're the healer."

Svante grabbed my arm and tugged me away. "Now, Destiny."

"It's not my place." She took a step back and bumped into the table holding her medical paraphernalia. She appeared afraid, but not of me. Her gaze kept going toward Svante standing behind me.

I took a deep breath soothing my anger. Approaching it from a sympathetic viewpoint might help. She was a healer and deserved respect, even if Svante and the leader didn't give it to her. "He's my grandfather. It's my place to know about his health."

"You'll have to talk to Grand Lord Justicar." Svante held the tent flap open.

Glaring at him, I gave Grandfather a final glance. "Oh, I will." I marched out of the tent planning to find out what had happened to him, what was wrong with him, and what was in the shot.

Stepping out of the tent, the cloudy day suited my dark mood.

Svante followed me and took hold of my arm to escort me. "Grand Lord Justicar is a busy man. He made a special visit to see your grandfather. Maybe I can help you?" His rough tone sent a shiver down my spine. "What did your grandfather say to you before I arrived?"

Shaking my head, I tried to clear my mind. "He was more coherent. Talking to me, trying to tell me something..."

Grandfather had been upset about the tattoo. He'd been trying to tell me how he'd tried to keep me away. Away from what? The palace, the banshee clan, or something else? Although he'd come to the banshees for help

I decided I wasn't going to tell Svante anything. I wanted answers. "I want to know what his diagnosis is and what the healer is giving my grandfather in those shots."

"Her job is not to explain a diagnosis. She's doing as ordered." Svante gripped my elbow a little too hard.

Passing the warriors in the fighting circle, two warriors faced off against each other. Their sharpened poles clashed as they fought and wrestled. Other warriors normally stood around cheering or jeering. It seemed to be an everyday occurrence. Today they watched while packing up the extra weapons and training items. They spied us and put their heads back down.

Svante gave them a tight-lipped grin. "Why don't we stroll around the camp and work off your anger. Grand Lord Justicar is busy."

"No." I broke Svante's hold. "I want to talk to him now."

"Women don't demand." His snide tone proved his real personality. No big surprise. He acted the bigot. "They obey orders."

He could stuff his philosophy. I'd force my way into the tent if I had to. I was tired of their chauvinistic ways. I ripped my arm out of his. "This woman doesn't obey orders."

His body stilled, shocked by my words and actions. I was in too much of a hurry to laugh. I'd catch the chauvinistic Grand Lord Justicar by surprise. Except I couldn't waltz past the guards on duty at the leader's tent.

Svante caught up to me and told me to wait a second and disappeared into the leader's tent while I stood outside by the guards. Why does the leader of this small clan need guards by his door? Was it to protect him from his own people?

Even though I'd been raised a hermit, I felt more at home with the other majiks in the dungeon than I did with my own kind. Sadness mellowed my anger. The banshee ways were different and unequal. Majiks had always feared banshees and I'd always believed it was because we signaled death. Maybe there were other reasons. Like their secrecy and sexism. I might've agreed to become one of them so I could heal my grandfather, but I'd never conform.

"Destiny, what a pleasant surprise." Charmig scuttled out of the tent. "You missed my father."

My shoulders sagged. "I really need to talk to him." I scowled at the tattoo on my wrist and the pain brought my anger levels up again. "About several things."

"I know where he went. Can I take you to him?"

I stiffened and took a step back, remembering last night.

"I can tell by your expression that I upset you." Now, who was the mind reader? He led me away from his father's tent, probably so the guards couldn't hear. "I want to apologize for last night."

"Go ahead." I wasn't one to hold grudges. I did remember them. I refused to make his apology easy.

His brows furrowed. "I just did."

Chortling at his arrogance, I wouldn't let him brush his attack aside. He'd probably gotten away with a lot since he was handsome and the leader's son. "That wasn't an apology."

He angled his head and considered me. He believed he could brush the attempted kiss and nakedness aside.

I crossed my arms and tapped my foot. "You said you wanted to apologize so go ahead and actually apologize."

He cleared his throat and took hold of my hand, making a big production out of a simple act. "I'm sorry."

Uncomfortableness crawled across my skin knowing others watched. "For?"

"For attempting to kiss you and getting into your bed." He spoke the last part louder, wanting others to hear he was in my bed.

Svante had just stepped outside the tent and growled. He disappeared back inside.

I ignored the ugly accusation in my mind. I wanted to make a point with him. "And?"

"And?" He arched his brows as if this was a joke.

It wasn't. I snatched my hand away. "And you won't do it again."

"I won't ever do it again," he winked, "unless you want me to."

Fisting my hands, I wanted to tell him never. But I didn't need another enemy. "Now, will you take me to your father?"

His cheeks reddened and he seemed taken aback. Had he expected me to immediately let him kiss me? Never going to happen. I loved Stone and I needed to find out what had happened to him. Because I hadn't killed him like in my dream.

Maybe Charmig didn't know where his father was and this was an excuse to be seen with me.

"Yes, let's go find my father." He went to take my hand and I yanked it away. He pouted. "I thought you forgave me?"

"I've been walking since I was two years old. I don't need assistance." I hated how they escorted me everywhere. I could find my way.

We trekked past the same group of warriors. I knew they noticed us because they immediately peered in the other direction.

My ribs tightened. I'd wanted to make friends of my own kind while staying with the banshees. I'd wanted to learn their ways and their history, even if I didn't agree with them. The only ones who really tried to get to know me were Svante, Charmig, and Lykke. Although she might be forced into being nice. "Why do the banshees avoid me?"

"They must not see you passing." Charmig's glib answer was wrong. I knew they'd seen me.

"When I pass, they look away." Acceptance was important to me, especially if I planned to change things around here. For example, the way they treated women and the brownies. I was now officially part of their clan, and yet I didn't feel like I belonged. How could I make changes if they didn't accept and respect me?

He took a few seconds to answer. "Banshees are known to be shy."

Shy or secretive? Or ordered to look away?

"You're not shy."

"They don't know you well and want to respect your privacy." His excuses kept piling up.

I didn't believe any of them. "The one warrior who did talk to me called me Lys Destiny. You and Svante have said it too." And I'd heard it in my dreams. "What does *Lys* mean?"

"Light." Charmig spat out. "It means you are the light."

My blood lashed through my body setting off electrical pulses. The deference, the servant and large tent, and the crown head-piece started to make sense. "What?"

Charmig waved his arms around as if reciting a prophecy. "Our hope. Our future. Our destiny."

CHAPTER NINE

No pressure or anything.

I didn't feel light. Darkness and shadows crossed my soul.

And what did he mean by *our Destiny?* I wasn't his—regardless how he'd tried to make it happen last night, and I wasn't the Skjult Banshee Clan's. I was my own person, and I decided my own destiny.

My mother's grandmother had given me the name Destiny for a reason. I'd never been told why. Was this the reason? Did she, and the other banshees, believe I was here to help them secure their future? What exactly did that entail? A loss of my freedom and rights? Leading them into the future? Having banshee babies?

Bile rose up my throat and I wanted to barf. To have banshee babies, I'd have to be with a banshee. Charmig and Svante both acted possessive toward me. Between the two of them and Lykke, I barely had any time alone. Any time to think about Stone and my friends or figure out what to do about Grandfather once he was healed.

"Destiny. It's wonderful to see you've fully recovered from the initiation." Gorig snuck out from the healer's tent, followed by Svante.

Weird because he'd left the tent a few minutes ago. And why was he visiting my grandfather again? More shots? I frowned, ready to throw accusation after accusation. I had to handle one thing at a time. I'd worry about the Lys thing later.

"You didn't warn me about the tattoo." I held up my wrist and shook it. I hadn't had time to confront him about this in the healer's tent.

"It's an honor to be marked as part of the Skjult Banshee Clan." Svante's offense seemed fake.

"My grandfather wasn't happy when he saw it." Or had he even seen it? Maybe he was upset about something else. It was difficult to tell.

"He recognized it?" Gorig squeaked. Then he smiled in a benevolent way making my shoulders tighten with discomfort. "He is getting better."

Grandfather was the most important thing to discuss. "What is the healer giving my grandfather? He was coherent and talking to me one second and then she gave a the shot and he was unconscious."

Charmig's expression pinched and so did his father's. Svante glowered. I didn't trust any of them to tell the truth. I had to keep asking questions, I had to keep pushing.

Gorig pointed at the campfire area. "Sit down and have tea with me."

A brownie scrambled to put a blanket on a log before he sat down. Another brownie servant carried a tea tray. Was this little talk planned or were the brownies always prepared for a spot of tea? Another thing I didn't appreciate about this clan. If I was going to be their future, I'd free the brownies from servitude.

I took a seat and a steaming cup. Waiting until the leader took a sip, I blew on the hot brew. I'd been poisoned by them before and I remembered. Bitterness filled my mouth.

The two brownies who served us were the only ones not rushing around the edge of the encampment, carrying things or being yelled at by banshees. In fact, every banshee was busy too, darting about camp. Except for the four of us.

"The warrior who found your grandfather described him as...how do I put this delicately?" He took another sip of tea.

"I don't need delicate. I need the truth." I slammed the cup into the saucer and it clattered similar to my nerves.

He took another sip, contemplating what to say next. "Senile."

The bile rose again in my throat. Grandfather was smart as a fox, sly. He'd never shown signs of dementia. "I want to know everything."

"When the perimeter guards found him, your grandfather was talking to a rock and mumbling incoherently. His clothes were ripped and dirty. His face and hands hadn't been washed. No injuries were visible."

My heart wept, picturing the scene. He'd been alone and afraid. Desperate to help me. He must've been lost for a long time.

"Your grandfather fought against the warriors, but his demons appeared to be invisible." Gorig took another sip of tea as if discussing a crazy banshee was normal.

Was it? And if so, why?

Dehydration could cause hallucinations. "Are you saying my grandfather is permanently crazy?"

Charmig had hinted at the same thing. I straightened my shoulders. I didn't believe it. Grandfather was an intelligent and strong man. He'd been coherent for a few minutes and hadn't lost his faculties. He knew the mountains and the city of Lindenhamn. He never would've gotten lost. So what happened?

My pulse raced thinking of his struggles.

Gorig patted my thigh, sympathy oozing from him. "The healer didn't know what to think when he was brought to us. She believed keeping your grandfather calm was the best thing so he didn't hurt himself or anyone else."

"Is he being sedated?" I quirked my head. She said she took orders from him.

"A combination of drugs to heal and pacify."

Grandfather must've been kept sedated for a long time, which wasn't good for him mentally or physically. "I think the healer needs to stop giving the medication so he's conscious long enough to use his muscles. To talk to me."

Charmig scooted in next to me on the log. "Once your powers are unlocked you can help him."

His father stood. "We'll push up the Unlocking Ceremony to tomorrow. Afterwards, we will stop your grandfather's medication and you can talk to him yourself."

I really wanted to talk to Grandfather before taking another step. He hadn't been happy about the tattoo. Or that's what I thought he meant. "What if we don't have the ceremony tomorrow, the healer stops giving Grandfather the shot, and I talk to him before I take another step?"

The leader shook his head in a slow back and forth motion. "We tried taking him off the medication and your grandfather went...crazy again. Whatever this illness or malady is, it is affecting his mind. Plus, we're relocating and it's best if he sleeps through the journey."

I gulped down air. "Relocating can't be good for him."

"We must relocate for the ceremony and we're meeting others." The leader set his teacup in the saucer, indicating this wasn't negotiable.

The ceremony was necessary for me to help Grandfather. He had shouted at me, telling me he didn't want me near him. His yells had been mostly incoherent and he fought when he was restrained. I sighed. The sooner I completed the Unlocking Ceremony, the sooner I'd have all my magic, and the sooner I could heal him. And find out what happened to him. I wanted my magic and my memories.

"What does the Unlocking Ceremony entail? What will happen to me?" I glared at the unwanted tattoo.

"Very simple." He handed the cup to a brownie without saying thanks. "The ceremony unbinds your locked magic."

"And my memories?" Because my past would help me to unlock my future.

"Of course." He stood, dismissing me.

Unsure, I didn't see any other path forward. According to him, I needed my magic unlocked to heal Grandfather. And if the leader lied, I'd use my powers against him. "I'll visit with Grandfather again. Maybe the shot has worn off and he'll be able to tell me more."

"Yes, wouldn't that be wonderful." Svante's sarcasm wasn't directed at me. He seemed to be throwing shade at the leader.

I didn't care about their relationship. The three of them were the leaders of the clan. They didn't need me. Although from the brownies' servant status and Lykke's subservience, maybe the clan needed me.

Back inside the healer's tent, I took a seat by my grandfather. Ursee had stepped out, maybe to talk to the leader. I picked up Grandfather's wrist and felt his steady pulse. His old-fashioned watch ticked in a similar beat. At least he was getting plenty of sleep. Exhausted, I slumped back in the chair and closed my eyes for a second.

The information I'd been provided by the banshees twisted and tangled in my mind like a treacherous winding path up a mountain. My head lolled.

Visions of ringing bells, white dresses, and flowers filled my head. The rich scent of roses tickled my nose as I straightened the old-fashioned white dress I wore. A lace veil covered my face. I peered down the aisle and recognized Stone standing at the end. The urge to run down the aisle to be by his side charged in my veins. His long blond ponytail hung past his broad shoulders and down his back. I couldn't see his face, but I knew he'd be beaming.

Music thronged. Flower petals fell from the sky.

Nerves spiraled inside. I hadn't told Stone I loved him yet, but we were committing to each other for life. A step was missing. The step where we actually spent time together, where we made up after our argument, where we told each other how we felt.

My legs trembled as I walked down the aisle. My heart told me to hurry, while my head wanted me to stop, stop, stop. Banshees from my clan lined the aisle. They wore their finest shulas and lots and lots of jewelry. The warriors slammed the ends of their weapons in a perfect rhythm as if being controlled by a puppet master. The thronging music changed to a drum battering and a horn wailing.

Reaching the front, I smiled at Grand Lord Justicar. As leader, he had the right to join the two of us together. I turned to my future husband.

Stone faced me. His hair darkened and his attractive grin morphed into a smirk. His green eyes changed to black. He winked.

My lungs shriveled.

Not Stone. Charmig.

I tilted away. "What's going on?"

"A wedding, of course." Charmig grabbed my left hand.

"No. No." My empty chest echoed. "Not to you."

"To me." The hands holding mine changed, becoming longer and thinner. Svante. He shoved a gaudy gold ring on my finger.

"No!"

My scream woke me and I bolted up in the chair. Panting, I scanned the tent.

Grandfather snored deeply, resting comfortably. By the light in the tent, I'd been here for hours. He wasn't going to wake up any time soon.

Standing shakily, I wiped my wet cheeks and scurried out of the healer's tent. I needed air to clear my head from the dream.

Because what if it hadn't been a dream? What if it was my future?

"Hello, Destiny. How is your grandfather doing?" Lykke asked the second I entered the tent.

Maybe she did care. If only she knew what had occurred this morning. I shuddered. "He's sleeping. All he does is sleep."

He hadn't said another word. Melancholy drifted through me. At least he'd been peaceful, unlike my nightmare.

"I'm sorry." She flipped the covers off the bed and folded the comforter.

Brownies dashed here and there through the room, not even trying to hide from me any longer. Iban dragged a trunk.

I picked up the side of the trunk and helped her get it next to the bed. "Where are we relocating?"

Lykke shrugged. "Grand Lord Justicar does not tell me these things. If I had to guess, we're headed higher up the mountain for your ceremony."

He'd said he wanted me to complete the next step tomorrow. "Why do we need to relocate for a ceremony?"

The two combined ceremonies had happened at this location just fine. Well, at least according to Grand Lord Justicar. I still got mad at the thought.

"It is not my place to know." She ripped off the sheets ending the questioning.

I gave up asking her about anything important. "How can I help?"

"You can't help. It is not your place."

Tired of being told about my place, maybe she could help me sort out the meaning. "I've been told I'm Lys. You've used the term yourself. Is that why I can't help?"

She stopped mid-fold of the sheets and perused me warily. "Why do you want to know?" A bit of fear edged her tone. Did she think she might get in trouble for my knowledge?

"Charmig said something to me."

She let the sheets fall onto the mattress. "Oh."

Was she upset that I had questions or that Charmig had told me because she was jealous? I huffed. She had nothing to be jealous about me and Charmig. My mind flashed back to the dream.

Avoiding my gaze, she finished folding the sheets and put them in the trunk.

Lykke assisted me and talked me through things. I wanted, no needed, a friend in the banshee clan. I'd learned the importance of friendship.

She shoved my pillows into the trunk, slammed it shut, and sat on the top to latch it shut.

I sat down on the trunk next to her, helping to hold it closed. "Is your family part of the clan?"

Her eyes drifted shut, and a pained expression crossed her features. "They were." Standing, her face went pale.

"What happened?" I sensed her sadness.

She licked her lips. "My parents died. And my brother..." she glanced around expecting someone to eavesdrop.

Was it a big secret?

The brownies continued to scurry back and forth, getting twice as much packed as us. If they paid attention to us, I couldn't tell.

She placed a hand on my shoulder. To support herself or comfort me? "My brother lost a warrior battle...and was k-k-died."

I'd seen majiks die in the dungeon and die in the fight against the guards. If I hadn't been kidnapped, I'm sure I would've seen more majiks die fighting for the prince.

"I'm sorry." Sadness wove through me.

"It was years ago." She lifted her hand and sidled to a half-filled trunk. Taking clothes from a pile, she sorted and folded.

I shuffled to her side and started working silently. I took a gorgeous shula from the shelf and refolded it to fit better in the trunk. I noticed a white cloth. My hands faltered on a white lace veil and I pulled it out. A veil just like the one in my dream. "Wh-what is this?"

She grabbed the item, folded it, and shoved it into a trunk. "A veil for a ceremony."

"A w-w-wedding ceremony?" I slapped my palm to my chest.

"The veil is passed down generation to generation." She steered me to another section of the shelf. "Would you mind folding these items?" She was awkward asking for my help.

Opening my mouth, I wanted to ask again about the veil.

"The outfit you wore on your arrival was interesting." She'd burned the clothes. She obviously didn't want to talk about the veil.

"You said it was hideous." I crossed my arms. Was she lying now or then?

"It was unusual." Turning her back, she folded a long white item, not letting me get a glimpse. "It wasn't banshee clothes and not approved by Grand Lord Justicar."

He was the fashion police too?

"The outfit was human and given to me by someone special." My voice cracked with emotion.

"I thought your grandfather was your only family." She knew more about me than I knew about her.

Interesting that she believed only certain, special people could be family. "Grandfather is my family. I have friends too. Good friends."

"Friends." She twirled the word around her tongue.

"You must have friends." She was beautiful and helpful and had lived with the clan her entire life.

Angling her head, she rotated toward me. "It is not really a banshee concept."

Nerves pinged in my gut. In time, I could see us being friends. Asking might be awkward, but I wanted to have her companionship.

"I want you to be my friend." I held out my hand, hoping she saw it for what it was meant to be. A pact. A promise of friendship.

Smiling, she placed her hand in mine. "I would enjoy being friends."

"Good." Satisfaction settled in my center. I didn't completely trust her. But I believed we could talk. Trust would come. "Tell me more about yourself."

Her mouth dropped open. Bewildered, I couldn't believe no one had asked her this question before. "What do you want to know?"

"What are your goals and dreams?"

Her hands paused in the process of folding. She angled her head. "What do you mean?"

"Well, right now you're helping me." I didn't want to say servant or even ladies' maid because I didn't want to offend her by pointing out her current situation. "What do you want to do next in life?"

"This is my role." She swirled away and went back to folding things in the trunk. "I serve whoever Grand Lord Justicar tells me to. I'm happy to do so."

She tagged on the last part. She wasn't happy. She rarely smiled and only talked when spoken to.

"That's sweet of you." I didn't know what to say to get her to talk. She said she didn't have friends, but I saw the way Charmig and several other males ogled her. "What about a boyfriend?"

Her cheeks reddened. "I told you, we don't have the concept of friendship."

"I mean a boy who is a special friend. Or a girl. Someone you're connected to."

Her cheeks went redder, and she stared at the floor.

"You do." I grabbed her hand and tugged. We could bond over guys. "What's his or her name?" I had an inkling I already knew.

Guilt flashed on her face and her red cheeks went pale. "No. It's not that way. It depends on your status. Either you have an official partner who you are bonded to and intimate with, or you are free for whoever."

"I don't understand."

"Do you have a boyfriend?" Her tongue tripped on the last word and she let out a slight giggle.

I enjoyed seeing her laugh. She normally acted too serious. Was Stone my boyfriend? I didn't know what to call him. My cheeks heated. He was someone special.

"You do." She pointed at me. "Is it Charmig?"

"No, of course not." I spat out. "We've just met."

"Last night I walked in on you two, and you were about to be intimate." She peered at the floor again and I couldn't read her expression. She sniffed. "He blames me for interrupting." She sniffed again. "He'd wanted to follow the Warrior Initiation Ceremony with a partner bonding."

"Excuse me?" Outrage flared to a peak remembering last night and the dream. "He took advantage of my exhaustion."

"Took advantage?"

"When someone doesn't want to kiss another or do anything else, and he or she forces you." My outrage escalated and I strangled the cloth I held. "It's wrong."

"It's wrong?"

"Of course, it's wrong." Now I was angry for her, remembering how many males ogled her. "Everyone has a right to say no and should be respected."

"Your ways are strange." She shook her head slowly, exhibiting her disbelief and sadness.

What was sad was that she believed the way she was treated was okay. "My ways are right."

How many times would I need to tell her to make it sink in? She wasn't the problem though. It was the male banshees. I needed to talk to Grand Lord Justicar about the injustice.

If I was Lys, I wanted to use my position for the short time I was here to make a change for good.

Chapter Ten

The packed and loaded banshee encampment started on their journey in the guise of a circus parade. Drums pounded as we moved. The perimeter guards ran ahead, followed by Grand Lord Justicar traveling in the small tent perched on top of the eleram—the animal the banshees used to travel. The leader journeyed in the same tent that Charmig and I had when he'd kidnapped me.

Charmig and Svante followed behind on elerams of their own while Lykke and I shared one, which had been another whole confrontation.

Surrounding us were the most fierce warriors, holding their sharp halberds and jogging. Ursee rode on her own eleram with a pallet dragging behind. Grandfather was asleep on the pallet. They'd strapped him down to keep him in place.

Frowning, I glanced behind me as I held Lykke's bare waist. I hated that they'd forced him to relocate. Of course, we couldn't leave him behind.

His pale face and dark shadows proved he wasn't having a restful sleep. Worry gnawed at my insides. He must be tortured by dreams, or demons. No. I refused to believe he was crazy. His loose hand flailed, resembling a leaf being blown by the wind. Blankets were wrapped around his body, swaddling him tight.

Behind him came more animals packed with the possessions of the banshee clan. Which reinforced my opinion that the clan should find a permanent home or have less stuff. Behind the animals came the women and children, struggling to keep up. Many of the women carried the smaller children, adding to their burden. At least the clouds kept the sun out of their eyes.

I shifted on the saddle. The unfair logistics bothered me. None of them complained, except Charmig. I twisted my lips remembering the ruckus when we'd begun the journey.

Lykke had led me to my eleram near the smoking campfire. "Do you know how to ride?"

The wide animal wore a beautiful saddle with beading. Its long nose scratched at the curled horns on its head. Its tail swished in time to some internal beat.

It was big. My stomach clenched. I'd been half-drugged and excited to see Grandfather the last time I'd rode on one, plus I was in the tent. "No."

"Destiny will ride with me." Charmig led his beast toward us. His shula rode high on his thighs. He winked.

I hated the wink. Did he believe one sly action would make me fall in a swoon?

Svante rode up beside us. "Destiny will ride with me." The authority in his tone insinuated the leader had given him permission.

No one had asked me. I hated being fought over like a wand or a wishbone. "I want to ride with my grandfather."

"No." Svante shook both his and the beast's head.

"Your grandfather will be carried on a pallet." Charmig's hand yanked on the reins. "He is not fit to ride."

"Especially if you don't know how to ride yourself." Lykke's explanation made the most sense.

Pivoting to her, I asked, "Do you know how to ride?"

"Yes." Her gaze darted between the two males.

"I will be riding with Lykke," I mimicked Svante's authoritative tone.

Her smile widened. I couldn't tell if she was happy or panicked.

"Her station doesn't ride." Svante's upper lip curled. "She doesn't have a designated animal."

"I do. And she's my friend." I sent her a reassuring grin and then I faced both of the males. "I'm Lys," I was learning it meant I was important, "and I say Lykke rides with me."

There'd been no more discussion and satisfaction thrummed through me. Now, if they'd just listen to my demands about Grandfather. I'd work on it once we arrived at the new camp. We'd mounted and been on our way. I'd have to remember to demand next time I wanted or needed something.

I leaned forward in the leather saddle large enough for two. "Why does the clan move around so much?"

"Banshees are nomadic. Safety and hunting are the usual reasons." Doubt clung to the edges of her voice, and she peered back at me for a second before looking forward again.

"This time?"

We traveled several seconds before she answered, "Besides your ceremony and a planned meet up with someone, a perimeter guard found evidence of a small group traveling toward our encampment."

"More banshees?"

"A scouting party of some sort." She glanced around and whispered, "Majiks or humans, maybe both."

My nerves tingled with excitement. If Stone had survived the battle with the prince, would he search for me? Of course, I was moving on with the banshees. "Who spotted the clues? I want to talk to him."

She shivered. "I don't know and it's not our place to ask."

My body tensed. "I'm Lys. I deserve to know."

Shrugging, she indicated that was my prerogative. A prerogative I'd take as soon as I got the chance.

The air grew chillier as we traveled away from the areas with the steam rising through the ground and climbed higher up the mountain. I was glad I had a heated cloak. Lykke must be cold with her skimpy outfit and thin cloak. So must the women and children hiking behind us. We'd reach snow soon.

Yanking my cloak across both Lykke and me, I pondered how they could own advanced technology like the heated cloak I wore and the transport I'd flown in after the kidnapping, but still rode beasts and lived in tents. Helping them modernize would be one way to help while I stayed with them. That and changing their expectations about roles and places. Especially the stations of most women.

Lykke tried to toss off the cloak. I fought to hold it over the bare parts of her skin. "The cloak is not for me."

"You're cold, aren't you?" Maybe common sense could convince her.

"Yes." Her teeth chattered.

"You keep talking about what's expected of you and of me. If I don't understand, how can I do what's expected?" I tugged the cloak back around her and she didn't resist. "Besides, no one important is watching. They're in front of us."

"True." She cuddled into the cloak. "You know Grand Lord Justicar is the leader of the clan. Charmig," her voice softened, "and Svante are the next highest in rank."

"They're Elders." I could tell by the fact that they were riding as opposed to hiking that they were important. Plus, they'd both told me their titles. And yet, they hadn't told me mine until recently. "They're not very old."

"It's not about age. It's about proving your worth."

My mind jumbled. "No one is very old."

"Grand Lord Justicar has every right to get rid of his challengers and to groom the next leader." Her teeth gritted.

She didn't believe what she said. Had her brother been killed challenging the leader? Maybe that was the reason she had no family left. If so, why was she willing to serve?

"What do you mean by get rid of?" The term didn't bode well.

Her back stiffened again. "Warriors prove themselves in the Proving Sphere every day. Any challenges to Grand Lord Justicar's leadership are taken care of in the circle."

It was an animal kingdom where a leader must fight to survive. My forehead furrowed. "Is that why Charmig and Svante are Elders? They've beaten their challengers?"

"Correct."

"Where do I stand in the hierarchy of the clan?"

"You are Lys." She heaved. "You are important to the clan's future."

How important? Guilt churned in my gut. Even though I didn't rejoice in the banshee clan rules, they'd taken good care of me. I stayed in one of the finest tents and had Lykke helping me. They'd rescued my grandfather. And while I didn't trust their care, I didn't believe it was negligent, more of a lack of knowledge. I needed to get him to a real doctor with real medical technology.

And I needed to find out what happened to Stone and my friends.

Tugs in several directions ripped at my insides, tearing my future plans apart. I wanted to help yet knew I couldn't stay. The big question, would the clan let me go willingly?

Rubbing my hands together, I stood before a small campfire warming myself. The caravan had taken a break for an early dinner, except for the perimeter scouts who continued forward to check the path ahead. Grand Lord Justicar sat on the elaborate chair from his tent by the fire which the females had had to unpack. Svante stood by the fire drinking from a flask.

While Lykke did an errand for me, I wanted to take advantage of her absence to follow up on an earlier question. I scuttled next to Svante. "I heard the reason we moved locations was because outsiders were snooping around."

He glared down his long pointy nose at me. "Where did you hear a tale so ridiculous?"

"I heard it somewhere." I shrugged and stared into the fire. If he wasn't going to be forthcoming, I'd have to goad him into it. "I guess it's probably not your *place or station* to know."

"I know everything." The left side of his mouth lifted in a half-amused smile.

"So you know whether or not the reason we're moving is because a group was scouting our encampment?" I held my breath waiting for the answer.

"Why would you care?" He took a long slip from the flask. "We're moving for your Unlocking Ceremony."

"I was thinking my friends might be searching for me." I bit my lip. Maybe being honest wasn't the best policy.

"Banshees don't have friends." His response was similar to Lykke's except he seemed disgusted by the idea while she'd sounded wistful. "We can't even take care of our families."

I took a step away from him. "Too bad because I thought we could be friends."

He grabbed my arm and jerked me back to his side. Leering, he pursed his lips. "Friendship is not what I want from you."

The pulse in my wrist skyrocketed. I knew what he meant. It was the same thing Charmig wanted. The wedding dream spiked in my brain. No! I didn't want either of them.

"Here it is." Lykke trudged through the snow and handed me another one of my cloaks.

"Are you cold even with the heated cloak?" Svante ran a finger down my arm. He didn't seem as forceful as Charmig. "Ride with me and I'll keep you cozy."

I jerked from his hold and took the purple cloak. "No. I'm not cold." Handing the cloak back to Lykke, my lips twitched. I wanted to prove to both of them that banshees could have friends. "This cloak is for you."

"What?" She hugged the thick material while shaking her head. "No, I couldn't..."

Svante's body stiffened and he watched us with narrow eyes.

"It's cold out. I have plenty to share." My heart felt warmer than my body. I'd never owned many things and now that I did—at least while I was with the banshees—I wanted to share.

"What is the meaning of this?" He tore the cloak from her hands.

I gasped. He couldn't possibly be so stingy. I clamped a hand on my hip. "She's cold. Why wouldn't I give her one of my extras?"

"This cloak was paid for by our clan. You can't give it away." His reasoning made no sense. Lykke was part of the clan too.

I ripped the cloak back. "If it's mine, I can do what I want with it." I handed it back to Lykke. "And I want to give it to her."

"Would you help every cold banshee no matter their station?" He challenged.

"What a great idea." My smile grew into a mischievous grin. "In fact, I presume the clan purchased or made all the clothes packed away in those heavy trunks."

Lykke gave a quick nod.

"They did." Svante's voice rose, guessing what I'd do next.

"The clan should benefit." I clapped my hands, unable to hold in my excitement. I wanted to help the banshees and this was a perfect plan. "Lykke, take out my cloaks and anything else that will help people stay warm and hand them out to the women and children."

Her wide eyes appeared shocked and her lips trembled. "It is my pleasure to serve."

She hurried away to do my bidding and probably to get away from the furious expression on Svante's face.

His thick eyebrows slanted and his nose pinched. "You are unbelievable."

I smirked and gave him a slight bow. "Thank you."

He stomped away, obviously annoyed. Hopefully, he'd never ask me to ride with him again. A definite bonus to the situation.

Staying by the fire, I watched Lykke hand out items of clothing to the women and children. Exclamations and expressions of disbelief were followed by shy and grateful glances in my direction. My heart warmed even more. I may not have met them, but I still felt something for them. I didn't appreciate how they were treated in this male-dominated society.

I wished I could do more. The women and children suffered the most in the clan. The leaders and I had so much. An abundance of comfort and clothing. The warriors were next in line. They were well fed and respected. Their jobs were the most dangerous, although some of the danger was brought on by themselves.

Grand Lord Justicar strolled around the encampment. His gaze narrowed each time he spotted a woman wearing more than the minimal amount of clothing granted to them. He talked to Svante and they both scowled at me.

Holding my head higher, I refused to cower. This Lys thing was important, which meant I was important. Lykke said I was essential to the clan's future. While I didn't know exactly what that meant, I'd take advantage of my status to help others. That's what a true leader would do. I choked. Not that I was a leader. I wasn't planning to stay around long enough to find out the full meaning of Lys.

"You can't give away the special clothes of the Lys." It was the first time Gorig acknowledged this title I didn't understand.

"Aren't the clothes mine?" I inquired mischievously.

Gorig huffed. "Yes, they are."

"Then I should be able to do what I want with them." Holding back a smug grin, I nodded with knowledge and satisfaction. I'd learned that banshees are offended if a gift is given back. Charmig had reacted poorly when I'd tried to return the sandals he'd given me when we first arrived. "And since I gave them as gifts, the women can't give them back."

Grumbling, he glowered at the sky. I could tell he was trying to think of a response.

I didn't understand how he could claim to be a good leader when he and the Elders received the benefits of their positions while the common people suffered. He wasn't cold or tired from hiking. He might carry a lot of responsibility, but he didn't do the physical labor. And he didn't seem to understand the extra work caused by his heavy trunks and his luxurious tent and furniture.

My tent was luxurious too. I hadn't realized it was my tent until recently. I planned to do something about the difference between the haves and the have nots.

I placed a placid smile on my face and challenged, "Don't you want your clan to be comfortable on the journey? As their leader, don't you want what's best for them?"

"Traditional ways have helped the Skjult Banshee Clan survive for centuries." He sneered. "No, upstart Lys is going to change everything."

Chapter Eleven

"Let's walk around," I said to Lykke. "I want to stretch my legs."

After questioning Gorig's leadership skills, I needed to get away from his furious expressions and piercing glares. If looks could kill... I shuddered and grabbed Lykke's arm, leading her away from the fire. The dinner break would end soon, and I didn't want to spend more time with the leader or Svante.

Dusk had fallen and the journey would become more hazardous in the dark. Why couldn't we wait until morning for my next ceremony? The hike would be easier for the clan. I hadn't seen the brownies since we departed and wondered if they hurried ahead.

"Some of the women want to thank you properly." She led me toward a group of women at the edge of the encampment, far from the male warriors.

"I don't need thanks." The banshees had purchased or made everything I wore. I should be thanking them. "I would love to meet them."

At the other encampment I hadn't met many banshees. I'd barely seen the women and children. Now, they scrubbed the pots and pans used to provide our meal. They'd probably cooked the food too. And after packing the camp and hiking the entire afternoon. Compared to them, I'd been a sloth.

When Grandfather and I had lived in the tiny mound home, he'd been the one in charge. I'd cooked, cleaned, and scavenged for food. Nothing like the work these women performed. Grandfather had never thanked me. He'd taught me how to take care of myself. How many male banshees knew how to take care of themselves?

"Saann." Lykke approached a woman bending over a large pot of soapy water.

The woman wore a tattered skirt and bikini top with a piece of cloth hanging from the bikini portion covering her midsection. She also wore one of my heated cloaks. Her dark, leathery hands scrubbed at a bowl made of gold. She handed the dish to a young teen girl who held a small piece of towel.

The girl wore a short shula and her breasts pushed up in the bikini top. One of my beaded scarves wrapped around her neck. She hit the woman's arm, almost dropping the bowl. "It's her."

"Reitha." The chastising tone changed to one of amazement when the old woman spotted me. She bowed deeply. "Lys Destiny."

I wiggled my shoulders. I hadn't come for thanks or attention. I took her arm and helped her stand. "Don't do that."

The woman nudged the girl, and the girl dipped into a bow.

I waved my hand. "Please stop. I came by to say hello."

"Thank you for the cloak." The woman drew the garment closer around her neck and smiled with crooked, yellow teeth.

"No thanks necessary." I noted how many of them wore a new piece of clothing. Their other clothes appeared old and dirty in comparison. "What good were the cloaks and other items doing stored in a trunk when it's freezing outside?"

"My granny's bones ache in the cold." Reitha unwound the scarf, twirled around, and giggled. "I love my new scarf because it's beautiful and attracts attention. The warriors will want me now."

My smile fell at her antics. Is this what she lived for? To be wanted by a warrior? She was probably twelve or thirteen. Disgust shivered across my skin. She had so much more potential. "Instead of being wanted by a warrior, why don't you become a warrior?"

She stopped twirling to stare.

The old woman gasped.

Others nearby paused what they were doing. They'd heard me and were just as shocked.

Frowning, I reviewed what I'd said. Nothing atrocious. I surveyed the snow on the ground, not wanting to be the center of attention. And yet, as Lys I supposedly would have some say in ruling I hoped. I'd start by raising the status of female banshees.

"I'm a warrior." I fisted my hand and held up my wrist with the tattoo.

It was what the male warriors had. Ashamed of being tricked into the mark, I flaunted it now. Better to use the tattoo to make a point, then hide it away. If I could get the warrior tattoo so could other females.

"You are Lys." An older version of Reitha grabbed her hand. "Most of us cannot aspire to be more. We have no magic."

My gaze widened. None of the females had magic? I'd wondered why they did the tasks by hand or with the brownies' help. If female banshees didn't have magic, why did I?

I peered at Lykke remembering how her thoughts of oppression were similar—that women were lower class and meant to serve. This gospel must be ingrained on them from when they were small girls.

It was the wrong gospel.

I let my hand drop, keeping the fist. Anger pumped through my fingers, charging with a need for equality. I was furious on their behalf. "What's your name?"

"Dore." The girl's mother dropped into a bow.

"I used to be ashamed and afraid." My anger coalesced and quieted around memories of being treated poorly because I was a banshee. "My grandfather and I hid from other majiks because *they* were afraid." We'd hid when we could've shown our strength with a simple wail. "I thought less of myself and believed I'd never accomplish anything."

Being taken by the palace guards was the best thing that happened to me. It changed my life and my belief in myself. Now, I needed to bestow the same belief on the female banshees, especially the young ones.

"When I was in the dungeon beneath the palace, I got to know other majiks. They were no longer afraid. In fact, they counted on me to help them escape. They became friends."

Lykke's smile broadened, causing joy to cascade through me. We were friends. If I could change her mind, I could change others.

The large group of female banshees edged closer. They listened to me. Expectation shown on their faces. I held my breath knowing I had the responsibility to make their lives better, but it had to start with believing in themselves.

"From the experience, I knew I could be more. Banshees could be more." My soul ached for them and what they could do for the clan and the kingdom. "Women could be more."

The females were silent. Not one of them moved, or even blinked.

Had they heard anything I said? Did they understand? Did they believe? Not in me, in themselves.

Reitha put her hands together in a single clap. Saann followed. Others joined in and soon they were clapping and hugging. Aspiration stamped on their faces.

My chest wanted to burst with pride. They soaked up my words and seemed to immerse themselves in what the future could bring.

The clapping stopped and the women parted in the middle. A path opened and Charmig strutted through the center. His fur lined shula was longer to keep him warm. His cloak also had fur around the collar, although his torso was bare. He flashed his trademark white-toothed grin.

The women fawned, touching his arm or chest. Some of the younger ones beamed and fluttered their eyelashes. They treated him like a god.

My shoulders deflated. After my speech, the female banshees still wanted to make an impression on a male.

Lykke's posture straightened, and she pushed the cloak back to display her body. Her tremulous smile told me she didn't fear him, she cared about him. And not just his position.

"What was everyone clapping about?" Charmig settled in front of me.

"Nothing." I answered before anyone else could. "I was getting to know the women."

He waved his hand dismissively and tilted closer. "There's no need for you to know them. They only need to know you."

The women dispersed going back to their cleaning and packing. Lykke disappeared in the crowd, but not before I noticed her disappointed expression.

"I want to get to know them." Glaring, I hated how the males assumed the females were subservient. If that's what they expected from me even though I was Lys, they were in for a rude awakening.

"My father was not pleased with your actions." He took my arm and tramped back to the campfire.

Not sure which action he referred to, I asked, "Getting to know the female banshees?"

"No. Giving away your garments." His tone hardened and he gripped my arm tighter.

"Doesn't your father want his clan members to be comfortable?" Or was the leader upset I'd verbally challenged him?

Charmig stopped, bringing our bodies closer. "I thought it was brilliant."

Surprise ignited a flame of hope inside me. He was a future leader. Once I left, maybe he would carry on with changes. Raise the women up, free the brownies. I relaxed, glad I didn't have to debate him too. "Thanks."

Charmig took my arm again and continued ambling. "Did you enjoy the journey riding on the back of the eleram?"

"It was different."

"Riding inside my father's tent was much cozier." He angled toward me and winked. His smile heated as if remembering how we'd slept side by side.

An ickiness crawled across my skin. My goal was not to get any more attention from him or Svante or any other male banshee. My goal was to get my magic restored and heal Grandfather so we could be on our way. Then I could find Stone.

"Charmig, I'm not like the banshee females. I'm not looking for any kind of relationship." The dream and the similar white dress and veil in one of the trunks haunted me. I didn't see any of the women wearing those white clothes. "I want to be friends."

"Friends?" His hand pressed against my waist.

Swallowing, I remembered Svante's response to my request. "Is that okay with you?"

Charmig glanced around and I noticed banshees watching us, including Reitha and some of the others I'd lectured.

"Let's seal our friendship with a kiss." He leaned toward me.

I tilted away. "Friends don't kiss on the lips."

"What makes you such an expert on friendship?" His lips upturned with a coaxing smile. "Banshee friends kiss."

I placed my hands on my hips and took a step back. He lied. "Banshees don't have friends."

"Until you." He lowered his voice seductively.

It didn't work on me. Not his charm or his smiles or his flirting. Not his lies. His constant charm assault made me unsteady. Still, he'd agreed with me about giving away the clothes. I needed a friend who had the ear of the leader.

A loud wail pierced. Another followed. And another.

My body tensed. "What's going on?"

More banshees joined the scary chorus.

"They're banshee warning screams. Must be from the perimeter guards. It means trouble." He gripped my arm and pulled me toward the other end of the camp.

Others ran frantically.

Adrenaline spiked. "I thought it meant death."

"With so many wails it could mean many, many deaths." He yanked me toward the animals clustered together. "We're not staying around to find out."

Confusion rattled in my head. If there was trouble, we should stay and fight with the warriors. Where was Grandfather? Darkness had completely fallen. An orange light flashed in the sky.

"Dragon." Charmig yanked my arm harder.

"Dragon?" My knees knocked together. I'd heard horror stories about the beasts.

The camp reacted. Banshees ran around like crazy. Warriors hustled Grand Lord Justicar toward the eleram with the traveling tent. They moved in unison without anyone yelling out orders. They must plan for dragon attacks. Then, why were they running away?

Svante ran behind and leapt on his mount, staying beside the leader. He peered back as if wanting to stay and help. For some reason he didn't. Or couldn't.

I couldn't stop watching the sky. Tripping as Charmig pulled me forward, my eyes widened following the destructive path.

A shadow fell over us, blocking the sky. The dragon soared lower, a large, orange, scaly creature. Small, knobby dark eyes gleamed and the snout opened. Flames poured out of his mouth.

A tree nearby caught on fire. Smoke filled the air.

"Ahhh!" A banshee hit by fire screamed. She fell to the ground, her skin a crispy red.

Terror slashed at my chest. Panting, I couldn't breathe. I stumbled to the ground. We shouldn't run away when so many needed saving. We needed to help the others get away and hide.

Charmig yanked me to my feet. "Let's go! We have to go!"

Frantic, I struggled against his hold. "What about Lykke? And the others? What about my grandfather?"

Charmig placed a strong arm under my legs and lifted me onto his animal.

I listed across the saddle, trying to catch my breath. Infuriated, I pounded against him with my fists. "What about Reitha and her mother and grandmother? What about the other women who are hiding in the burning forest?"

They'd looked up to me with hope.

He swung a leg up and positioned himself behind me on the saddle, trapping me. He grabbed the reins with both hands. His father and Svante's animals were farther ahead of us. Warriors ran behind them, their job was to protect the leaders.

Who protected the normal banshees?

I clutched the saddle, knowing leaving was wrong. "The banshee warriors are cowards." I struggled against Charmig's hold. "Why don't they defend the females?"

"Because my father ordered the warriors to protect him."

"All of them? I didn't hear him shout a command."

"He doesn't need to." Charmig flicked the reins and the eleram started to trot.

"No!" I screamed, even though my throat scratched with pain. "No, stop! I need to go back."

"You're crazy." He stared at the dark path ahead.

"I can help." I contorted to slip off the animal.

He grabbed my waist, nothing flirtatious about the action this time. "Stop fighting me! You're more important than any of those banshees. Our clan needs you."

My jaw dropped and I turned to stare at him. I didn't see the suave Elder, but a terrified boy. He acted selfishly. I didn't have time to argue with a child. "You're right. The clan does need me."

His hold on me loosened, totally misunderstanding my meaning and believing he'd won.

"And *they* are the clan." I pointed at the destroyed camp, tucked in my arms, and shoved against him.

He dropped the reins and I slipped off headfirst toward the ground.

Oxygen whooshed out of my lungs. I could die in a jump from the animal. My head could hit a rock. There'd be no saving anyone then. I cleared my fears. I couldn't think that way. Tucking, I hit the ground with my shoulder and rolled away from the animal's hoofs. I laid still for a second assessing my body. A cut stung my arm and my ankle was twisted.

"Destiny." Charmig pulled back on the reins and stopped. "What're you doing?"

I stood on shaky legs and glared. "I'm fighting for my clan."

Limping toward the camp, I tried to run as fast as I could with my bum ankle. Good thing we hadn't gotten far.

Most of the area had been torched. Blackened trees and burnt leaves floated. Thick smoke filled the area making it difficult to see. I caught glimpses of banshees running and hiding behind boulders or anything they could find. I tripped on a dead body.

My stomach revolted and I yelped.

I hunched, knowing I couldn't help the dead. I could only help the living. Charmig didn't understand my powers. Because I hadn't told any of them everything I could do. And neither had Svante. He'd seen me push the warrior across the circle.

Rolling my shoulders, I concentrated.

The dragon circled around coming back my way.

I raised my arms and focused on a large boulder. A boulder big enough to kill the dragon or at least injure it enough that it might fly away. I narrowed my gaze.

The boulder rocked and lifted an inch. It fell back to the ground.

I wanted to fall down too as doubts pelted me from the inside.

The dragon flew closer. I spotted its luminescent scales and large claws reaching out. With my arms raised, I was a clear target.

"I can do this." I raised my arms again.

With another glance, I noticed minute details down to its spiked tongue and smelled the rotting stink of its breath. It would be on top of me soon, shooting fire and scorching me.

Perspiration formed on my upper lip. I fixated on the boulder. I remembered the feeling of almost losing Stone and how I'd obliterated the rocks and boulders in the cave collapse under the palace dungeon. This was the exact opposite.

I needed to keep the boulder together. I had to throw the bulk of the rock high and fast at the dragon.

If I didn't, I'd be fried.

Chapter Twelve

S tretching my fingers, I focused on the rock. Energy percolated in my veins.

The boulder lifted higher. It hung in the air as if time were suspended.

Trembles quivered through my body, starting at my ankles and working to the top of my head. Sweat pooled on my lower back. Nerves attacked me from the inside while a dragon attacked from above.

The dragon flew closer. Flames licked the top of my head.

"Lys Destiny!" Reitha's shout didn't distract.

Blowing out a breath, I stopped the quivering. Stopped the doubts and the fear. I had to maim the dragon to save her and the others close by.

The dragon opened its wide mouth and a wave of heat and stench hit me. Flames spewed out and scorched the ground in front of me.

My body shook with exertion. I had seconds to make direct contact before it set me on fire. The boulder rose higher, about tree height. My arms quaked and it hurt to hold them up. Perspiration dripped off my face. Drop by drop. From the strain or the dragon's fire? It was hard to tell.

Everything happened in slow motion. The dragon dipped down. He headed straight in my direction.

I choked on the smoke and lost my concentration.

The boulder smashed to the ground.

My pulse sped up. The dragon was a few feet away. I'd lost the height advantage. Could I throw the rock like a slingshot? Doubt turned to determination. Firming my muscles, I glared at the rock. I stood with my arms to the sides. My fingers spread wide. Magic sparked through my bloodstream resembling electricity.

The dragon swooped. I was in its sights.

Forcing my magic into my hands, I thrust my arms upward with all my might. Power cascaded through me, coursing and gushing through my body.

The large rock followed my movements. It flung in the air and whacked into the dragon's skull. The sharp edge sliced through the dragon's scales. Blood poured out of the wound. The dragon's fire died.

Relief and exhaustion formed a puddle in my center. I'd stopped the attack.

The dragon wobbled in the sky. His humongous eyelids flickered and closed. He started falling.

My body wavered with weakness.

The dragon plunged down and would land on top of me.

I tried to shift my feet. I couldn't. Shock and tiredness left me unable to run, unable to think.

"Lys Destiny!" Reitha charged. She wrapped her arms around my waist and tackled me out of the falling dragon's path. We hit the ground with a hard bounce.

My body went numb. Not from the hard hit, from shock. I lay there trying to catch my breath. "Is it...is it dead?"

She rolled off me and we both sat up.

The dragon's eyes were closed. Its tongue lolled out of its mouth. The huge chest went up and down. Blood poured from the wound I'd given the animal, but it was alive.

My body sagged. I hadn't killed the dragon. My muscles tensed, going on high alert. I hadn't killed the dragon. It was still alive. It could still shoot fire.

Saann tiptoed toward the front of the dragon. She took a rope previously used to tie up luggage and slipped it beneath the dragon's snout. Reitha jumped up and grabbed the end, tossing it back to the old woman. She tied a knot and yanked it tight, closing the unconscious dragon's mouth.

"Can it breathe?" If the creature hadn't died in the battle, I didn't want to kill it now. What I'd done, I'd done to protect the banshees.

"Through the nostrils." Reitha stood and held out a hand. "What did you...?"

It wasn't a complete question so I didn't answer. I couldn't explain right now. I didn't know if I could ever explain. My banshee magic was supposed to be locked down but I'd accessed powers before. She knew, as did the others who'd witnessed, that I'd lied about my magic. I put my hand in hers and let her pull me to my feet.

Other female banshees came out from their hiding spots. Their stunned expressions showed shock and comprehension. Of me and my powers, or the wounded dragon? They did what needed to be done. A couple of women took a canvas tent and wrapped it around the dragon's spiky tail. Others tied up the front and back legs so it couldn't move. A group of five women braved the animal's body by climbing onto the beast. They took ropes and material and fastened down the wings.

No way was the dragon escaping. I felt bad for the animal because I could relate.

"Destiny." Charmig hurtled to my side now that the danger had ended. He grabbed both my arms. "What did you do?"

"I..." My head grew woozy.

"She saved us." Reitha placed her hands on her hips. Her expression was more fierce than any male banshee warrior.

"The boulder...you have magic..." He couldn't wrap his head around the idea.

I didn't understand. Some banshees had magic, didn't they? My head went from woozy to pounding. Why hadn't any of the other banshees used their magic to stop the dragon? Why had Grand Lord Justicar ordered the warriors to run away?

"You told my father you could only read human minds." His words cut in accusation.

"That's true."

"There's more you didn't tell us." He gripped tighter. "Even while under the magic lock."

I held my throbbing head. The more he yelled the more it hurt. "I..."

Lykke slapped his hands off me. "Leave her alone. She's about to pass out."

Warriors marched back, led by Svante and Grand Lord Justicar.

"Is it dead?" the leader asked from the safety of his tent on the animal.

Charmig glanced at Lykke and she shook her head. He wheeled to his father. "No. It's alive."

"The females secured it," Lykke whispered to Charmig.

"I've had the beast secured." He stood taller. "And saved Lys Destiny."

I gasped quietly, wanting to argue but knowing I shouldn't say anything. I wasn't ready to explain the magic I'd used. He could take credit for what I did. His lie gave me leverage.

Lykke kept her head down. She wasn't going to correct him, not in front of his father. Neither did the other females.

Frustration wove through me and pulled the cords tight. These women demonstrated their bravery. They needed to be strong enough to stand up to the males.

"Warriors," his father waved his hand and said nothing else.

The warriors jogged toward the dragon and secured it even more.

"Warriors have their orders." Grand Lord Justicar crossed his arms and glowered. "The rest of you, pack what's left and meet us at the site."

"What orders?" I worried the warriors would kill the dragon. "I didn't hear anything."

Charmig bent too close to my ear. "You didn't need to hear anything. Not yet."

His nonsensical explanation annoyed.

I squeezed my eyes tight picturing the body I'd tripped over. "What about the dead?" I whispered to Lykke. She better give a straight answer.

"The women and the warriors will say something over the bodies. Nature will take care of the rest."

By nature she meant scavengers like vultures and wolves. Not a respectful way for the end of life. It wasn't the right time for me to argue about their traditions and customs. I swallowed the lump in my throat. "And the wounded?"

Would they leave them behind for animal food?

Lykke had moved away and didn't answer.

"The women will render aid and help them walk or carry them. If there's room on one of the pack animals, they might be able to ride." Reitha shrugged. This must be a common theme.

I didn't want to leave the wounded behind. "Keep my eleram for the wounded."

"What about you? I can tell you're weak after saving us. You expended much energy doing...whatever that was." Her voice rose with astonishment.

I didn't want her to be astonished by me. I wanted her to be fond of me and rise to the woman she could become.

"Destiny will ride with me." Charmig announced in a tone brooking no discussion.

What choice did I have? I wanted to leave my animal behind. I couldn't walk. I could barely stand. It would be better to ride with Charmig than his father or Svante. Charmig had at least believed he was saving me by trying to carry me away.

"Fine." I nodded.

"I'll help you to his mount." Reitha let me lean on her as we took a step.

"No need." Charmig grabbed me around the waist and legs and lifted me into his arms like a sack of potatoes. "Get to work."

He dismissed my young friend without a thought. My neck tensed. I was too tired and weak to argue. He placed me on the animal and swung a leg up behind. Grabbing the reins, he kicked the sides of the beast and we were off.

Closing my eyes, I slumped against him for support. The body I tripped on haunted me. The many injured banshees tore at my heart. But it was the pain in the dragon's eyes that caused a single tear to run down my cheek. Something about the fire-breather called to me. I didn't want him tortured or killed. I wanted to set him free.

⤐⤐ ⫷⫷

"Drago! Drago, where are you?" A young fairy wearing a tiara searched through a snow-covered forest. She flapped her wings as she flew higher up the mountain. "I need you Drago."

I sucked in a breath. I recognized the girl. Princess Ellery, a friend of Stone's and in love with Prince Zacharye. With her royal status, what was she doing alone? If the prince had lost the battle, had he lost the whole war? The banshees said he'd been executed. Was the princess in hiding and searching for a lost pet?

My mind bunched with imaginary images. I wished I knew more about what had occurred in the battle against the regent. Who had died? Who was captured? Who had run away and escaped with their lives?

The scene changed. A dragon lay in a deep mound of snow. He was tied up and listless. A deep cut on its head oozed a puffy pus.

This must be the dragon I'd brought down. Sadness wafted through me. I hadn't had a choice. The dragon was attacking the clan. I hated how it was tied down and no one had cleaned the wound.

A banshee warrior approached the dragon. He poked it with his sharp halberd right in the belly, and then again and again. The dragon winced.

I winced too.

I wanted to rip the weapon out of his hand and crack the handle in two. The warrior was being mean. The dragon was injured and couldn't defend itself. Yes, I understood the dragon had attacked the banshees. There must've been a reason for the attack.

The dragon's shallow breath proved it struggled under the tight ropes. The green pus from the wound poisoned the animal's blood. I sensed it didn't have much longer to live. Another power? My mother foretold the future, not me.

A wail built inside me. I didn't know banshees screamed for dying animals.

Princess Ellery had been searching for a pet. Could it be…?

"Drago." The name hushed between my lips. "It must be Drago."

The dragon quirked its head as if hearing me.

"Wake up, Destiny." Charmig shook me. "You were dreaming about the dragon attack."

I was dreaming about the dragon *being* attacked. And teased and tortured.

"It was a nightmare." He rubbed a gloved hand against my waist.

I jerked fully awake and knocked his hand away. "What're you doing? You can't touch me whenever you want."

"Yes, I can." His smug attitude had me smacking at his fingers beneath my cloak. "Ouch." He removed his hand.

Smashing my lips together, I hadn't really hurt him, but I wanted to.

"If you don't want to snuggle, let's talk." Charmig's persuasiveness didn't work on me. His logic did.

We did need to talk. He'd witnessed my powers. None of the other banshees had used magic to help me. Something wasn't right. I straightened with suspicion.

Scanning the area, I noted the heavy snow and how the eleram trekked slower because of the icy path. Shivering, I tucked my cloak tighter around me. Once my powers were released, the first thing I'd do is create a heavy winter coat with wool pants and a sweater. For me and every other female banshee.

"What do you want to talk about? How you lied to your father about what really happened with the dragon?"

He hadn't secured anything. He'd run like the rest of the banshee leadership.

His fingers gripped my chin in a threatening action. He forced me to turn my head and look at him. "What if instead we talk about how you lied to my father about the magic you wield?"

He reversed the circumstances on me, making my head spin. I flattened my lips. I was in enough trouble already, no need to contemplate punishment from Grand Lord Justicar.

"My father didn't see you use magic. Others did. The information will get back to him unless..."

Charmig held out the hope that he could control the information to his father.

My gaze narrowed. Frowning, I tried to control my raging imagination, especially since he kept fondling me. We were on the back of the animal so I couldn't push him away. There was nowhere for me to go.

I asked the question I knew I'd regret. "What do you want for keeping my secret?"

CHAPTER THIRTEEN

"Unfortunately, I can't keep your secret. Many females have relationships with my father. They'll tell him what happened." Charmig bragged. "Better to tell me everything so I can twist it to your advantage when I tell my father why you lied."

"I didn't lie. I left a couple of things out." I jerked my chin out of his grip and stared ahead. "Besides, you lied about what happened too."

"A couple of things?" His hand gripped my waist tighter and he brushed my comment about his lies aside. "What else can you do?"

I shrugged and surveyed the passing scenery. It was difficult to see with the surrounding darkness. We were higher than the tree line, nothing shielded the wind or the blowing snow. Only a couple of stars could be seen in the night sky. If it wasn't for the hi-tech light on the leader's tent atop the eleram, we could've easily dropped off a cliff.

Shivering from the thought—not the frigid temperature—I clung tighter to the animal's saddle. The eleram carrying the healer and dragging the litter with my grandfather rode behind the leader. Svante followed behind him. Warriors ran between and around us.

"I'll explain if you tell me something." I wanted to understand the structure of the clan leadership. Svante hadn't clarified everything.

Charmig stiffened behind me. "That's not how this is going to work. I know you lied. I saw you use magic. You will tell me."

"You said you're an Elder. You're always at your father's side." To learn what I wanted, I needed to feed his ego. "You're awfully young for such an important position."

"I'm eighteen. Not too old for a sixteen-year-old." The leering voice gave me chills and I was tired of his insinuations. "Not ancient like Svante at twenty-five."

I shuddered at the thought of being with either of them. Why were they the only two presented to me? To talk to me and escort me. Is that what Prospectives meant? My heart thundered. The one I wanted to be with was Stone, and even now I traveled further away from him. My lungs contracted causing my cold breath to shatter.

"I don't mean this as an insult to your capabilities, but why isn't there anyone older than you and Svante helping your father rule?" Remembering how Grand Lord Justicar treated the females, I tensed. He was a terrible leader and having someone older by his side might help him see things more clearly. "Someone more mature and with more leadership experience."

Someone like my grandfather. Pain tore through my chest. I couldn't lose him.

I hadn't seen anyone older in camp. The warriors appeared to be in their teens and twenties. The perimeter guards were around the same age. There were no middle-aged men or senior males. I'd noticed the discrepancies before but never thought much about it.

"No reason for you to concern your pretty little head about how my father rules." He scoffed. "All you need to do is use your magic as my father demands."

A scream built inside me. I'd refuse to let the leader use me. The magic was mine. I'd use it for what I deemed necessary. Not to keep the brownies as slaves or the females as chattels and servants.

"I've answered your silly question, tell me what magic you can already do."

Charmig hadn't answered, and yet he believed I'd confess everything when I planned to say only a little. When my magic was released, he wouldn't know the difference between what magic I possessed now and what I'd gained.

"I told your father I could read human minds." I peered at the dark sky trying to finesse my lie.

"Not banshee minds?" Nerves trembled in his tone. What evil thoughts did he possess?

"Correct." I wasn't going to share how I sensed something in his father's head when I forced him to stop tattooing me, or how I could make humans do things. I did have to explain the rock event. "With the dragon, it was the first time I'd lifted a boulder and tossed it. The reason I knew to try..."

"Yes?" He leaned forward pressing into my back.

I used my elbow to jab him. "When I was in the palace dungeon I was forced to work in a mine. There was a cave-in and a...friend was going to be crushed by huge boulders. I was upset and not really thinking. A powerful emotion overtook me and a wave of magic vibrated out. It demolished the falling boulders into tiny pebbles. My, um, friend was saved."

My pounding heart refused to settle even knowing I'd saved Stone that day. I'd lost him anyhow. At least for now.

"The magic you displayed tonight was amazing." Charmig didn't sound amazed. He sounded as if he was plotting something.

"It's not a big deal." My thoughts grew dark. He schemed to use me as did his father. "All banshees have some kind of magic."

Except the females.

"Of course we do." His response rushed out.

"What can you do?" I hadn't seen anyone perform magic since I'd arrived. I twisted around to face him, wanting to see his expression. "You do have magic, don't you?"

"I do." His voice deepened into solemnity. "Not every banshee does."

"Is that the reason for their status or place? How much magic they possess?" I turned back around, not wanting to continue looking at him or show my emotions about this issue on my face. That must be why the females have such a low status.

"One of the reasons." His response didn't really explain anything and my frustration built.

Those in front of us stopped. His father dismounted and warriors scrambled around setting up lights on a flat plateau. A bluff protected us from the wind.

My brow furrowed. If the female banshees didn't have magic, how did they control the brownies? My friend Pith was a brownie and he might be bashful, but he wasn't subservient.

Grand Lord Justicar blew a horn, calling our small group together. "Elder Charmig and Lys Destiny," he enjoyed partnering our names. Too bad we'd never be together. "Elder Svante, Healer."

I went to get off the animal and Charmig stopped me. My muscles tightened and I wanted to slug him. How dare he force me to stay beside him. Riding together was the closest we'd ever get.

Svante stayed on his animal and positioned himself next to us. I shivered. Even he wanted to get closer. The healer dropped behind us on her animal in a choreographed dance. Grandfather's pallet was no longer tethered to the eleram.

My pulse jolted. "Where's Grandfather?"

"He's being taken care of." Ursee's serene expression didn't calm me. "Your grandfather will be the first one in a tent after Grand Lord Justicar."

My back stiffened. Gorig believed he should get everything first, that he deserved the best of everything. Grandfather was ill. He should be made comfortable before anyone, especially after enduring the grueling journey. I pressed my lips together. Speaking out would get me in more trouble.

Do the ceremony and get my full magic, heal Grandfather, help the female banshees especially after being saved by Reitha, free the brownies, and then leave to find Stone. My to-do list was getting longer.

Warriors hurried to build the largest tent of the encampment.

"Lys Destiny," Grand Lord Justicar continued, "You are about to embark on a prophetic journey."

I thought I was already on a journey. A journey where he forced his people to relocate on a whim, where they marched in the cold and snow, where they were attacked by a dragon, and possibly other things I didn't even know about.

"Charmig and Svante," respect ground in the leader's tone, "will escort you to the Obsidian Precipice. With the healer's spiritual guidance, they will set you on course. Then you will be on your own."

Really on my own? Was the banshee clan finally letting me go? Realization zapped my entire body. Gorig would never willingly let me go, especially once I received full magic.

I'd cross that bridge when I came to it.

What he must've meant was that whatever I was headed for, whatever this ceremony entailed, I'd be on my own. Yay, no surprise tattoos. Suspicion leaked into my mind. Why were Charmig and Svante accompanying me then?

"This deep freeze ceremony will be the opposite of the ceremony that locked your memories and your magic."

Charmig gave me a side glance.

Did he know something about the ceremony or was his look an insinuation about the magic I already possessed?

"Once your magic is liberated, you will assist the Skjult Banshee Clan in their goals and assist in fulfilling their agreements." Gorig mumbled the last part. "Do you accept this duty?"

I'd be thrilled to help the banshees fulfill their goals. I wanted to help, especially the females and those of lower status. I didn't want them to always be cold and hungry and working. I accepted this responsibility. Even when I left to find Stone, I'd make sure the banshees were doing okay. I'd find a way.

My mind filled with thoughts of helping the family I never had. "I do."

"Then let you be off." He handed the hi-tech light to the healer and blew the horn one final time. "Safe travels. Safe journey. Safe Unlocking Ceremony."

"We're here." Charmig stopped the eleram several yards from the edge of the highest peak. The animal had stumbled several times up the treacherous, steep, narrow, and icy path and I'd thought we were going to die. The wind howled and blowing snow obscured my vision.

"Where are we exactly?" I clutched my cloak closer, wishing for the warmth of the banshee campfire.

Snow hit my face and I pulled the cloak over my head. Grand Lord Justicar had said this would be the opposite of the locking and blocking ceremony. He'd been right. I wished for the boiling water and steam now.

Charmig dismounted and the snow came up to his thighs. He held his arms up to help me.

"I'll stay on the animal." The body heat from the beast kept the chill off.

"Soon you won't even notice the weather." He put his arms at my waist and brought me down.

Shivering, I marched my feet in the high snow trying to keep moving. Pain shot up from my injured ankle. I inched to the ledge and peered down. My stomach cramped and I took a step back. I had a nonsensical fear of heights. The abyss below the peak was nothing but blackness. I knew the fall would kill.

The healer tied up the animals against the cliff out of the wind. She pulled a shiny blanket across them. The royal guards I'd tracked with at the palace had something similar they used to keep warm.

Svante trampled up behind me and I took another step back. What if he pushed me off? "Afraid of heights?"

"No." I lied.

"Good."

The wind blew harder, whistling a high-pitched resonance and biting through my cloak. Now, I wished I'd kept my extra clothes.

"Why did you and Charmig come with?"

"We are the Elders of the clan and your Prospectives. We're here to make sure everything goes smoothly." Svante's determination came through in his cold tone. It sounded as if he forced himself to take part.

I wanted to ask Prospective what, but I wasn't sure I wanted to know the answer. "Grand Lord Pain-in-my-bu...Justicar said I'd be taking this journey alone."

"You will be." Svante's lips twitched, knowing what I'd been about to call the leader. He turned his head and stared at an icy precipice sticking out from the edge.

Charmig trudged over and put his arm around my shoulders. "Get a good look?"

"Can't see much." I appreciated his body warmth, not his proprietary manner. Maybe I could play them against each other and get the truth. They seemed to be in a competition for something and I couldn't tell if it was the leadership of the clan or me. "I was asking Svante why the two of you got stuck escorting me."

"I don't know about Svante, but I wanted to stay by your side." Charmig pulled me in closer and Svante huffed. "I want to make sure you survive the ceremony."

Cold screeched through my throat. I swallowed the frozen lump. "Survive? What do you mean? What might happen?"

"Lys Destiny will discover her truths and her power on her own." Healer Ursee struggled through the snow. She held a bottle and a plain wooden box. "Drink this."

I tensed. "What is it?"

"Dragon blood."

"Disgusting."

"It's magic and part of the ancient ceremony. Banshees have been drinking dragon blood for centuries in many different rituals." She held up the bottle apparently making an offering.

The frozen lump in my throat threatened to come back up. "Is that why the dragon attacked us? Because banshees stole his or his friends' blood?"

"Dragons don't think like us majiks, or humans." Svante grabbed my arm.

"They're animals," Charmig added.

"They're living, breathing things." I felt sorry for the misaligned dragons. The princess had one as a pet. I understood hunting animals for food, but not to drain blood. "And banshees aren't vampires."

Charmig chucked his arm tightly around my shoulders, becoming a shackle. "Such an imagination. The visions you have will be emotional and vibrant."

My nerves lit up in a frenzy. I had enough nightmares. I didn't need more visions.

"Let go." I scrunched trying to break free of his hold. My pulse raced against my fear. I tried to stomp on his foot. The high snow made the struggle impossible. Between the journey, the fight against the dragon, and now this, I was exhausted.

While Charmig held my body, Svante grabbed my wrists together in a vice grip. He pried my mouth open.

The healer chanted a few words and held the bottle toward my mouth.

Jerking my head, I angled my chin to prevent the unpreventable. I clenched my jaw, trying to get my mouth to shut. Svante was too strong. I couldn't move. Dread pressed, resembling the squeeze of his hand.

Ursee poured the dragon's blood into my mouth.

The thick liquid tasted coppery and metallic.

"Spftt." What dragon had the blood been taken from?

I gagged and tried to stop the blood from going down my throat.

The healer rubbed my neck and I couldn't stop it from going deep inside of me. She stepped away and I spit out the remnants from my mouth. Red dribbled down my chin.

"Gross." I kept spitting trying to get as much of the liquid out as I could.

Turning my head, I used the force of my anger to spit at Svante. How dare they force this upon me? Just like the tattoo. He didn't loosen his hold on me. I resented the leaders of this clan and couldn't wait to get away from them. The regular banshees I cared about though.

Magic first. Heal Grandfather second. Banshee females' freedom third, and the brownies. And then I could leave and find Stone.

I'd keep repeating that to myself through this entire awful ceremony.

Ursee opened the wooden box and took out an old patterned wool blanket. She waved the blanket up and down and spun around in the high snow. The entire time she chanted.

Shaking my head, I realized she must be crazy. Or I was, for going along with this ceremony.

She plowed through the snow to the icy precipice and continued to chant and dance and wave the blanket.

"She's getting a little close to the edge." I voiced my concern. I knew I wouldn't get that close.

She spread the blanket on the icy crag.

I tensed. The crag couldn't be sturdy. It might be able to take a blanket, but not a person. And why waste a blanket on a rock?

Charmig and Svante, who still hadn't let go of me, lifted me off my feet.

The surprise weightlessness had my stomach dropping. I kicked out, jabbing at their knees and thighs. "What're you guys doing?"

They carried me toward the healer and the edge. Their tight grips told me I wasn't going to escape.

Alarm rang in my head. I kicked some more. "Put me down."

They said nothing as they carried me closer to the healer and the edge by the jutting icy precipice.

My alarm buzzed louder creating static in my head and chest. I took in short breaths of the cold air which cooled the burning in my throat but not in my lungs. "I'm not getting a good feeling about this."

My skin crawled beneath the heavy cloak. My eyes grew wider and wider as the precipice got closer and closer. My panting became shorter, more panicked. I was going to pass out. I struggled harder, twisting my body and jabbing my elbows into them.

Fighting them wasn't going to work and it might even cause them to drop me to my death.

"I'm afraid of heights." Stilling my body, I raised my gaze to Charmig and beseeched him. "Please let me go, Charmig."

Ursee took a step back and the guys set me down past the spot where the crag connected to the cliff. My feet slipped on the ice. Startled, I braced myself. They held me there.

"This isn't a joke." I peered behind the edge into the blackness. Pressure built in my chest. "This isn't safe."

"This Obsidian Precipice has not fractured accidentally for centuries." Ursee waved her arms around and spread her fingers wide. "If you stay still and quiet."

The warning didn't register. I tried to shift under Charmig and Svante's hold. I was too afraid to push too hard. What if I fell? "Maybe time is up."

Charmig released my shoulder and unbuttoned my cloak. He tugged it off me with a swish. Svante used a key to take off the anti-magic bracelets.

"No! Wait! It's freezing." I lurched and slipped. Dizziness swam in my head. Did they want me to die? "Is this some ancient sacrifice?"

"Banshees have used the Obsidian Precipice for ceremonies since the beginning of time." Ursee handed me a sharp piece of black glass volcanic rock.

Desperate, I grabbed onto her wrist, clinging to her.

The crag was old which meant it could break off.

"Please let me go." I hated the pleading in my tone. "I thought this was about my locked magic and memories. I don't need to do this. I don't need to be here."

She slipped out of my grip. "Your memories, your magic." She took the bottle again and dribbled the dragon blood where the precipice attached to the edge of the cliff. "Plus, additional power siphoned from...the newly dead."

Sucking in a breath, I had to wonder who had died. Did they kill the dragon?

I rubbed my hands against my bare arms. This stupid bikini top and skirt did nothing to protect me from the cold. Hypothermia, falling, simply being scared to death—there were many ways I could die. I'd come so far to save Grandfather and now I couldn't see it through. "I don't want to be Lys. I just want to heal my grandfather."

"You have no choice." While holding me down, Charmig waved his free hand mimicking the healer.

My skin burned and went numb from the cold. Sweat formed on my lower back and would turn to ice. My heart pounded and fell into my middle with a solid thump. Just like I was going to fall.

Svante made the same motions. "You have been destined to be our Lys since your birth, Destiny."

My stupid name again.

"You can't keep me here." I crossed my arms. "As soon as you step away or go into your comfy tents, I'll walk off this ledge and destroy it."

"No, you won't." Ursee got to her knees and blew on the wet dragon's blood.

The blood spread out. The crag trembled and I braced myself. A crack formed where the cliff ended and the icy precipice began, in the exact place the blood had been spilled.

My pulse pumped. "You said the crag wouldn't break?"

Svante and Charmig stood on the other side of the crack. They let go of me and I bent low, ready to charge them, leap the crack, knock them down, and run.

The fissure widened. Darkness and nothingness were visible through the fracture.

My entire body stiffened. Afraid to move, I fortified my stance. "What's happening?"

The precipice detached from the edge of the cliff. The space grew bigger and bigger. I got further and further away from solid ground.

"Destiny is fulfilling the prophecy." The healer shouted across the chasm forming between us. "The Obsidian Precipice is where you will emerge from your chrysalis and your personal, magical, powerful journey will begin and end."

Chrysalis as in a butterfly? She was insane.

The crag drifted further out. How could it be floating? How could I?

Terror scraped across my lungs, shredding them to pieces. "If I don't end."

And by end, I meant die.

Chapter Fourteen

The precipice continued to drift away from the ledge.

Away from the ground. And away with my sanity.

I peered down at the bleak darkness. My eyes bugged and my body stiffened as if frozen—like I would be soon. My lungs shriveled and I couldn't breathe. I couldn't see anything. My entire body trembled while my skin went numb. This wasn't going to end well.

Above was the dark night sky dotted with stars. Below was blackness. I knew way, way, way down was a valley with trees and rocks and hard, hard, hard ground. If I fell, I'd smash to pieces. If I didn't die of fright from the fall.

Or freeze to death.

The crag remained steady even though the wind blasted trying to blow me off. The snow pummeled my bare skin. The frigid air sunk deep into my bones. I was so cold I couldn't even shiver.

"Charmig!" I crouched, trying to stay steady on my feet. I threw the black rock Ursee had handed me. "I thought you cared about me. Why would you do this?" At the very least he cared about my status and magic.

"You're already powerful." Yelling, he pounded his fist to his chest. "This will make you more powerful than any Lys before. You will fulfill your name Destiny and you will fight for..."

The precipice floated further away. I couldn't hear the end of what he said. I really didn't want to. The crag drifted into a cloud and fog surrounded me. Now I couldn't see or hear. The dampness of the clouds wrapped me in a moist cold. The opposite of a hot spring. Shards of ice pierced my skin, real and imaginary.

I couldn't jump. My powers could only throw or shatter the precipice which would cause me to fall. My scream wouldn't reach the three of them standing on the ledge, if they were even still there. I couldn't see them anymore. They'd brought shelter to stay warm.

While I froze to death.

How was this going to save Grandfather?

And how were they going to get me back to the side of the mountain? Preferably, before I fell off or died of hypothermia.

Confusion stampeded in my brain. I didn't know how to save myself.

Taking a seat on the center of the floating rock, I wrapped the old, woolen blanket around me. The moldy smell comforted, reminding me of the small mound home I shared with Grandfather. Another more pungent stink mixed with the mold and burned my nostrils.

At least one body part was warm.

I would've been better with the hi-tech, thin silver blanket draped over the animals or my heated cloak than this old quilt.

My thoughts frosted and wandered. I went into a daze with my body still. Why did the banshees believe in ancient, torturing ceremonies while owning technology-modified clothing, gadgets, and the modern transport I'd traveled on? Where did they get these human items when banshees were hermits and didn't even associate with other majiks?

So many questions and I'd never learn the answers. Because I'd be dead.

The snow stopped, but the wind continued to howl. Similar to a banshee scream. The clouds broke apart and the moon shone low in the sky. It must be about halfway between midnight and dawn. The stars blinked brighter.

If I wasn't so terrified, it would be beautiful.

With the clouds clearing, I squinted at the cliff where Charmig, Svante, and Ursee had stood. They were gone. They'd abandoned me and wouldn't be coming to my rescue. I gathered my guts and peered over the edge of the rock. Tiny lights blinked below. Could it be the new banshee clan encampment? How was my grandfather doing after the journey? Dark shapes of varying-sized cliffs and outlines of tall trees wavered in the strong wind. A thin line of blue wended through the valley. Beauty and danger laid out before me.

One slip and I'd fall to my death.

Settling on my back, I closed my eyes and tried to calm myself. I hoped the healer had a plan to get me back to the ground before I became encased in ice. I was so cold that I didn't feel cold. Which meant I was delusional. My heavy eyelids flickered closed.

"I can't believe we missed her." Stone kicked the log I'd sat on with Grand Lord Justicar hours ago in the last banshee encampment.

My chest squeezed. Stone had missed me by hours. Was this wishful thinking or a vision?

"There are large animal tracks leading this way." My friend Lukas prowled around the area where we'd mounted the elerams. His brown hair stuck up in tufts and his clothes were dirty. "We'll follow the tracks."

"Oh my stars." Cassia pulled her dark green hair back into a ponytail. "We don't know when they left or how far ahead of us they are."

Pith, my brownie friend, jumped on the log. "The banshees won't welcome us."

Trolgar yawned as he searched the abandoned campsite.

My heart warmed with love and friendship. They were searching for me. At least five of them had survived the battle against the triumphant regent. Or was I delusional and just needed to cling to hope?

"I'm going to send a message to Princess Ellery and see if she can help." Stone pulled out a device and pushed a bunch of buttons.

"That could take awhile." Lukas continued to prowl around the old banshee campsite, stopping here and there to examine something on the ground.

"In the meantime, we continue to track her down." Stone stomped his foot. He slung a backpack across his shoulder and faced the others. "You each have to make your own decision if you want to continue with me. I understand you were in the dungeon for a long time and want to get back to your families."

"Destiny is family." Cassia snapped her fingers and a ball of light shone in her hand.

Pith jumped off the log. "She saved us from the dungeon. If we'd still been imprisoned, we would've been killed during the battle against the regent."

"Or tortured in the auraguillotine," Trolgar added.

Gratefulness filled my soul. My friends stuck up for me and believed in me. They'd escaped after the battle, and instead of heading home or hiding, they searched for me even now.

Or so I thought.

I jerked awake. My entire body tensed. It was a dream, and I was still freezing on this stupid rock. I gnawed my bottom lip and rubbed my arms. If I kept falling asleep, I'd die sooner. Now that I'd had a dream about Stone and my friends, I needed to fight to stay alive so I could find them and heal Grandfather.

The fairy princess strolled in the forest with Prince Zacharye at her side. Were they hiding from the regent? She studied a device similar to Stone's.

Was my stream of consciousness like a story with chapters, each scene unfolding in my mind?

"Stone needs our help." Princess Ellery waved a hand. "Drago!"

I waited for the dragon, waited to see if it was the same dragon I'd injured.

When the dragon landed, Prince Zacharye pet the scaly beast. The dragon didn't have the wound from the rock I'd thrown. Unless this was before the attack. Was I seeing the future or the past?

Or was this just part of the floating-above-an-abyss-in-the-freez-ing-cold nightmare?

"Is Stone searching for the lost girl who has the prophecy?" the prince asked.

Me? I thought he searched for me because he cared. My heart cracked with reality.

"Yes." She stroked the dragon's snout. "I need you to help me find a female banshee. Search the west side of Drage Mountain. Be safe and always be on the lookout for Regent Theobald."

I convulsed at the mention of the evil man. The prince and princess must be hiding from him. Hopefully, fighting against him. If I survived and got my magic, I was going to heal Grandfather, help the female banshees, find Stone, and join the fight against the regent with my newly-released powers. The list kept getting longer and longer.

I needed Drago to find me. I hoped he wasn't mad I'd hurt him. He could fly out here and rescue me from the precipice. "Drago!"

My scratchy voice woke me up.

There was no Drago and no rescue. Another dream. I was adrift in hopelessness.

If the prince and princess were fighting against the regent, they didn't have time to worry about me. My eyes prickled as if I was about to cry, but I was either too dehydrated or my tear ducts were frozen because no tears flowed. The cold infiltrated through the old wool blanket and my skin. The freeze permeated my soul. Rolling, I peeked over the edge and lost my breath.

The beautiful view spread out below me. The clouds were completely gone, and I could make out the cliffs and the trees and the river more clearly. I searched for a dragon in the sky.

Regent Theobald sat in a gold chair. It wasn't a throne chair, although it was difficult to see in the darkness. No modern lights blazed, candles and flashlights barely lit the dark room.

A few guards wearing ripped and splattered uniforms watched the wide-rounded doorway. The entrance resembled a cave opening. A drumming came from outside.

A woman with curly blonde hair strutted in. "They are approaching."

"Are we ready for them, Bee?" The regent straightened in his chair and rubbed his hands together.

"Oh, I'm ready." Bee wrapped her arms around the regent and kissed him on the cheek. Standing, she tugged the tight dress she wore. "The negotiations will be a Binding Promise."

The term sounded familiar.

"They believe they will have rights and partial control, but once they hand her over, the prophecy will be destroyed. We'll kill them all."

The regent's wicked smile made me tremble. "So glad we hid another auraguillotine to complete the job."

Another auraguillotine?

The drumming grew louder.

My teeth chattered, waking me up. That must've been the drumming in my dream. The beat reminded me of the banshee drums while traveling and in celebration. I rubbed the goosebumps on my skin. At this rate, the bumps would become permanent. I was so cold.

Curling into a ball, I tried to keep my core warm. My heavy lids blinked a couple of times and closed again. If I wasn't saved by Drago or the healer soon, I'd be joining my parents in death.

Grandfather plodded into the impeccably designed room with antique furniture and grand paintings on the wall. Vi and I sat at a checkered table with marble chess pieces.

"Check." Vi, also known as Lord Vitor and Stone, moved a rook into position.

I harrumphed. Since receiving the chess set for my seventh birthday, he'd beaten me at the game every time we played. My pulse stilled. It was the same chess set he had in his suite of rooms as Lord Vitor. He'd kept my game.

"Vi, you need to go back to your family's suite now." Grandfather's terse tone held a note of sadness.

"We're in the middle of a game." I didn't want him to go home yet. I saw a chance to win against my friend this time.

"I'm sorry." Grandfather's eyes appeared red and his cheeks puffy. "Vi needs to go now."

Tension filled the room. I sensed something was wrong and tried to see inside Grandfather's mind.

"Stop, Destiny." He glared and proceeded to his bedroom.

Vi pushed back his chair showing his full height. He flashed a special grin at me. "See you later."

"Bye." I stood and shuffled to my grandfather's bedroom and knocked on the open door. He had a suitcase open and was throwing things inside. "What's wrong, Grandfather?"

He sank into a chair and patted his lap. I climbed on and wrapped my arms around his neck. His labored breathing showed he was upset.

I couldn't take the silence any longer. "What?"

"We're going on a trip." He smiled but it didn't reach his eyes. "Pack one small bag with your most important possessions."

"Okay." We rarely went anywhere and this didn't seem to be a vacation. "What about Mom and Dad? Are they going on the trip?"

"No." His voice cracked and tears fell. "I'm sorry, Destiny. There's no easy way to say this."

A shadow fell across my heart. He didn't need to say anything. I knew.

My parents were dead.

My head nodded and I jerked awake. My body quaked. A memory from my childhood I hadn't remembered until now.

The cold hit me immediately. I must have fallen asleep again. Surveying over the edge, I shivered. Falling asleep could lead to falling, which could lead to death.

Like my parents.

A single tear leaked out and dripped down my cheek, freezing on my skin.

I remembered the day now. Too clearly. I'd been numb, similar to how I was right now except the numbness had come from grief. At the time, I'd also sensed something alive beneath my skin, something itching to get out.

Grandfather had packed a few things. Vi, my childhood friend, had stopped by one more time. We'd barely had the chance to say goodbye. Then Grandfather and I had traveled to the banshee encampment where they'd locked my memories and magic.

And now I was back with the banshees.

Possibly being murdered by them.

I moaned. Between the cold and the floating piece of frozen rock, I hung onto my life by a thread. I squeezed my eyes shut. Visions and images, dreams and nightmares, whirled like a fast-spinning, nonstop kaleidoscope making me dizzy.

The raging bonfire at the banshee camp and a young Charmig simpering. His father staring at me with greed.

Moving into the small house in the mound with Grandfather, becoming hermits, and rarely venturing outside. How I'd been basically catatonic for months.

Playing hide and seek with Vi in the palace and him shouting, 'I'm going to find you.'

These were not dreams, they were memories. Memories locked away for the past nine years. I tossed and turned with new-old flashbacks with minute details.

Grabbing my head, my mind filled up with past recollections. Memories and the clashing emotions coming with them. My heart sagged with the weight of conflicting feelings. Happiness and sadness. Warmth and terror. Fear and friendship.

I rolled the other way.

My mother rotated her hands and created a ball of light. She tossed the ball up. Not banshee magic.

Smashing a piece of chocolate cake into my mouth on my first birthday and remembering the sweet taste. Pride beamed off my parents and grandfather.

Turning the other way, I tried to stop the thoughts and recollections. I couldn't.

I tossed the other way and rolled off the edge.

A second of weightlessness had my insides tightening and disbelief dazzling my sight.

There was nothing sturdy beneath me.

I screamed, "Ahhhh!"

Flinging my arms up, I grabbed the edge of the precipice. My breath rasped. I didn't know what to do. I hung off the floating rock. My arms strained while my mind was bombarded by more images and visions. Every single detail came into focus. I remembered everything.

Everything.

From the moment I was born, to my strange naming ceremony, to being friends with Vi, to rushing out of the palace after my parents died. Renewed grief hit me in my center. My knuckles whitened and I repositioned my hands on the precipice. I refused to die from this fall. I was different. I had an important destiny, I just didn't know what that destiny was. But I now had the knowledge to move forward. I couldn't die.

If only I had the magic to rescue myself.

The sun rose over the mountain and light streamed onto my face. The clouds were gone, and I could see for miles in every direction. Banshee wails reached me from our encampment far below.

"Don't look down." I regripped the ledge.

Charmig, Svante, and Ursee stood at the edge of the cliff, jumping up and down. They wailed too.

My constricting ribs poked my lungs and oxygen leaked out. Were they predicting my death?

Not if I could help it. I wasn't going to die today. I struggled to pull myself back on the floating rock. My muscles tightened and strained. Sweat formed on my upper lip.

Ursee stopped wailing to speak into a communication device. Her animated motions told me she was excited.

I wasn't excited. Blackness surrounded my brain in a thundercloud. Static currents crashed through my heart. A squeezing pressure built in my chest.

"Ahhhhhhhhhhhhh!" I joined the banshees in their wailing. "Ahhhhhhhhhhhh!"

The precipice crumbled beneath my fingers. The icy crag splintered and blasted into pieces.

And I dropped into the abyss.

Chapter Fifteen

I was *falling, falling, falling.*

Panic skittered across my skin while air rushed from my feet to my head making me dizzy. My fear of heights was nothing compared to my fear of hitting the ground. A cold draft whizzed past me on my way down. My lungs deflated and I couldn't breathe.

This was it. The banshee wailing had predicted my death. I'd predicted my death.

Raising my hands, I hoped it would be quick. When I hit the ground, I wanted to die on impact.

Except...my falling pace slowed. In fact, I seemed to be moving upward.

Confusion rattled in my dizzy brain. So much had happened to me in the last few hours I didn't know which way was up. That was the only explanation.

However...I was definitely headed higher.

The cliff Charmig, Svante, and Ursee stood on didn't appear as tall. The ledge wasn't as far away. The ground below became smaller.

My stomach lurched. I was going up. I was flying.

Without wings.

I tensed. How was flying even possible? What sorcery was this? *Magic. My magic.*

My locked banshee magic now set free.

Power shimmied through me. Finally, all my banshee powers had been released. I imagined them thrumming and pulsing through my veins, bringing me strength and taking away my fears. If I had magic, I couldn't fall. I could fly.

I twirled around, trying to get my bearings. If I could fly, I didn't have to stay where Ursee had put me, I didn't have to listen to Svante or Charmig. Or his father. I could do what I wanted, help who I pleased, heal Grandfather.

Soaring upward, I enjoyed the exhilaration and weightlessness. Triumph ran through my bloodstream. This was more than old magic locked away. I'd never heard of banshee with flying powers. We didn't even get wings.

Squinting down, panic shrieked through me. I was so high. I dropped my arms.

Not for long. I went *down, down, down*.

My brain buzzed. I pointed my arms back up and I went up. I didn't know how I was doing this, but I didn't want to fall.

Keeping my hands raised, I pointed toward the ledge where the banshees stood. It's how I focused my power for the heks scream. Maybe this was the same. I moved toward them. It wasn't exactly flying, more like floating. Or rocketing because I was going fast.

Their incredulous expressions broadcasted even this far away. They weren't expecting this to happen. Angling my head, I wondered what they had been expecting. Did they even know how I was going to get off the precipice? Or did they want me to die?

Glaring, I hovered above the three of them. Ursee read from a book, murmuring a chant. Charmig's face whitened. His body swayed and he fainted. His body hit the ground. Svante's lips twisted and his gaze narrowed. He watched me as if I was prey.

Maybe because I was flying like a bird.

Exhilaration flittered through me, spreading lightness and joy. I held in a giggle and lowered my arms to descend. I raised my arms quickly and flew straight up. Without wings, I controlled my flight with my arms.

"I can't believe it's real." Ursee waved at me. "Land here."

Her telling me what to do rubbed against my nerves. She'd tricked me, forced me to drink dragon blood, and left me out on a freezing crag to die. "Why should I?"

"Because you want to heal others, don't you?"

Grandfather.

Lowering my arms, I directed my body toward the spot she pointed. My body hit the ground and I landed in a crouched position. Good thing the snow comforted my drop. I'd have to learn how to land. Maybe the princess could teach me since she knew how to fly.

I stood on quivering legs. "What happened to me?"

Svante helped Charmig stand up.

"She is more than Lys." Ursee referred to her book. "Her background and upbringing and..."

"I don't care what I am." The new power jolted through my body. "I'm alive and you said I'd have the power to heal. Heal Grandfather."

The thought brought a smile to my face. The first step in my multi-step plan. I was alive and had my memories and my powers. What did they think was next? And would I go along with it?

The three of them exchanged glances. The healer shook her head warning them against something.

Wariness tamped down on my excitement about my magic. "What?"

"Nothing." She tucked the communication device into a coat pocket. "Let's try some spells."

Svante pulled out an energy bar and gave it to me. "Eat this for strength."

"Nothing toxic or a gross animal byproduct?" I still tasted the dragon blood on my tongue.

"No." He better not poison me like Charmig.

I sucked down the food, not realizing my intense hunger. "What do you mean by spells?"

"She means your natural banshee magic." Charmig's quick tone told me he was hiding something.

"Yes, um," she thumbed through the ancient book. "We'll start with something simple."

"We'll start by heading back to the encampment." After eating, I felt stronger. I didn't want to waste time. I'd practice by healing Grandfather.

Charmig put an arm around my shoulders. "She's right. We should get back. There's a celebration taking place."

"What's being celebrated?"

"You."

The celebration, supposedly for me, had started before we arrived at the camp to drumbeats, music, and dancing. How could it be for me when they didn't know what had happened? Of course, Ursee had a communication device so she could've told them. If they were celebrating me, shouldn't they wait for me?

I'd wanted to fly back to camp. She'd convinced me I shouldn't because it would make me too tired. She was right. I needed energy to heal Grandfather.

The music halted. The warriors stopped dancing and drinking immediately. The rest of the banshees followed their actions.

My face heated. I didn't enjoy the attention or the atmosphere of expectation. Expectation about me. Ursee must have communicated to Grand Lord Justicar. He normally didn't share information with the other banshees. A sense of dread chilled my bones.

"Lys Destiny!" A single loud clap sounded. "Lys Destiny!" Another clap and another. The warriors clapped in a slow pattern giving more emphasis to the applause.

Male warriors marched over to me and lifted me off the eleram. They carried me, and this time I wasn't afraid of the height. Charmig and Svante dismounted and joined the procession. Were they celebrating my new powers or the fact that I'd survived the night?

My pulse skipped a beat. What was the earlier banshee wailing about? Whose death had been predicted if not mine?

The warriors carried me to the leader's chair. Ursee stood by his side.

"Lys Destiny!" He saluted me.

I dipped my head, proud and embarrassed about the attention, and also mad they hadn't told me what was to come. Mad about the cold. Mad about the fear they'd instilled.

"Lys Destiny! Lys Destiny! Lys Destiny!" The crowd cheered and slow clapped with enthusiasm. I saw Reitha standing on a rock trying to see. Her grandmother stood beside her.

Shaking my head, I didn't deserve this recognition. Not until I did something worth the praise like saving my grandfather.

"Lys Destiny." He quieted the crowd with a hand gesture. "Warrior of the Skjult Banshee Clan."

The warriors set me on my feet. I wasn't sure how to respond. "Um, thank you."

Thank you for sticking me out on a precipice which broke off from the ledge and floated to the sky in freezing weather. I couldn't believe I'd survived. Now, it was time to get to work. "Where's my grandfather?"

Women and children shimmied around me. They raised their voices in song. The drums played and music chimed in. The females swayed, blocking me. A drink was pressed into my hand. Taking a sip, I thought about the last thing I'd drank—dragon's blood. I swished the liquid around in my mouth. Realizing it was alcohol, I spit it back in the cup.

The dancers pranced away from me and gathered around the large bonfire. Swaying, the seemingly drunken warriors hit on several of the young females. They laughed and flirted. Svante drew the leader aside and whispered. Maybe he was describing the spectacle he'd witnessed. Charmig had pulled Lykke behind a tent. I wondered what was happening between them.

It didn't matter. Nothing mattered except healing Grandfather.

The new campsite sat in a valley between cliffs. The tents had been arranged in different positions. The biggest tent had the best location, followed by the next few biggest ones. I couldn't spot the healer's tent.

Fighting against the crowd, I grabbed hold of Ursee's arm to stop her from walking away. "Is my grandfather in your tent? Which one is it?"

"This is a party for you. There will be plenty of time to talk about your grandfather later." A smile didn't change her hard expression. She ordered me to have fun.

"I don't want to talk about him. I want to see him." The dread I'd experienced upon arrival grew into a misshapen ball in my stomach. Something wasn't right.

"You haven't learned the basics of magical healing." She tried to free her arm in a wild dance move and avoided my gaze. "We'll start in the morning."

I gripped her arm tighter. Determination ramrodded through my spine. "We'll start now."

"Very well." She nodded and glanced at the leader.

I didn't know what they silently communicated but I didn't appreciate it. My feet quickened.

No guards stood outside the small healer's tent. A foreboding sign, or maybe they'd been allowed to go to the party. The ball in my stomach grew and dragged to my chest, weighing heavily on my spirits. I snagged the tent flap and rushed inside.

Grandfather laid on the small cot similar to the last time I'd seen him inside the tent.

Something was different.

No life force exuded from him. No aura.

My body tensed and I didn't want to go forward. I didn't want to know.

But I had to. I approached slowly, noting everything about him. The gray skin on his face appeared to be carved in stone. His lips were purple. His eyes were closed.

"Grandfather?" I called to him.

Deep in my gut I knew he wouldn't respond.

I took hold of his cold hand, colder than I'd been out on the precipice. Dead cold.

My heart ripped in two. My lungs shredded and my eyes went dry. I threw myself on top of his lifeless body. "Nooooo!"

Coldness from his body infiltrated my soul. Memories of him floated through my mind. So many memories. The ones I'd always remembered, and the ones locked away for years. The images assaulted me and I couldn't find a space of calm.

We'd always been together. When my parents were alive, he worked at the palace too. Grandfather was always there. He'd watch me when they went on missions. He'd been a second father, a protector, and a guide.

The good and the bad. The conversations and the laughs. The fights and the love.

Sure, he'd been stubborn and tough and hidden me away. But now I understood why.

A sob welled and a cry burst out of my mouth. I cried for the things we'd had together that I didn't appreciate. For the love I never expressed enough. For the life he'd given up to keep me hidden. I took a raspy inhalation. He'd never again comfort me when I was sad. He'd never hug or kiss me. He'd never console me after a nightmare.

Disbelief morphed into rage and lanced through me, bringing so much agony I didn't know where the pain began or ended. I lifted my head and scowled at Ursee. "What happened to him? You said he'd be fine."

She twisted her hands together. "I thought he'd be fine for the short time I was with you."

"He wasn't." I lunged and grabbed her shoulders.

She gripped my arms, trying to pull me off. "It was a long journey and—"

"An unnecessary journey." Fury brought force to my tone.

"We needed to bring you to the Obsidian Precipice for you to get your powers before...before—"

I knocked her hands off my arms and stalked toward the cot with my dead grandfather. Slipping the watch off his wrist, I clutched it in my hands. Something to remember him, though I'd never forget.

Grand Lord Justicar had made a big deal of my powers. Not me. And certainly not my grandfather.

I held Grandfather's hand again like it was a lifeline and sent a glare toward the healer. "Is that all you and the leader care about?" I wouldn't call him by his real title.

"You cared about your powers." She used a persuasive voice. "You needed your unlocked powers to heal your grandfather."

A dark chortle erupted out of my mouth. "Well, a lot of good it did me."

She placed an arm around my shoulders. "Your grandfather was old. He lived his life. He'd want you to have his powers."

My jaw dropped. "What?"

She released me and took a step back. "What I meant was, he'd want you to have your powers that have been locked away for years."

I furrowed my brow while watching her through a narrowed gaze. Something was off. My grief-stricken brain couldn't fully process. I needed to be by myself. "Leave me alone."

"Everyone is celebrating tonight. We'll begin the grieving process tomorrow. Come and have a drink."

"I don't want a drink." As if I could put my emotions on hold.

The brownie who normally served the healer opened the tent and let the leader in. Wearing more beads than normal, he placed a hand on my arm. "Are you okay?"

I swiped his hand off. He couldn't comfort me. No one could. Fury built and boiled, stirring and whirling, about to explode into action.

"You knew he died." I rushed him and grabbed the beads hanging around his neck and yanked. "Why didn't you send a messenger up to the precipice or use the communication device? We could've done the ceremony on another day."

Two guards stepped forward and stood next to the leader. Their expressions hardened in a threatening manner.

So much for being celebrated.

The leader shook his head and placed his hands on mine. He didn't try to remove them from his torso. "It happened at dawn while you were in the midst of your ceremony." His lowered tone vibrated hollow. "There was nothing you could do."

Couldn't I? My mind flew in a million directions but landed at the same place. "You said I'd be powerful." How powerful? Powerful enough to do the impossible? "I can bring my grandfather back to life."

Ursee gasped.

The leader jerked back and gentled his expression. "You have very powerful magic, but not enough. And no one should bring the dead back to life. It's sacrilegious."

My hope flew, resembling my thoughts, never to return. Someone could bring the dead back to life, just not me. Glowering, anger settled at him and the healer. If they hadn't dragged Grandfather on the long journey, if the healer hadn't left him alone to escort me. There must be something I could do, but I'd never get answers from them. I stormed out of the tent.

Sound assaulted my ears. The noise of celebration. Laughter and music. Drums and horns. Jangling jewelry from the dancing. Joyous shouts. I scrunched down, not wanting any part of the celebration. I had nothing to celebrate.

Only grief.

Pushing my way through the raucous, drunken crowd, I dodged flailing arms and dancing bodies. The stench of sweat, smoke, and alcohol mixed together making me feel sick. I didn't see Lykke or Charmig, or even Svante. That was okay. I'd rather be alone.

Hardening myself against their jubilee, I shoved my way through the crowd. I couldn't handle everyone having fun when I was devastated. I needed to get away from them and the clamor and the smell. Spending time in my tent would be claustrophobic. Grabbing a blanket off a pile, I headed toward the nearest bluff.

Another dead end.

I moaned. If I couldn't go further away, I'd go up. Scanning to the top of the bluff, I figured it was nothing compared to the ledge I'd been on earlier. This was only thirty feet high. I could handle it, and if I didn't, I could fly.

Flying would end my fear of heights real quick.

Putting Grandfather's watch around my wrist, I lifted my arms. Floating up, I picked a spot at the edge and sat down, dangling my legs. The muted noise from the party below soothed. The blazing bonfire competed with the hi-tech lighting scattered around the perimeter of the encampment. I could make out banshees moving, but not anyone specific.

I was surprised no one had followed me. Although they couldn't follow me into the sky. I wrapped the blanket around myself and contemplated the sky. A burning sensation crawled up my chest and into my throat. My body trembled and not from the cold. I blinked several times trying to stop the telling prickling sensation in my eyes.

Taking a shattered breath, I let myself cry.

Cry for the loss of my grandfather.

Cry for missing Stone.

Cry for me.

Grandfather was my anchor and now I felt adrift. Stone was my protector and comforter. He made me feel capable and strong, and now I missed him even more. And for myself, now I didn't know what direction to turn, where to go or what to do. I had my list of things I wanted to accomplish. I'd failed at healing Grandfather. What else would I fail?

I rubbed my fingers together, trying to get control of my emotions. I couldn't fail again. I rubbed my fingers faster and fiercer.

Little sparks shot out from the tips.

I halted the motion. Part of my new magic? I might not know how to yield the new power, but the sparks of light comforted me. Made me believe I was less alone.

Swirling my finger around, a circle of light formed in the sky.

The light gleamed off something shiny and orange. A scaly orange.

I squinted, trying to distinguish why the orange boulder was different from the other rocks around. The orangish boulder was stuck between the cliff I sat on and the one across the way, shoved into the hidden spot. The orange boulder had white rope tied around the bulk as if someone had used the lines to climb to the top. The front of the boulder had a snout shape and pointed teeth.

Gasping, I realized this wasn't an odd colored boulder. It was a dragon. One of my dream-visions was true. He had come to find me. "Drago?"

Chapter Sixteen

Scrunching low, I peered at the dragon from the cliff on the other side. Only two banshee guards patrolled the area around the large dragon, marching between the dragon's mouth and tied tail in the narrow passage between the two cliffs. Similar to my vision.

Did they tease and torture the beast as well?

I sucked in. If part of my earlier dream-vision was accurate, all of them might be. I'd had another dream about Stone searching for me. Had that dream been real? And if the more recent dream about Princess Ellery and a dragon was correct, it meant this dragon was her friend and pet, Drago. And I'd hurt the poor guy.

Only one way to find out.

Scooting down the cliff on my knees and elbows, rocks scraped and dug into my skin. I didn't care about the pain. Hopefully, I could heal the wounds. A trickle of rocks released and rolled down. The clatter had me stiffening. I couldn't be spotted.

The beating of drums and music still rang. The clan partied on. The guards patrolling around Drago didn't pause or switch directions. The noise of the party worked in favor of my current mission.

Reaching the bottom, I noted the passage around Drago and the two cliffs was only wide enough for one person at a time to slip through. Just enough room for one guard to patrol as they circled the animal on a regular pattern.

With my pulse charging, I bent down by the side of the dragon. My fingers fumbled on the rope as I slipped one end through the knot. I uncoiled the free end and passed it around the anchor point. I left the knot lying there as if it was tied.

I tiptoed to the next rope, untied it, and slinked to the next.

A guard rounded the dragon's tail, coming my way.

My muscles tensed. My gaze sought an escape and found only one way to hide. Up. Placing my foot between a scale, I patted the animal. "Sorry, Drago."

I placed my hand on a scale and pulled myself up. Hand over hand, I climbed to the top.

The guard glanced up and I pressed myself against Drago's body. The slick scales emanated with the dragon's body heat. My chest pounded faster and faster. If I got caught, they'd probably lock me up. The guard moved on and I waited for him to reach the snout of the dragon and turn. I only had a little time until the next guard rounded the animal.

Staying low, I crept forward and stopped near the open wound I'd inflicted. Sorrow passed through me. I hadn't wanted to injure the dragon, just save the helpless banshees. Now, it might turn out that I'd injured the dragon trying to rescue me.

I patted him. "Drago. I'm a friend of a friend of Princess Ellery." *Kind of.* I hoped he understood what I was saying. "I'm sorry I hurt you with the boulder. I didn't realize you were searching for me." Still wasn't positive. "I'm going to set you free."

The animal's scales shimmied sensing my amicable stroke and words.

I patted him again. "Will you tell her to tell Stone that I'm okay and I'll find my way back to him soon."

If Stone came for me, I didn't know what the banshees would do to him. They weren't kind to strangers. They weren't even kind to their own.

I slid off the dragon and paused, listening for hurrying footsteps. My message was long, and I hoped the dragon understood at least part of it. Especially the part where I didn't mean him harm.

I rounded the dragon's front. The snout wasn't tacked to the ground like the rest of his body. A rope had been wrapped several times around his snout, keeping the mouth closed tight. He could only breathe through his wide nostrils.

Which meant the dragon couldn't shoot flames.

Even though he'd attacked the former campsite, Drago didn't deserve this cruel treatment. I now realized he hadn't meant harm, he believed he was protecting me. Because of his connection with the princess, and the fact that banshees drained dragon blood, he must've had a reason to attack.

His large, dazed gaze followed my movements. He didn't seem scared, but I didn't want to frighten him with my actions.

"Be patient." I worked on loosening the knots keeping his mouth shut. I did not remove the rope completely, hoping the guards wouldn't notice and the dragon wouldn't act until I was ready.

Following the pattern of the guards, I rounded the other side of the dragon, untied the first rope, and stopped.

A clear rubber tube stuck out between Drago's scales. Blood drained through the tube into a pump that throbbed faster than a heart. Below the pump a large container collected the blood.

My stomach churned and I squeezed my eyes shut for a second remembering a similar device in the healer's tent. A coppery taste filled my mouth. Saliva gathered. I spat on the ground and fisted my hands, wanting to punch something. This was cruelty. The banshee ceremonies were archaic, forcing me to drink dragon blood, giving me a tattoo without my permission, most likely expecting me to marry someone they picked.

Never going to happen.

If they knew the dragon was a friend of the princess, they wouldn't treat it this poorly. I hung my head. It was me who'd thrown the rock at Drago to bring him down. The leader and his mighty warriors had run. I snorted.

I couldn't tell the banshees who the dragon was. Somehow they'd find a way to use the information against the princess.

I'd already brought the mighty dragon down. I didn't want to be responsible for him being held for ransom.

Shaking out my fists, I had to stop this. Now. The more blood Drago lost, the weaker he'd become. He wouldn't be able to fly to safety. I wrapped my hand around the tube. Blowing out a calming huff, I didn't know whether to slide the tube out slowly or yank it. Doing it quickly seemed to be the best option. The guards could round the beast at any second.

"Sorry, Drago. This might hurt." I tugged on the tubing. "Don't howl and give my position away."

With a plop, the tubing jerked out of the dragon. Blood poured from the wound.

"Ew."

Drago's body trembled.

Worry settled into my gut. If he couldn't fly, I'd risked releasing him for nothing.

He was losing more blood than before. I had to stop the flow. I took a hold of my cloak and ripped the garment, tearing off a piece. Holding the cloth to the wound, I pressed against it. The cloth became saturated with his blood.

I skimmed the area, hoping the guards didn't see. They'd definitely notice the loose tubing and piece of cloth. They might even recognize it as coming from my cloak. Although I'd given away my other cloaks and many clothes. Maybe they wouldn't be able to pinpoint the sabotage to me.

Shrugging, I didn't care. I was glad I was freeing Drago.

I tucked the cloth between scales to hold it in place and hurried down his belly, untying ropes as I went.

The tail wouldn't be so easy.

Stopping to assess, I noted how the women had wrapped the tail in a canvas tent to cover the spikes. They'd used ropes to tie the canvas on and more ropes to tack the tail to the ground.

How was I going to get the tail untied without the guards noticing or Drago mistakenly swinging his ferocious tail and hitting me?

Magic was my best option.

Clearing my mind, I focused on what I wanted to do. I'd never used magic to do anything like this before, but all my magic was available to me now. In the past, I'd been filled with emotion when performing magic I didn't understand how to use. Surely, I could do something simple. I peered back and forth. A guard would round the beast soon. It was either now or get caught.

I rubbed my fingers together and a spark lit. The flicker gave me an idea.

Rubbing my fingers harder, I stepped closer to the tail. Sparks kindled and ignited. I set my hands on the edge of the canvas and blew gently on the tiny flame.

The fire would serve two purposes. The flames would loosen the canvas and ropes around the tail and weaken the construction. Drago's scales would protect him from being scorched. As the fire grew bigger it would signal Drago that it was time to fly away.

Flames caught and grew. Smoke filled the area. The fire went higher and higher.

Too high. The fire had grown out of control.

I took a step back and bumped into the cliff.

Dismay trickled through me. I was trapped between a rock and a hot place.

"*Skreeeep. Skreeeep.*" Drago's tail swished, almost catching me with one of his sharp spikes.

My breath caught and I jumped. High, really high. I pointed my arms up and flew like I'd done on the Obsidian Precipice.

"Fire!" A guard ran toward the back of the dragon and stopped.

Worry jabbed. Had he seen me? Although I'd set the fire intentionally, I hadn't figured out the rest of my escape plan.

The high flames flicked in front of me. Smoke filled the space between the two bluffs.

"The dragon is on fire!" the other guard shouted.

Drago's wings flapped, creating a draft. Now, I could see him clearly. His tail swished, ridding himself of the blazing canvas. He opened his mouth and shot out a small flame. His wings flapped again and he sprang into the air. "*Skreeeep.*"

His roar sounded relieved and happy. He was free.

Smugness solidified in my bones. Floating above the cliff, I watched Drago rise with the disappearing smoke. He lifted a claw and saluted me before he flew away, moving slower than his original attack. He must be weak and in pain from the injury and the blood draining. Once he was away from here, he could land and rest somewhere safe. He'd heal.

Startled, I noted that the salute had been at eye level. Which meant I was at the same height as him. I gaped at the ground below, way below. The nausea and shakiness I normally experienced with my fear of heights was gone. I guess being able to fly meant I could never truly fall.

I felt free. Light and breezy. A grin lit my face. I could truly be free. There was nothing holding me here. Drago might lead me to the princess who could take me to Stone. I'd feel terrible about abandoning Reitha and the other female banshees, but I needed to be safe myself before I could figure out how to help them.

The drums, the music, and the celebration stopped below. They must've spotted the smoke, or more likely the flying dragon. The banshees stared.

Not at Drago. At me.

If I was going to leave, now would be the time. The only goodbye would be from a distance. I lifted my arm to wave.

A flaming arrow swooshed into the sky.

My veins sizzled. I dove to the right.

Another flaming arrow flew.

They were trying to kill me. I dove to the left.

Banshee warriors shot several more arrows into the sky. The arching patterns of light crisscrossed the dark night. The image would've been beautiful if it wasn't so deadly.

Deadly to me.

My temples pounded and agony spiraled through my head. They tried to shoot me down. They didn't care about me. I careened right and left again. Up and down. The weaving and dodging threw me off balance. I didn't know which way was up.

An arrow hit my forearm. Sharp pain pierced my skin and the flame sizzled.

Losing control, I started falling. This time it wasn't like when I'd fallen off the Obsidian Precipice. This time I couldn't raise my arms to stop the fall. Alarms rang and echoed in my body. The arrow must've done something to my muscles.

I screamed.

My entire arm went numb. My mind went cloudy. I squeezed my eyes tight, trying to control the random thoughts in my mind.

Dragon. Fire. Goodbye. Stone.

I fell and fell. My body flopped right and left. Feet first then head first. Opening my eyes, I didn't fear and it wasn't because I was no longer afraid of heights. Rationally, I knew I'd smash to the ground and probably die. Or be seriously injured, and I didn't trust Ursee to heal me. The arrow tip must've had some drug on it. Why else wouldn't I care about falling to my death? I drew ragged pants in and out. I'd never be able to help the female banshees or the captive brownies, never be able to help the prince. I'd never get to tell Stone I loved him.

I tensed and closed my eyes, awaiting impact.

My body hit. Except it wasn't the cold, hard, deadly ground. Warmth wrapped around me with strong arms. Not able to shift my arm, I quickly analyzed my other various limbs and body parts. No real pain. No burning injury. No blood.

No death.

Opening my eyes, I gazed into Svante's concerned expression.

He held me in his strong arms. His mouth gaped open, trying to suck in more oxygen. His wide eyes zeroed in on me. "Are you alright?"

"Yes." I sounded faint and unsure.

"Lys Destiny! The prophecy is true," the banshees chanted. "Hail Lys Destiny!"

The chanting bombarded. They were talking about me, hailing me. My body curled in on itself and I buried my face in Svante's chest. I didn't want them to think of me as some type of hero or prophet. But they'd seen me fly. And fall.

More murmurs reached my ears. Not as loud, but somehow more tormenting. Something about sorcery and evil. I couldn't make sense of what they said.

Before I could protest, anti-magic bracelets slapped around my wrists. My numb arm couldn't fight the restriction and my other arm was pinned against Svante. He set me on my feet. Two armed guards immediately took hold of my arms, stopping me from doing anything.

Panic streaked through me and I struggled. "Why are they doing this?"

"I ordered them to." Grand Lord Justicar's brows thundered in anger.

I hadn't heard a command.

"Why did you free the dragon?"

Firming my lips, I glared at the man. Prickles of banshee gazes stuck in my back. I sensed their stares. At least they'd stopped the awful chant.

Shifting my feet, I couldn't tell them the truth.

Grand Lord Justicar stood tall, glowering. "Why would you free an animal you'd brought down?"

His throwing it back at me was a slap. "Why were you torturing Drago—dragon, the dragon?"

I didn't want them to know that I knew the dragon's name. They'd really flip out if they thought I spoke with the animal or knew about my accurate visions.

Or knew I'd intended to fly away with him.

"You injured the dragon." His accusation-explanation didn't work on me.

I tamped down my temper. How dare he blame the dragon's state on me. "While saving banshees. Your clan." I emphasized the last part. If he wanted to toss around accusations, I'd join in. "While you ran from the danger."

His gaze darted around in a nervous sign. He judged what the other banshees thought of my reckless yet truthful allegation. "Or maybe you didn't mean to free the dragon. Maybe you were playing with magic and it went wrong."

The accusation stabbed deep.

"No." My magic had gone exactly right. Well, until the falling part. "Did you drug me with those arrows?"

"Ursee." The leader stepped back from me as the healer lurched closer. He never answered my question, but I knew by the way he avoided my eyes it was true. "See to her wound."

I tried to step away, not wanting to end up dead like my grandfather. The two guards held me in place.

The leader stood on his grand chair and raised his voice. "Destiny set the fire by accident. The dragon freed itself and almost killed her."

His easily-told fib made me wonder what else he'd lied about.

The crowd shouted, "Hail Lys Destiny. Pray for Lys Destiny. The prophecy is true!"

I couldn't shout over the crowd to correct him, and what they said confused me. What prophecy? Something tingled in the back of my brain.

The leader stepped off his chair with the help of his son. He leaned into me. "The truth of you freeing the dragon and trying to escape will be our secret. You wouldn't want your people to believe you'd abandon them."

The guilt trip didn't work. I was proud that I'd freed the dragon. But if everyone in the clan learned I'd planned to fly away, there would be more distrusting eyes always watching me. It would make escape harder. "I'll keep the secret if you tell me what prophecy they're yelling about?"

The healer had said something right before I'd drifted away on the Obsidian Precipice, and I'd heard about this prophecy in my dream-visions. Did everyone know about a prophecy involving me, except me?

Loneliness surrounded me in a black cloud. Or was it the drugs? I felt lost in my own life.

The banshees went quiet. They watched our exchange with expressions of awe and terror. Were they more afraid of me or their leader?

"Your magic will be quite powerful." His gravelly tone made me think of greediness. "But unapproved magic is not allowed."

I huffed. Being treated as a child dug at me. I'd simply set a dragon free and flew. What the banshees wanted or approved of didn't matter to me anymore. Grandfather was gone and it was time for me to be on my way. I'd figure out how to control my magic on my own.

"Take Destiny to her tent," the leader ordered the guards who held me. "Make sure she stays there."

I jostled my shoulders. I wasn't a prisoner, and it was too late to leave tonight anyway. "I can walk there myself."

"I'll escort her." Charmig stepped from beside his father and took hold of my arm.

The crowd parted around us. I tried to spot Svante to thank him for catching me. He was deep in the crowd talking to a young girl. Was that my friend Reitha?

Narrowing my gaze, I turned and studied Charmig's expression. "No funny business."

"I promise." He placed his palm on his chest.

Charmig walked me and the guards followed close behind. The anti-magic bracelets rubbed against my wrists, reminding me I couldn't fly or start a fire or do anything else. Which meant I couldn't leave yet.

Lykke must've pushed through the crowd because she stood by my tent. "I'll help you prepare for bed."

Additional guards took positions around my tent. Were they afraid I was going to sneak out in the dead of night?

Angling my head, I thought about the idea. The temperature was already below freezing, and it would get colder. I'd almost froze once today. Plus, I didn't know where we were or which way to go. And I wore these stupid bracelets.

I held up my wrists. "Will you get them to take these off?"

"You know I'd do anything for you, darling." Charmig kissed my wrist at the spot where the bracelet dangled. I held back a shudder. "But until your magic is controlled, those need to stay on."

The shudder changed into a slow quake of anger. "Until my magic is controlled."

Controlled by whom?

Chapter Seventeen

My hand hit something and a crash jolted me awake. I sat up and noticed a glass had shattered on the ground and water spread on the rug. I must've thrashed in my sleep and hit the glass.

"Elves bells." Throwing back the covers, I got out of bed and stepped on a piece of glass.

Pain cut my bare foot. Though the injury was less sharp than the emotional anguish and terrible thoughts I hadn't escaped in sleep.

Grandfather was dead. I was locked in these anti-magic bracelets. I missed Stone. And the banshees treated me like a prized prisoner. Doom settled around me in a gloomy fog. I didn't even have the dragon to talk to anymore. Being alone was the worst way to grieve. A shattering sob leaked out and I held my head in my hands, not caring about the pain or the blood staining the carpet on the tent floor.

Iban scurried in and wrapped a towel around my foot.

"Thanks." I held the towel so I wouldn't create any more work for her.

The brownies hurried in and out, cleaning and delivering items every day. I'd tried to speak to them. Only Iban had spoken back. I needed a friend, someone I could trust, someone who wasn't a banshee.

"Let me help. It was my clumsiness that caused the mess." I got down on my knees, bringing myself to her level.

Fear flashed on her expression. She bent down to pick up the broken pieces of glass. "Combined magic," the brownie mumbled.

"What?"

She scanned the tent expecting spies. "Combined magic."

I shook my head slightly, not really understanding but happy to have someone to talk to. Maybe she meant my magic combined with my grandfather's. I knew banshees became more powerful when older members of the family died. My eyes prickled and I swiped at them.

She patted my thigh in a comforting action knowing I grieved.

"You're sweet." I sniffed and tried to smile. "You know, I have a good brownie friend named Pith."

Her heavy brows slashed up. "You have a brownie friend?"

She spoke as if it was impossible for a brownie and a banshee to be friends.

"Yes. We were both in the palace dungeon and shared a cell. We worked together to escape." My eyes prickled again. This time because I missed my friends. "I wonder where he and my other friends are now."

"Other brownies?" Her motions slowed showing interest in my story.

"No. An elf, a witch, a troll, a goblin, a werewolf, and a fairy," Frowning, worry for Violet increased. Had she ever become un-frozen? I sort of understood how it felt. "And a half giant."

My voice cracked. Those dreams of him searching for me were wishful thinking. Even though a vision had come true, I couldn't pin my hopes on a rescue. I studied the bracelets and my doubts doubled.

Iban finished picking up the broken glass.

"I'd hoped my friends would come after me. They probably believed I'd run away, not realizing I was kidnapped." Or they'd been killed or imprisoned in the battle.

"Kidnapped?" She tilted her head and studied me. "You don't wish to be here?"

"Not anymore." Determination firmed in my bones. "I mean, Charmig kidnapped me. When he explained Grandfather was here, I wanted to come. And Grand Lord Justicar told me I could heal my grandfather by releasing my powers and my memories, but first I had to be initiated." I rubbed the tattoo on my wrist. "The only reason I did those things was to save my grandfather. And now he's gone."

"I'm sorry."

Despair at the loss crumbled my determination. "I don't agree with the banshee customs and traditions." I huffed. "I don't want to be part of this way of life."

She stared at her hand on my thigh. I'd been talking about only myself. "What about you? I don't understand how you put up with the way you're treated. You seem to be busy all the time."

"Very busy." Nodding, she removed her hand. "Brownies are busy preparing for new guests tomorrow and someone very important in a couple more days." She removed her hand. "Lots of work for us to do."

"New prisoners?" Bitterness cooled my emotions because that's what I'd become. A prisoner.

Before she could respond, Lykke strutted in the tent carrying a tray. "The stupid brownie neglected to tell me you were awake."

Iban scurried out of the tent afraid of getting in more trouble.

The comment poked. "Iban's not stupid." If I said she was helping me clean, the brownie would get in more trouble for letting me help.

Lykke dropped the tray on the table. A new piece of jewelry hung around her highly decorated neck.

I took a seat at the table. "Is it true we're expecting guests?" I used the word guest lightly, not believing it after my treatment. "Because if you need this tent for them, I'm going to be leaving soon."

"How did you hear?" She didn't deny.

I wasn't going to tell on the brownie. "I overheard someone talking on the other side of the tent."

"The guards?" She squinted at me suspiciously and I nodded. "I don't think you'll be leaving anytime soon."

Her comment ripped through my midsection. I'd feared the banshees wouldn't let me walk away. I couldn't avoid the truth any longer. It was time to confront Grand Lord Justicar.

I jumped up from the table, threw a cloak on top of my nightgown, and stormed out of the tent. The guards standing outside didn't stop me. The suspicious non-action almost made me halt.

"Hello, Lys Destiny." Charmig hurried to catch up.

So that's the reason the guards hadn't stopped me. He was waiting for me. Not the person I wanted to see. "Leave me alone."

He continued to saunter beside me.

Annoyed, I ignored him and picked up my pace. This camp didn't have the steam vents puffing through the sharp rock. It was higher and colder and more desolate. Cloudy skies and strong gusts of wind. Running away without help or provisions would be difficult.

I could do it. I had to do it.

Warriors standing around the Proving Sphere stopped to scowl. They made an unfamiliar gesture and murmured something. Fear showed on their expressions.

So much for being tough warriors. Afraid of a dragon. Afraid of me. Hurt sliced through me. They never liked me and now they feared me.

The murmurs continued from a few women hanging clothes to dry. "Sorcer...evil...proph..."

Stopping, I reeled toward Charmig. "What are they saying?"

"Nothing." He grabbed hold of my hand and the stupid anti-magic bracelet clinked against Grandfather's watch.

I snatched my hand back and continued walking.

A group of children stopped to gape. Their murmurings were louder and clearer. "Evil sorceress."

Charmig whistled trying to cover it up. It didn't work.

The hurt radiated spreading throughout my body. This was the exact experience of being a banshee in a forest of other majiks. Now I was with my own kind and even they called me evil. I was a banshee who happened to have magic similar to the leader and Charmig. I couldn't help it if my family hadn't lost their powers.

I stopped again. My pulse beat faster and faster. Is that what they thought of me? Not as a warrior of their clan, but an evil sorceress. Banshee magic wasn't evil. Or was it?

The whispering and murmuring carried through the crowd. *Sorceress* and *devil* and *prophecy*. I pivoted on my heel. The banshees had congratulated me after the Unlocking Ceremony, they'd celebrated. Maybe they'd been ordered to by Grand Lord Justicar. Now, they feared me.

"You're upset." Charmig grabbed my hand again.

Sniffing, I tried to hold the pain inside. "No."

He held our clasped hands up in front of the crowd near the firepit. "Destiny is our Lys. You will show respect. She will guide us into the future and fight with her magic for our cause." He clasped my hand tighter, still holding it for all to see.

My cheeks heated. I didn't want to be held up as good or evil. I wouldn't be fighting for their cause. Not after the way they treated me.

"Lys Destiny has committed to the Skjult Banshee Clan." Charmig brought our clasped hands down and kissed my fingers. I appreciated how he defended me, but not the kiss. "She will be partnered with me and as her mate I will direct her magical powers."

His announcement rattled me to my core. The worm niggling through my brain warning me about Charmig and Svante's intentions grew into a snake. A slithering poison-spitting snake. Committing to the clan meant committing to a male banshee.

No debate. No free choice. No opportunity to leave.

They wanted me to be a prisoner for life.

"No!" I shouted to the crowd gathering. Yanking my arm, I released his hold on my hand. "I'll never marry you."

Wheeling around, I ran from their gawking stares and Charmig's angered expression. I didn't care if I hurt his feelings. He never should've announced a fake engagement. There was one place to rant about the mistake, one place to clarify the truth and explain that I planned to leave the clan. Today.

I arrived at Grand Lord Justicar's tent. The guards blocked the tent flap, not allowing me entrance. My anger about Charmig's announcement drilled into me. It was time to make a few things clear.

Charmig grabbed my arm. "Destiny we need to talk."

Snatching my arm away, I was tired of him touching me without permission. "The only one I'm talking to is your father."

He studied me and nodded to the guards. The guards lifted their weapons and let us both enter the tent.

Grand Lord Justicar sat in his heavy chair, sipping from a glass cup, not actually doing anything. Svante sat on the chair beside him. Both startled when Charmig and I barged in.

"Thank you for taking care of my grandfather and helping restore my memories and magic." Speaking between tight lips, I wanted this conversation to start on the right foot.

"You're welcome, Lys Destiny." He inspected me with a narrow gaze. "You are now part of the Skjult Banshee Clan."

"About that..."

Nerves jumped in my stomach. I rubbed my hands against my cloak. His son expected to marry me and control my power. I stumbled a step back. Everyone wanted to control me, even those protecting me like my grandfather and parents. And especially the leader sitting before me.

Gathering my determination, I needed to be forceful. "I will not be a prisoner and married off to whoever you choose."

"Whatever are you talking about, dear?" Gorig spoke, pretending to be a friendly father figure. He waved at Svante to stand and patted the chair. The leader wrapped his fingers around the ceremonial halberd.

"No, thanks. I'd rather stand." I paced in front of him and noticed the guards gripping their halberds a little tighter. "Charmig insinuated that he would be marrying me." I held in a cold quiver.

Charmig slunk into the chair Svante had vacated.

"Your son said he'd be in control of my magic." Right now, I wasn't even in control of my magic.

The leader chuckled. "Past customs. It does not mean it will continue to happen."

Charmig and Svante exchanged a look.

I paced in the other direction. The banshee clan clung to their ancient ways. From the Proving Sphere to the ceremonies, to the treatment of female banshees, to the slavery of the brownies.

"Charmig proclaimed to the warriors he'd been chosen to marry me." My voice rose higher. I couldn't marry him.

"Nothing has been decided yet."

"Nothing will ever be decided. I *will* decide." And I choose Stone.

"Of course, you'll have a major part in the decision." The leader's commiserating tone didn't work. I didn't trust him. "Obviously Charmig is my favorite because he's my son. Although Svante saved your life yesterday."

Charmig smirked, his expression smug. Svante's gaze lightened as if he had hope.

I'd douse any hope. "Neither is my favorite."

I crossed my arms afraid I might try to attack the leader. With his guards standing next to him it would do me no good.

The leader's lips shifted upwards, but his gaze narrowed. "There's no need to decide anything at the moment. There are more pressing matters."

I shook my head. "It doesn't matter. I'm leaving. I have friends...and others who miss me."

"I understand." His calm and complacent tone didn't reassure. Between his orders, the anti-magic bracelets, and shooting me down last night, I understood he wanted to dominate and rule me. "I also understand your banshee magic is completely undisciplined."

Guilt twisted in my gut and my cheeks heated. I'd tossed a warrior across the ring, set a dragon's tail on fire on purpose and it had gotten out of control, and flown without realizing. And I'd done other uncontrolled magic before arriving here.

"Wouldn't you feel better about going into the kingdom if you could control your banshee magic?" He angled his head and gave an understanding, commiserating smile.

He didn't understand what I was going through, and I hated him pretending that he did.

"I can control it." My voice trembled with the lie. I didn't even know what I could do. Only one thing mattered. "I need to find my friends."

"Will your friends be safe from you if you can't control your magic?" His question attacked my doubts.

I fisted my hands and crossed two fingers. "I won't hurt my friends."

"How do you know? If you can't control your magic, you might." His pitch rose with conviction as if he understood my predicament.

Uncurling my hands, I rubbed my fingers together and ignited an unwanted spark. "I can control it."

The entire tent quaked. The guards stumbled and drew their weapons. The brownies fell to the floor. The unpacked glasses shuddered. One crashed to the ground and broke. Red liquid soaked into the round carpet.

"That's not me." I lifted my arms with the anti-magic bracelets.

"Not me." Charmig held up his hands.

Svante's brow furrowed, appearing confused. Must not be him either.

"Even with the anti-magic bracelets you cause trouble." Grand Lord Justicar attempted to broadcast empathy and concern.

"I can control it." If I kept saying it, maybe it would be true.

He set his glass on the table with a thump. "Arriving tomorrow is a special banshee magic trainer. The trainer will help you learn to use your magic and control the power. Just meet the trainer."

I'd planned to leave. I wanted to find my friends and help the prince. But the banshee leader might be right about one thing. If

I couldn't control my magic, how much help would I be? Maybe I'd be a hinderance. Loneliness echoed deep in my soul knowing I had to make the right decision for everyone. One or two more days wouldn't be too awful. I'd meet the trainer and get a clear assessment of what I could do or what havoc I could create while plotting my escape.

I nodded.

"There is a prophecy related to you, Lys Destiny." His deep timbre boomed in the tent.

My muscles tensed. The prophecy the banshees had chanted last night, the one whispered about this morning. The one tickling my memory. "What prophecy?"

"I haven't heard the exact words. I just know the damage you could cause." He poured another glass of the red liquid and took a sip. "Which is why the banshee trainer will arrive tomorrow for you. The trainer will assist you, teach you, train you to control your banshee power. Once we know you won't injure anyone accidentally, we'll remove the anti-magic bracelets and you'll be free."

The word meant different things to different people.

Did he mean free from the bracelets or free to leave?

My shoulders sagged. "My friends..."

"What's more important?" He challenged me to do what he thought was right. "Finding your friends or keeping them safe from your destructive nature?"

The man had a point. Before leaving the tent, I agreed to meet with the banshee trainer, to discuss my powers with them, to learn what I was capable of. Sadness flowed in my veins as I inched toward my tent. I missed Grandfather so much. He could've told me about the prophecy. Why hadn't he? I'd hoped the banshees might become family, but I understood with their strict rules and protocols, with their places and statuses, I couldn't stay with them.

Svante stepped next to me. "Interesting meeting."

"Was it?" Discontent tinged my tone. I shouldn't take my upset out on him. "Thanks for catching me when I was falling."

"You're welcome. I'd hate for our Lys to die." A bit of sarcasm wove through his words.

"If the banshees didn't want me to die, they shouldn't have shot me down."

"True." His agreement threw my mind in a tizzy. "They believed you'd save yourself."

"Hah." I hadn't even realized I'd been flying. I might've returned to the ground. Or flown away.

A dark thought hit me. Would Grand Lord Justicar rather have me dead than not under his control? Maybe that was the reason he gave the order to shoot. Or if the banshees believed I could save myself, why didn't I? Was my magic defunct?

We walked in silence. It was amazing how I'd been with the banshee clan for weeks and didn't understand how it operated. The hierarchy was obvious though.

Grand Lord Justicar ruled with an iron fist. Charmig and Svante helped rule while vying for his leadership spot. The favored warriors were next. Teinn, the warrior I'd tossed across the Proving Sphere. He managed and disciplined the other warriors. Then there were the lesser guards. The ones Lykke frowned upon, insinuating that she was too good for them. They included the perimeter guards and the banshees watching the tents. And currently watching me.

The female banshees were next. I couldn't tell their hierarchy, although Lykke had a special place. And poor Reitha could be so much more than an ornament on a male's arm.

I spotted Lykke at the side of the leader's tent. She shifted toward Charmig and their heads bowed together. They spoke intensely. She had a distinctive position. Free to roam between the groups. Assigned to help me. Close to Charmig.

Awareness had me watching her more closely. Was Lykke only pretending to be my friend?

Svante edged closer to me. "I know the prophecy."

My skin electrified. If he knew, the leader definitely knew the full prophecy too and hadn't wanted to tell me. Big surprise.

Angling my head, I studied his profile. His sharp nose tilted upward. His intelligent eyes always darted around, watching and assessing everything. He had broad shoulders and must have won in the Proving Sphere or he wouldn't be in the Elder position. He stared straight ahead appearing neither impatient nor interested in my response. He knew I was desperate to know.

"The prophecy about me?" I wanted to confirm we were talking about the same thing.

"Yes." His expression gave nothing away.

I leaned forward. Anxiety twisted my muscles. "What does the prophecy say?"

He chuckled. "Why should I tell you?"

"Because it's about me."

Because I needed to know. Needed to know so I wouldn't hurt my friends or the kingdom. Needed to know so I could do the exact opposite.

Svante glanced around and considered me. "If I tell you the entire prophecy, what will you do for me?"

CHAPTER EIGHTEEN

"The Wicked End Prophecy has been written." A woman with a long thin nose peered deep into my eyes seeing my soul. "And her name will be Destiny."

"Why would you put such a heavy burden on a baby?" Grandfather's angry tone jerked me fully awake.

"It is not I who gave her the burden. I just foretell the future." The old women glared at my grandfather. "The Dark Angel chooses those who are worthy to handle the risk."

I watched the exchange with a baby's eyes but a teenager's knowledge. This was an important moment in my life.

"Gigi, you know the Dark Angel." Mom held me in her arms. "Are you sure?"

Mom's voice quivered with fear and trembled with vulnerability. Her gaze darkened in her beautiful heart-shaped face. A face without a mark on her forehead. She gazed at me, and love pulsated off her in waves.

"We will train her, watch her, teach her control." My father's handsome face hovered above. He put out his finger and I grabbed it with my tiny hand. "She is our child. We'll protect her."

"It's not her I'm worried about." Gigi, the old witch, cackled as she tickled under my chin. "She should live with me."

I didn't want the old hag touching me.

"She will not live with you." Grandfather slammed his fist on the table. Cups and saucers jangled. "You can't keep her prisoner."

Classic coming from him. In a way, he'd kept me a prisoner by locking up my powers and my memories, by hiding me away in the small mound home. After all I'd been through and with my memories returned, I understood he'd done it out of fear and love, but it still damaged.

Mom and Dad beamed and their smiles burst in my heart. I'd been wrong about them. I thought they'd put their careers over me, but now I understood. I'd had to make my own tough choices in life.

Gigi peered at me quizzically. "If her power is not controlled, she will destroy the kingdom."

"Destroy the kingdom?" I jolted awake. Moaning, I buried my head not wanting to face the day, to face the other banshees, to face the reality of my life.

Prisoner. An unwanted mate. And now destroyer of the kingdom?

How was that even possible? The banshees' murmuring had set off this particular dream. They believed I had some kind of sinister power. I didn't believe it. I was a banshee the same as them, although I understood my magic was stronger.

Studying my hands, I tried to see beneath the surface. How much power did I possess? Some powers had emerged before the ceremony like the heks scream, reading minds, and manipulating humans. If my banshee powers had been locked down until the ceremony, how was the other magic explained? The magic I'd shown had been in a fit of temper or a wallop of emotion. Uncontrolled.

I gulped. Was I uncontrollable? Would I destroy the kingdom? Grand Lord Justicar had blamed me for the small quake in his tent even though I'd worn the anti-magic bracelets.

Grunts and shouts from the Proving Sphere could be heard from my tent. The warriors were training with fights.

"Good morning." Iban greeted me, carrying a breakfast tray.

Lykke sauntered in behind her. How did she always know the second I woke up? Goosebumps traveled across my skin. Was she spying to please Charmig?

I grabbed the silk bathrobe and put it on before sitting at the small table.

"You'll wear a new outfit for the banshee trainer." She circled around the room. "Where's the new outfit for Lys Destiny?"

Shrugging, I had no idea.

She glared at Iban. "Find it!"

The brownie scurried out of the room without a backward glance.

The day hadn't started so good.

"Good morning, Lykke." I picked up a spoon, trying to change the mood.

"Lys Destiny." Her lips lifted yet I saw the stress on her expression.

The tent flap opened with no warning. I was glad I'd put on the bathrobe.

"Good morning." Charmig strolled into my tent as if he belonged there. He smiled at me and then noticed Lykke. "Leave us alone."

Her expression fell and she dropped her gaze. Her shoulders rounded trying to make herself smaller. Her lashes flicked up at him a final time before she strutted out of the tent, swiveling her hips back and forth. If she spied for him, it was because she wanted to please him.

Charmig ogled her the entire way out the door.

My knuckles whitened around the spoon. "Why do you treat Lykke so poorly?" While she was obviously besotted.

He waved his hand in dismissal and took the seat next to me. "She doesn't know her place."

"What is her place exactly?" She was one of the banshees I couldn't figure out. "What does she mean to you?"

He flashed a grin. "Jealous?"

My face contorted. I was the furthest thing from jealous. I wished he'd pursue her. "Not even close."

"You want closer?" He grabbed my arm, yanking me out of my chair and onto his lap. "I've got news."

"Stop." Stiffening, I wished I didn't have the stupid anti-magic bracelets on. I could've shown him. I shoved against his chest. "I said no."

The tent door opened and Iban dragged in a large trunk by herself.

Maybe Charmig would be a true gentleman and offer to help, which would also make him let go of me.

"How dare you interrupt us." He stood, dumping me on the ground. He picked up the breakfast tray and threw it at the brownie.

At least one of my wishes came true. I rubbed my backside.

The tray clunked onto the ground. The glass bowl shattered. The spoon hit the wall.

Shock rooted me in place. I couldn't believe his quick temper at an innocent majik.

Iban dropped the trunk and her gaze widened with fear. Her entire body scrunched, waiting for an expected hit. She was right.

Charmig stomped toward her and raised his hand to slap.

"Stop." How dare he? She was itty bitty and he was a monster in comparison. I scrambled to my feet and dashed to her side. "Leave her alone."

Her blue eyes swirled. Her cheeks reddened. Her body didn't move. She was terrified.

"Don't touch the filthy thing." Charmig scrunched his nose in distaste.

"Why would I listen to you when you don't listen to me?" Animosity flushed through my system and I helped her sit on the trunk. His treatment of both me and her was similar. He didn't respect either of us.

"Wash your hands with soap and scalding water before you touch me again. My father wants to see you." He stormed out.

As if I'd ever touch him. Too bad he'd already left, or I would've shouted the sentiment. He wasn't important now. Iban was. "Why do you put up with this treatment? Why don't you leave?"

Her mouth dropped open. "You don't know?"

Shaking my head slowly, I knew I wasn't going to like the answer.

"See this?" She lifted her tunic to show a triangular mark. "Long ago a relative in my family owed the clan a great debt. The price was our servitude. Each baby is born with this mark and is cursed." She tugged her shirt down. "I can't run away because of the Debtor's Mark. The only way to pay the debt is to work it off."

"How long will that take?" I braced at her stoic expression.

"Until we die."

The answer slugged me in the gut. The brownies weren't workers. They didn't want to serve and weren't paid. "You're a slave."

Chapter Nineteen

"The special banshee trainer has arrived," Grand Lord Justicar announced when I arrived at his tent after dressing in the new shula, bikini top, and cloak.

I smashed my feet into the thick and heavy carpet. The man had followed through on a promise. Finally, someone who could help me learn about my banshee powers.

"The banshee trainer has taken a vow of silence." His lips tightened. "She will only speak when training you. No idle chit-chat. You're to ask no questions about her."

Sounds fun. I wonder if it's because of the trainer's station. Maybe her level isn't allowed to speak unless spoken to. The sarcasm almost spewed out of my mouth.

"You will only discuss how to use and control your magic." His demanding tone put the onus on me.

"What if I hurt the trainer or do something wrong?" By wrong I meant dangerous.

"Don't." He waved his hand in dismissal.

I wasn't ready to go. I wanted to get information from him. Not about the banshee trainer. Now that Grandfather was gone, I needed to understand why my family left in the first place. I'd thought the banshee clan might become my family, yet my real family hadn't stayed. And neither would I. "Why didn't my family stay with the clan?"

"We are your family now." Gorig pinched his lips and spoke as if he had the final word.

I firmed my lips. "No, you aren't."

"We will be." He acted so positive. But I knew I'd never stay and marry either Charmig or Svante. "Your grandfather and your parents worked for King Jostein. After the king died, they stayed on."

"And worked for evil Regent Theobald." The man's name tasted bitter on my tongue. I didn't understand how they could stay and work for the sinister man.

"The regent isn't bad."

My eyebrows rose. "You've met him?"

"Not yet." The leader waved his hand, trying to erase part of the conversation. "Your parents planned to rejoin our clan until they were murdered by the regent's enemies."

This man casually tossed around the fact that my parents were murdered and turned it into an imaginary knife to my throat. "How do you know they were killed?"

"I'm the leader of the banshee clan. Information gets back to me." His expression soothed and he spoke with a factual tone. "Your grandfather knew foul play was involved so he brought you to us right after the deaths."

My head whirled as memories clashed with perceptions. "To lock up my memories and magic."

"You inherited your father's powers and your mother's..." Grand Lord Justicar trailed off. "Your grandfather didn't want you or others in danger and thought it best you forget."

The battle in my brain continued as my mind sorted through the pieces of my memories. I was seven and clearly remembered my parents going on a trip. Mom had known she or my father would die. I didn't realize banshees could foresee the future. Had she known both of them would die? Either way, the discussion brought back my grief about their deaths and the more recent death of my grandfather.

"Let me unlock those bracelets so you can begin training." Grand Lord Justicar signaled for a guard to remove the anti-magic bracelets. "The guard will escort you to your tent."

Dazed by the refreshed emotions, I went back to my tent, opened the flap, and halted.

Lykke stood by my small table and with her was...

Cassia.

My mouth dropped open and my pulse raced into my chest. I wanted to run to her and squeal.

Her surprised gray eyes flashed with fear. She tilted back and gave a slight shake of her head.

That's when I noticed the banshee mark gleaming on her forehead. The mark had ugly red welts around it as if it had just been forged.

I tumbled back. My friend Cassia was not a banshee, but this girl looked exactly like her except for the mark gleaming on her forehead. What sorcery was this?

She wore a drab brown shula, bikini top with no beading, and an old cloak. Pinching her lips together, she pleaded with her gaze.

Pleaded for what?

Smashing my lips tight, I didn't say anything or indicate that I knew her. Hope fluttered. This must be part of a plan to rescue me. Was Stone hiding nearby? My heart pummeled so hard I thought Lykke would hear. I was ready to leave, but what about learning how to control my banshee magic?

Lykke glanced back and forth between us. "Destiny. This is the special *banshee* trainer Grand Lord Justicar told you about. She's here to teach you how to use your *banshee* powers."

Gaping, I couldn't stop staring at the mark on Cassia's forehead. She wasn't a banshee and yet she had the mark of one. She wasn't sneezing either. I hoped she hadn't scarred herself for life just to rescue me.

She refused to look at me, keeping her head bowed.

"Her name is Cassia, a very common banshee name." Lykke pulled out a key and unlocked the anti-magic bracelets Cassia wore. "Grand Lord Justicar wanted me to emphasize that because of her banshee position, she only speaks of training issues. No idle chatter or gossip."

He'd said the same thing to me. Was this a rescue or were they trying to pass Cassia off as a banshee? They didn't know she was one of my friends. What were the chances they'd bring me a witch I actually knew? I knew so few majiks. My lungs lightened and I wanted to fly. She must've been nearby with Stone, Lukas, Pith, and Trolgar similar to my dream.

The questions tried to burst from inside. I tamped them down. I had to play it cool until I figured out what was going on.

"Hi? I'm Destiny." Even though an introduction was totally unnecessary.

"Certain banshees take a vow of silence." Lykke's stilted voice told me she'd memorized what to say. "Grand Lord Justicar persuaded Cassia to break her vow of silence to train you because of your lack of control over your powers. It's a great honor."

"Okaaay." I didn't know what to say. Confusion and excitement blended into a strong urge to shout. If this was my friend's ploy to rescue me, I hoped she had a way out of the encampment. Besides, wouldn't Grand Lord Justicar know all the banshees? If there really was a banshee trainer, what had happened to them?

"Don't try to make conversation." Lykke scanned over Cassia and me. "It's insulting to her station."

The word station snagged a sore spot. Some people grew into greatness. I understood the need for a leader and those who helped lead, but not everyone in a society should be assigned a place. Some changed and grew or developed later.

"You may begin." Lykke nodded at Cassia and took a seat.

If Cassia was supposed to be a high-ranking banshee, Lykke would never tell her what to do. Even their lies didn't make sense. Although I wouldn't point it out until I talked to Cassia in private.

"Are you going to watch?" I bit my tongue. The question might make Lykke suspicious. I didn't want to ruin Cassia's plan.

"I'll let you get started while I get a couple of the items Cassia, the banshee, requested for training." Lykke kept inserting the word banshee.

My stomach clutched. Did she suspect Cassia wasn't a banshee trainer or were they trying to fool me?

"Even though the anti-magic bracelets are off, don't even think about stepping outside. Guards surround the tent." If it was a rescue and Cassia was pretending to be a banshee, Lykke might not be buying Cassia's act.

Back up must be nearby. Excitement spiked. Stone could be right outside the perimeter of the camp. I'd be free soon.

"Grand Lord Justicar wants a progress report at the end of every day." She said before taking her leave.

I rushed to Cassia and hugged her. "I can't believe you found me. What's your plan to get us out of here?"

"I'm so glad you're alive." She hugged me back. "What plan?"

"Lykke called you a banshee trainer." Excitement shimmied across my skin. I'd be with Stone and my friends soon. "I assumed it was an act. Part of a plan to rescue me."

She hugged again, clinging to me. "Destiny, we've been searching for you since the night you left."

"We?" My heart tumbled. "Stone's with you."

"Stone, Lukas, Trolgar, and Pith. He—"

"How are they?" My voice rose. "They're here at the camp?"

"No." She grabbed my wrist. "I was kidnapped by a group of banshees."

"So was I." I couldn't stop my sarcasm.

"What?" Her jaw dropped. "At first Stone thought you left because you were mad about him not letting you fight in the battle. He searched for you and couldn't find you. Someone saw what happened and said you left with banshees. Prince Zacharye told us to go after you."

"You didn't fight in the battle?" Relief swished in my midsection. "I was so worried when I heard how horrible the prince's side lost."

"Lost?" She sounded confused. "He won. He's king of the kingdom. King Zacharye. I call him prince out of habit."

I filled with lightness. He'd won. Majiks would have equality. "Grand Lord Justicar told me that the prince lost and there were lots of deaths."

She shook her head.

Bewilderment shifted in my mind. I'd been lied to about the battle. I sank onto the floor. "What else has the banshee leader lied about?"

"Plenty." She sat down beside me and took hold of my hand. "He's threatened that if I don't pretend I'm a banshee, he'll torture me and kill Pith."

"Pith's here?" Anxiety flipped in my belly. Brownies were slaves for the banshee clan. It was dangerous for him. He could become bound like the other brownies.

A tear slipped onto her cheek. "Pith and I were gathering berries near where our group camped. We'd been following the banshees, trying to find you, and lost their trail at the river."

My body sagged and my heart broke. There was no rescue planned. If anything, my friends Cassia and Pith were in danger too.

"The banshees snuck up, confirmed I was a witch, and grabbed us. We didn't even have a chance to shout. They separated us here and told me that if I didn't do exactly what they wanted and pretend to be a banshee, they'd kill Pith. They're blackmailing me."

"Stone and the others have a fresh trail to follow. And if they find you, they'll find me." Even though I hated that they'd been kidnapped, I was glad she was here. And Stone was near. "What about Violet? How is she?"

"Helartha and Gnit took Violet to my coven to see if they could help her out of her frozen state."

"Why didn't you go?" The coven was her home.

Cassia shrugged. "I wanted to stay with our friends a little longer." She pointed to the tattoo on my wrist. "You got a new tattoo too."

"It's a banshee warrior tattoo." I traced a finger on her forehead. "Why did the banshees mark you?"

"It's a tattoo mimicking the banshee mark so you'd believe I'm a banshee."

"Oh Cassia." I hugged her tight as anger crashed through me. The mark hadn't been a ploy. It was a real tattoo. She'd have to wear the banshee mark forever and be shunned like I'd been for most of my life.

"There's a reason they wanted you to believe I was one of them." She pulled back and wrung her hands. "They didn't want you to know your powers don't just come from being a banshee."

My muscles tightened and I angled my head. "They don't?"

Her rounded eyes told me she was afraid to reveal the truth.

"I'm tired of the banshees lying to me." The anger crested and crashed. "Besides the fact that Prince Zacharye won and you're not a banshee, what else are they keeping from me?"

Cassia didn't flinch. She didn't blink. Whatever she was about to say was important.

I held my breath and braced myself.

"You're only part banshee." She took hold of my hands and squeezed. "And you're part witch."

Chapter Twenty

*P*art witch?

The foreign phrase as it related to me clanged in my head, plopped in my chest, and banged against my ribs like an ancient pinball machine. I wasn't a pinball wizard, and I couldn't be part witch. Both my parents were banshees. My dad had a prominent mark on his forehead. And mom had a mark on her forehead too, didn't she? The image of her from my dreams was fuzzy. In the photo I had, she clearly had a banshee mark. Grandfather was definitely a banshee. I didn't know much about his spouse. Or my mother's parents.

"No. Impossible." Standing, I paced across the room.

If I was a witch, I would have way more powerful magic. I might've been able to save Grandfather before receiving the banshee powers. I paced the other way. Or did I already have banshee powers and it was my witch powers released at the Obsidian Precipice? Iban had murmured *combined magic*.

Cassia got to her feet. "I don't know how, but I heard banshees talking about you and your combined powers. It explains why they kidnapped me."

My mind rattled and I paced back again. "How am I a witch? How is it even possible?"

She shook her head. "I don't know. Who in your family might have witch ancestry?"

My brain ached. "Not my grandfather." Had he realized the banshee clan lied?

"Who else?" Cassia wandered around the tent, picking up a gold bowl, running her fingers across the silk comforter, peeking into a trunk.

I didn't want any of those things. I didn't want this. My mind flipped through the old yet new memories. Grandfather's spouse had died before I was born. I'd never met her. My mother seemed to be estranged from her half of the family.

I jolted. In a vision, Mom hadn't had the banshee mark and she'd created a ball of light. A light turned on inside me.

"My mom." My heart swelled and I blinked back tears. She'd never talked about her family and Grandfather had been upset about the naming in my dream. "She must have witch ancestry. My great grandmother named me Destiny and said something about a prophecy. Some of the banshees have whispered about a prophecy too."

"Oh my stars." Cassia whirled around. "You're the one."

Fidgeting, I eddied out of the way of her stare. I had no clue what she meant.

"You're her." She backed away.

"I'm who?" Impatience thrummed creating static in my bones. "Tell me, Cassia."

"The Wicked End Prophecy." Her tone lowered to a whisper.

Wicked End? I gulped and the words pummeled my mind. I'd heard it somewhere before. The name was foreboding. "Wh...what does the prophecy mean?"

I held my breath fearful of the answer. My mind contorted and gnarled with the terrible things it might foretell.

Her skin paled and she moved her head back and forth. "I can't remember the details."

Svante knew. He'd said he'd tell me the prophecy if I returned a favor. We'd never discussed it again. How would he know about a witch prophecy? Then again, Grand Lord Justicar had known I was part witch because he'd brought Cassia to train me.

Before I could pull my thoughts together, Lykke tramped into the tent with a brownie carrying a tray.

A scream of frustration built inside me. I was finally going to get an explanation about the meaning of my name and the prophecy and was interrupted.

Cassia staggered back and gaped at the brownie. She must've thought it was Pith.

I peered at Lykke. Had she heard us talking? I'm not even supposed to know Cassia's a witch or the fact that she speaks about more than training. We could both be punished.

Lykke's gaze narrowed. "Are you two getting to know each other?"

"The banshee trainer barely talks." I needed to disperse her suspicion. I couldn't have her telling anyone about our relationship. "How is she supposed to train me if she doesn't speak?" I took Lykke's hands. "Why can't you train me?"

As a female, I knew she didn't have magic. I was just trying to throw off suspicion by asking.

Her cheeks reddened. "Most banshees don't have magic. That's the reason there are ranks and places. Grand Lord Justicar and the Elders don't show off their magical abilities." She sounded rote again.

I knew many of the banshees didn't have magic, Charmig had told me, but she'd just admitted that *most* banshees didn't. I had power and my parents and Grandfather had power. Was it because we weren't part of the clan?

"Here are the things the banshee teacher said she'd need to teach you." Lykke indicated that the brownie should set down the tray he'd been carrying.

On top of the tray lay a white feather, a rock, and an earthen pottery bowl.

"Um, I think it's for later." Running various scenarios through my mind, I made up things as I went. If we did anything spectacular, Lykke might be curious and stay. "Cassia said we'd begin with meditation."

I plopped on the ground and crossed my legs, hoping Cassia would realize what I meant and sit.

Cassia dropped to the floor beside me and crossed her legs. She turned her back to the banshee and winked at me.

I angled my head at Lykke. "Do you know what meditation is?"

"No." She leaned against a thick tent pole.

"It's sitting silently and being aware of your surroundings." I hoped she'd realize how boring it would be to watch and leave. "For hours."

"The warriors meditate as part of their training. It's as if they're in a forced trance."

"It's for banshees with power." Cassia spoke down to her and winked again. Good thing Lykke couldn't see my friend's jolly face.

Closing my eyes, I let my mind wander while waiting for Lykke to leave. How long would it take Stone to find us? My heart hammered with yearning to see him. Lukas would be overprotective and Trolgar would be tired and grouchy.

The tent opening flapped.

I slitted my eyes. "Lykke's gone."

Cassia uncrossed her legs. "Where did you learn meditation and why?"

"Meditation is helpful, but it was also a trick. Professor Nilsen at the palace used it to bore the guards so they wouldn't pay attention to what we were saying."

Her eyebrows arched. "You trusted him when he worked for the regent?"

"Technically, he wasn't on the regent's side. Similar to Stone." I knew Cassia had learned Stone was also Lord Vitor. "Do witches meditate?"

She stood and stretched her legs. "When learning we do need to focus, but so much of the magic comes naturally. We go to school, have spellbooks, and memorize incantations."

Fascinating. It was such a different world. First, I wanted to learn whether I truly was part witch. And if I was connected to the Wicked End Prophecy.

"How can we tell for sure that I'm part witch? And that I'm the one from the prophecy?" My lungs deflated and I struggled to draw in oxygen. I didn't want to be the center of a prophecy called Wicked End. "And what does the prophecy mean?"

I had so many questions. Now, I'd finally get answers. No more interruptions.

Cassia rubbed her fingers together and sparks shot out.

A spark lit inside. "I can do that." So could my mom.

Focusing on my hands, I rubbed them together and light flared.

"Can you do this?" She levitated.

"Kind of." I pulled my thoughts together and remembered how I'd felt when I'd saved Drago. He'd flown away and I'd flown higher. "It's more like flying and I'm not sure if I can do it on cue."

Focusing, I raised my arms and my feet lifted off the ground. My muscles clenched. When I'd flown after the Obsidian Precipice exploded it had been sheer terror, and when I'd flown beside Drago I hadn't fully realized what I was doing. This time I wanted to levitate and it happened. "I'm flying!"

"We can't go as high as flying." Cassia's comments confused me. She floated around the room and landed on my comfy bed. "Banshees can't do those things at all. You are a witch!"

My entire body tingled. Finally, something to explain the strange things. Incredible things. I spun around and divebombed next to her. My body plopped on the mattress.

We both laughed. It was good to let loose and have a bit of fun.

She rolled to her side to study me. "Levitating is an advanced tactic, and you haven't even been trained as a witch."

"I was never trained as a banshee either."

"I don't understand. You pulverized the rocks during the cave in to save Stone." Her expression turned thoughtful. "Was that banshee power or witch power?"

"I have no idea." I shrugged. "I tossed a boulder with my mind and started a fire to free a dragon. I can also read human minds and force them to do things. Are those witch powers?"

"Not anything I've heard of." She tapped her chin.

Anxiety tangled inside. I jerked upright. "Tell me the prophecy."

She sat up and straightened her cloak that she kept wrapped around her body. Then, she smoothed the comforter we'd messed up. "I don't know if I remember all of it."

"Cassia, are you stalling?" The tangling nerves tied into knots. It must be bad. "If the prophecy is about me, I have every right to know."

She shrugged. "You're right."

I fisted my hands, wanting to hear while also not wanting to know.

She kicked her legs against the side of the bed. "I know what the witches believe about the Wicked End Prophecy."

A chill ran up my spine and I shivered. Even the name sounded terrible.

"We believe the prophecy signals the end…"

"The end of what?"

"Of the kingdom." She considered me and took hold of my hands. "I know the head of my coven believed Regent Theobald would be the cause of the Wicked End."

"The prophecy is about him?" I could totally see him being the cause of destruction.

"No." Her emphatic response had me cowering. "It's about a majik who is part banshee and part witch."

My lungs shrunk. "How many of us are there?

Biting her bottom lip, she sized me up. "You're the only one."

The statement dropped into the shell of my soul. I was alone. Different.

"The coven leader believed you, or the person the prophecy is about, would join Regent Theobald on his quest to end majiks."

"Never." The single word rushed out with passion. Although, when I first started this journey, I wasn't on anyone's side. After landing in the palace dungeon, I realized how unfair and cruel the regent acted toward majiks. I was on their side now. Well, except maybe the banshees.

"The regent's restrictive laws against majiks, the arrests for no reason, and the torture machines he built was one of the first signs the prophecy was coming true." Her tone became more serious. "He planned to steal majik powers and kill the rest of us."

A whoosh of air came out. "Prince, I mean King Zacharyc stopped the process. The prophecy won't come true."

"The sinister man is on the loose." A warning rang in her voice. "If you're the one in the prophecy he might be looking for you."

I slipped my hands from hers. "He doesn't know I'm the one in the prophecy. He's never met me." Professor Nilsen had kept him away from me, but I'd sensed the darkness looming around the regent. "Maybe he's the one in the prophecy."

"That would be terrible." Cassia wove her fingers together. "And he's not a banshee or a witch. The regent could use your combined powers to release a dark force into the kingdom."

Bleakness stole over me, blanketing me in doom and gloom. I shook my head slowly as if already encased in evil sludge. "I'd never destroy the kingdom. I don't think it's me."

"They call the one from the prophecy a dark angel."

"I'm a banshee and a witch, not a dark angel." I jumped off the bed and paced to the other side of the tent.

Something about the term jiggled in my mind. I rotated the other way. Worrying about the name wasn't important. Cassia thinks I'm the one from the prophecy and she could be right.

"I don't want to control anything or destroy the kingdom." Chills raced across my skin. Grand Lord Justicar wanted to control me. I couldn't stay here and let him use my power for evil. "But I need to be able to control my powers." I spun around and stopped pacing. "We need a plan."

"I'm a prisoner. Pith is being held to keep me here." She threw her hands up. "And you're treated as royalty by the banshees. They want you to stay. What can we do?"

"I'm a captive like you." I pointed out the fancy furnishings and clothes. "I might be in a gilded cage, but I've lost my freedom. And I want to get it back."

She wrung her hands together. "We don't even know how to find Pith before we attempt an escape."

Determination rammed through me, straightening my spine. "I can find out. I've made a brownie friend. She'll help."

"How do you know you can trust her?"

"Because she, and the other brownies, are prisoners too. Slaves, really." And I was going to help them get away.

"Banshees are despicable." Cassia spat.

I gave her a scowl. Banshees always had a terrible reputation. I'd tried to teach everyone that banshees didn't cause death, just predicted it. Then again, maybe we did. "We're not all like that."

"Not you."

Or my grandfather and parents. Possibly Reitha and her grandmother.

"While we figure out how to find Pith and escape, you should teach me how to use my witch magic but Grand Lord Justicar will think you're telling me it's banshee magic." My spirits lifted. I'd learn to control my powers. No more mistakes. "That way you and Pith won't suffer."

I smirked as another scheme came to mind.

"So, what does your mischievous expression mean?" Cassia hopped off the bed and stepped by me.

My lips twitched. "I'll pretend to be terrible at magic to delay the process until Stone and the others get closer." I'd used a similar ploy when the regent had wanted me to track.

"What if they don't find us?"

Straightening my shoulders, I contemplated my bracelet-free wrists. I was done being kept in the dark by the banshees. Done being lied to. "We'll get Pith and break out together."

CHAPTER TWENTY-ONE

"You're picking everything up so quickly." Cassia's praise made me smile.

She'd been training me in witch magic, pretending it was banshee magic, for hours. The first thing I'd learned was how to create a sound shield to silence our discussions from anyone who might be listening outside. I also learned how to move an object with control, instead of just throwing a boulder or smashing things. When I did something correct, my blood sizzled recognizing the power.

"Try one more time." She'd been patient with me even while bearing the tattoo on her forehead marking her as a banshee for the rest of her life.

Guilt riddled the rush of power, and my body fizzled. I hated how she'd been marked because of me.

"You're not concentrating." The entire time she'd kept the drab brown cloak wrapped around the skimpy outfit she wore beneath.

"How can I concentrate with the noise coming from outside?" The grunts and clashing of metal had gotten louder and louder. "What's going on out there?"

She slit open the canvas door and peeked. "The warriors seem to be preparing for war."

Iban slipped in the smaller back exit used exclusively by the brownies. She halted when she spotted Cassia.

"Hi Iban." I got down on my knees. It was time to take a risk and trust someone else besides my close-knit group of friends. "This is my friend Cassia. She's not a banshee trainer as I've been told."

The brownie nodded, confirming she already knew.

"I need your help. Remember my brownie friend, Pith, that I told you about?"

Iban nodded again, shy and unsure around Cassia. Or maybe she just wasn't allowed to speak of certain things.

"Cassia is a witch. Her and Pith were kidnapped, and she's being forced to pretend she's a banshee because they're holding Pith as leverage." I told the short version even though so much more was going on. "Have you seen or heard about a new brownie prisoner?"

Iban's eyes widened and her gaze darted between the two of us.

"I'm really worried about my friend." My pleading tone pitched high. "Will you at least ask the other brownies if anyone knows?"

She hurried back out the tent.

"Do you think she'll do it or will she snitch on us?" Cassia wrung her hands.

I leaned back and stood. I could trust Iban. "She'll find out and tell me."

That night the bonfire blazed especially high in the clear sky. The warriors appeared merrier. The drinks flowed freely. Grand Lord Justicar sat in his opulent chair wearing a headpiece resembling a crown. Svante and Charmig sat on either side of him, bare-chested and buffoonish. Lykke sat at Charmig's feet like a slave girl.

Frowning, I scrutinized the three males. Guards had practically dragged me from my tent and forced me to stand for inspection.

"Show us what you've learned." The leader inspected me as if I'd changed with my new knowledge.

I hadn't changed on the outside, but I'd changed on the inside. Knowledge and truth were a powerful thing. Now that I knew the prophecy was that I'd destroy the kingdom, I planned to avoid the outcome, beginning with not being a powerful performing puppet.

I decided to fail at something simple.

I focused on the gold goblet sitting on the small table next to him. The glass had been refilled by a brownie slave. A ripple of acrimony went through my veins. The man didn't deserve the drink.

My fingers tingled with magic. I held my hand toward the goblet and my body quivered. The goblet trembled on the table.

"Well?" His one-word question prodded my anger. "What're you going to do?"

"I'm going to lift your goblet." And then I was going to dump the contents on the ground. Or his lap. A little oops followed by an apology should suffice to make him believe I was incompetent. Focusing again, I let the magic flow through me.

The goblet shook.

He had no right to question my ability. Anger at him and his demands pulsed through my system lighting my sizzling bloodstream on fire.

The goblet lifted and rocked. The glass tumbled onto the table and rolled to the ground.

The shaking didn't stop. The table and the ground shuddered. A rumbling filled my ears. The quaking earth moved beneath my feet, feeding into my fury. About how I'd been treated. How Cassia and Pith had been kidnapped. How the females and the brownies were ordered about by this man.

"Destiny." Grand Lord Justicar got to his feet. He lost his balance and stumbled. "What're you doing? Stop."

The ground rocked under the banshee encampment.

Male and female screams mixed. Everyone ran and hid. Tents toppled. Rocks from the surrounding cliffs tumbled down creating a *boom, boom, boom.*

Grand Lord Justicar took his index finger and swirled it over the tattoo on his wrist. The warriors surrounded him, protecting him from any falling debris without a word being said. They'd been with him for so long they must know what he wanted. He gripped the ceremonial halberd.

Lykke and Charmig hugged. Svante stared, his dark gaze burying deep into my spirit.

I jerked from my magical trance. I was causing the quake, and someone could be wounded. The cliffs could collapse and completely block us in like the cave in at the mines. This was similar to when the earth quaked in Grand Lord Justicar's tent, only worse. I'd had the anti-magic bracelets on and didn't believe I'd caused the shaking. Maybe I had. I didn't understand how my magic could break through the restrictions of the hi-tech bracelets.

I'd meant to fail in my magic demonstration, just not so spectacularly. Hurting innocents wasn't my goal. Taking a deep breath, I calmed my rage. I focused on the beauty surrounding me, on my friendships, on a good future now that I knew Zacharye was king.

"Bring me the wit—," Grand Lord Justicar twisted his lips, stopping himself from blurting the truth. "Bring me the banshee trainer."

Two guards ran to a back area filled with small tents. Some of the tents stood at haphazard angles.

I bit my lip. I hoped Cassia wasn't hurt. She'd warned me about letting my emotions get away while casting magic.

The two guards returned dragging Cassia between them. Her messy hair stood on ends and her gaze was wild. The cloak stayed wrapped around her tight.

"What have you spent the day teaching Destiny?" He shouted. "She could've killed us."

His eyes suddenly went wide. Was he thinking about the prophecy? Surely, he knew my forecasted future.

He lifted his hand to strike Cassia.

My stomach clenched. None of my friends would be hurt again because of me. I raised my hand, not even needing to think, and sent waves of power toward him.

His fist stopped midair. He adjusted his stance and tried to hit her again. His fist couldn't pass the invisible wall I'd erected.

"Put those anti-magic bracelets on her," he demanded. "Put them on both of these two."

Trying to hide my smirk, I studied the ground. At least I'd protected her.

Svante studied me with a knowing expression. Tension tangled in my gut.

Cassia gave a final glance before the two guards bundled her off to whatever prison cell they held her in. I hoped she'd be okay. As long as I needed training, the banshees would keep her safe.

"If she can't control herself maybe you should, Father." Charmig's casualness belied the tension in his tone.

He was right about me losing control. I hung my head.

"The hunt has been put off long enough." He slammed a glass on the arm of his chair.

"What's the hunt?" If Charmig wanted it to happen, it couldn't be good.

"Every banshee warrior must show allegiance to Grand Lord Justicar." Svante's voice trembled. He didn't seem to be the anxious type.

Grand Lord Justicar puffed his chest out. His smugness made my palms grow clammy. He pounded the ceremonial halberd into the ground. "Tomorrow morning Destiny will go on the hunt." He shot a pointed look at Svante. "It's normally done right after a banshee becomes a warrior. Svante believed you should be trained in your banshee magic first."

My tension gnarled into knots. I didn't want to kill an animal and I'd use any excuse at my disposal. "I'm female. I thought my warrior status was figurehead only."

"Correct." Grand Lord Justicar's smug smile broadened into a knowing grin. "You will serve your husband and me."

The clamminess spread throughout my entire body and changed into cold shivers. I wouldn't serve a husband. I wouldn't have a banshee as a husband. He'd said I'd get to decide. Another lie.

"Don't worry. My warriors will hunt and trap for you." He must've misinterpreted my expression. "All you have to do is make the killing blow."

My brow furrowed. They were taking it easy on me. It must be because I was female, and they didn't think I could hunt successfully. I quirked my chin, trying to act brave. "What kind of animal is considered big enough to make my allegiance to you?"

"Animal?" He chortled with one side of his mouth tipping higher. "Who said anything about an animal?"

My bones felt as if they'd shatter.

"You will kill a majik." Grand Lord Justicar dropped his jolliness. He leaned forward and observed me. "And bring back the heart."

Chapter Twenty-Two

The tent flap closed behind me and I flopped on the bed stunned by Grand Lord Justicar's request. *Kill a majik? Cut out the heart?* I couldn't imagine doing a more evil task.

Iban scurried in the back exit. She had a helper.

I jerked up in bed. "Pith?"

He waved his small hand.

"Pith!" Excitement pinged inside me. I jumped out of bed and ran to him. "Are you okay?"

The small brownie nodded and hid his head. His pointed ears wiggled. He appeared the same, yet different. Bandages were wrapped around his head and leg.

I hugged him tight, trying to reassure myself. "Are you okay?"

"Fine." Breaking my hold, he stubbed his foot into the carpet.

Would I ever be fine? Many of the decorative items had fallen in the tent. A chair was on its side. My cheeks heated. I'd done the damage and more. Worry gnawed at my insides. If I couldn't control my magic, how could I *not* destroy the kingdom?

"Cassia told me you were kidnapped with her." The earlier flush of excitement at seeing him waned and our predicament punched. Now that he was here and I had an idea where they kept Cassia, it was time to make our move. "We need to find her and get out now."

"Cassia is locked up and under heavy guard. You'll never get her out without magic."

I glared at the bracelets. Could I find a way to sneak my magic past their restraint? I'd done it before.

"Destiny," Pith's deep frown should've been a warning. "Iban's brother works for the healer."

Iban nodded but didn't speak.

"Because of the Debtor's Mark she can't tell you, but she can tell a fellow brownie." He pointed at himself and slid a shy smile toward Iban. "Ursee wasn't giving your grandfather anything to help him heal. She was giving him a sedative until the day he died."

An immediate sense of loss darkened my insides. I knew she'd kept him sedated while also giving him medicine to heal. "It kept him sleepy so he wouldn't feel the pain."

Iban shook her head. "No medicine. No painkillers."

"Just a sedative so he couldn't talk to you," Pith added.

My earlier anger brewed into a rage. I'd yearned to talk to my grandfather, to ask him why he'd come to the banshees, to tell him about my new friends, to get his advice about what I should do. Now that I knew about the prophecy, I had even more questions.

Questions he'd never be able to answer.

"There's more." Pith patted my knee.

Wariness shifted inside me. She'd brought my friend Pith here for a reason, not a reunion. She'd brought him to possibly soften a blow.

Iban pulled out a syringe with a bright red label.

"What is it?"

The two brownies exchanged glances. They were afraid to tell me. My world spun. Whatever it was, it was bad.

He took my hand. "It's poison."

My thoughts raced. No. It couldn't be what I was thinking. My grandfather had lucid moments and tried to tell me things, warn me. He'd died right after I got my full power.

Pith took hold of my hand. "The banshees killed your grandfather."

I felt as if I'd lost Grandfather all over again.

A sock in the gut of denial. The jagged anguish in my chest of guilt. The flash of fury across my vision. The emptiness in my soul. Grandfather had come to the Skjult Banshee Clan to get help and rescue me. He'd died because he'd come here for me.

No! The fury brewed inside as I adjusted my take on his death. He'd been murdered.

Murdered by the clan that said they were my family.

They weren't family. Families didn't kidnap. Families didn't kill each other. Families didn't enslave innocents. Families didn't ask you to kill.

The clan didn't care about me. They wanted me for my power. When Grandfather came to them for help, it was the perfect situation to find me, kidnap me, enslave me. They'd killed Grandfather because they didn't need him any longer and his powers would transfer to me when he died.

They thought they had me. But I refused to be enslaved.

Whirling around, I stepped out of both brownies' reach and marched toward the door. I wanted to march into Grand Lord Justicar's tent and tell him my real thoughts and plans, how I really felt about him and his clan. I knew I couldn't. The anti-magic cuffs locked my power down. All I had right now was my righteous anger.

"It's one thing to want your power." Iban's serious tone caught my attention. "There has to be more."

She was right. Some of the banshees had powers of their own.

"What do you mean?" Pith let his arms drop to his sides. He realized I wasn't going to do anything rash by rushing out.

"Brownies work around the entire camp. In every tent. No one takes notice of us as long as we're doing our jobs." Iban's high voice filled with anger and softened at the end. "Except for you, Lys Destiny."

The title rubbed against my already raw nerves. "Don't call me that."

Lys was what the banshees called me, and it wasn't an honor. I wanted my friends to call me by my name.

"The warriors are preparing for battle, Grand Lord Justicar is constantly electronically messaging someone important. The tension among the regular banshees is high."

The leader had more tech at his disposal. Communication devices, weapons, the transport vehicle.

"What're you saying?" I flopped onto the floor and crossed my legs. This way I could be at the same level as them.

"We listen while we work." She flopped down next to me. "I think the banshees are preparing for war."

Cassia had said they appeared to be training for a war. Both of them had come to the same conclusion meaning it was most likely true. According to Cassia, the war had ended, and King Zacharye was now in power. "A war with who?"

Iban raised her hands in surrender. "I don't know, but they're planning to use your powers to win."

Her statement sliced across me. I jumped to my feet. "I'll refuse."

She stared at the floor. "I've heard brownies are arranging for the hunt tomorrow."

Grand Lord Justicar killed my grandfather and now he wanted me to kill. Is this why banshees had such a bad reputation? They were supposed to predict death, but this clan...this clan was different than what I'd been brought up to believe. A shiver ran up my spine and landed in my head, freezing my brain. I'd claimed to my friends that banshees didn't murder or kill, they only warned of death.

I was wrong.

"I don't want to kill anyone." Moaning, now I understood the banshees' reputation. The leader didn't just want me to kill a majik. He wanted me to cut out the heart.

"They won't give you a choice." Iban sounded sure. She'd been with the banshees her entire life.

"I'll refuse." I grabbed a frilly, decorative pillow off the bed and threw it. Banshees were chauvinistic. They didn't believe in female warriors. I was the exception. "I'll tell them the sight of blood makes me sick."

"They won't care." Iban darted to the pillow on the floor and picked it up. It was her job as a slave. "Brownies help with the hunt. I've been told the other warriors will force the initiate, even if they have to wrap their hands around the initiate's hand and force him to shove the halberd into the victim."

A burning sensation crawled up my chest and into my throat. The thought of senseless violence made me sick. "Why would they do such a cruel thing?"

The brownies shared a glance. Pith took hold of Iban's hand and nodded for her to continue.

"If you sport the ritual warrior tattoo..."

I scowled at my wrist and the unwanted mark.

"...and kill for him, Grand Lord Justicar controls you." Her face tightened with tension. "Physically."

My eyebrows practically jumped off my face. "Say what!"

"He can compel you to protect him from enemies, to fight suicidally, to jump off a cliff." Her voice rose higher with each exaggeration. "And in your case, Grand Lord Justicar will control your powers."

Chapter Twenty-Three

Cassia arrived early the next morning and put up the sound shield. She must've realized what terrible shape I was in by the fact that I still laid in bed. I quickly updated her on the current situation. Iban nodded along with my explanation.

"So the warriors on the hunt will hold the weapon in your hand to force you to kill?" Cassia curled her lip in disgust.

"Grand Lord Justicar doesn't realize how strong and powerful I am." I slid out of bed and paced across the room. I'd do the worrying for both of us. "He doesn't know that I know I'm a witch or that I also know about the prophecy." Heaviness sunk in my gut. "What if that's how I stop the destructive prophecy from happening? My destroying the kingdom will only come about if I do his bidding."

Cassia put her arm around me. "Then you can't make a kill. Because if you do, he will control you and your powers."

"Exactly." The controlling tattoo explained why the warriors always acted in unison without Grand Lord Justicar saying anything.

"Many brownies will be on the hunt to help track and do the manual labor." Iban tapped her tiny finger against her chin. "Maybe there's a way we can help."

Lykke stepped into the tent and glanced around the room. She carried a bundle of clothes and set them on the bed. "Good morning." She scowled at Iban.

Iban hurried out the back door before she could explain what plan she was devising for the hunt. How could the brownies help me?

"I've brought clothes for the hunt." A combination of jealousy and disgust edged her voice. Did she want to be a warrior or just be with the males?

"I hardly need to be fashionable while killing an innocent majik." Horror leaked out in my sour tone. I hated how I had clothes and a nice tent and other luxuries, while most of the female banshees had little to nothing.

Cassia stepped to the other side of the bed. She knew Lykke supervised her activities with me.

"You're lucky you get to go out with the warriors, including Charmig." Lykke sighed.

Why wasn't she mad at him? He was supposed to marry another. Me.

"I don't feel lucky." Not with the prophecy hanging over my head and the demand that I kill a majik, which I now knew would make me obedient to Grand Lord Justicar.

I got dressed in a long black tunic. The anti-magic bracelets clattered on my wrists, a cloak was placed around my shoulders, and I was ready. Yet, so not ready. I didn't have a plan. I didn't know if Iban had a scheme to help.

Nerves fluttered through my veins and took residence in my mind. Between being forced to kill an innocent and not knowing if the brownies could help, my entire inside twisted in a knot.

We headed off on foot on the cloudy day. It always seemed to be cloudy. A group of brownies ran ahead to track. I tried to catch their eyes to no avail. Warriors followed them at a more leisurely pace. They talked and laughed, giving the impression of being happy away from camp. I was stuck between Charmig and Svante.

I huffed. That was always the case.

The steep downhill terrain wore on my knees and I found it difficult to breathe at this altitude. While with the banshees, I hadn't been able to do much physical labor or exercise.

I rattled the bracelets. "If you take the bracelets off, I could fly to the top of this hill."

"No." Charmig didn't glance at me.

The tramp-tramp of our feet echoed between the bluffs. The warriors' grumbling carried back to us. The brownies had gone around a curve. How would anything be caught with the noise we made?

Large birds swooped overhead and cawed.

I wished it was Drago. Wrapping the cloak tighter, I squinted up at one of the sheer cliffs. The trail we hiked on was narrow, dropping away to one side. The powerful wind gusts could blow one of us off the steep drop on the other side. What type of majik lived this high?

The knot that was my body pulled tighter. Every tendon went taut. Every muscle constricted. Every bone rattled. If Iban wasn't able to get the hunting brownies to agree to a plan, how could I pull this off? Maybe I could say I killed and that the body disappeared by magic. Different majiks had different death processes.

When Svante and I dropped behind the group, he took my arm and bent his head closer. "We never finished our conversation from the other day."

"I've been a little busy." I bit my lip, not wanting him to realize I already knew the prophecy. Picturing him having an intimate conversation with Reitha, I accused, "So have you."

"Have I?" His dark brow rose and a flash of fear shown in his gaze.

I didn't know what he feared, but I wanted to warn him away. "You should leave Reitha alone. She's too young for you."

His lips twitched. "That might be difficult." He scanned around, checking to see whether Charmig and the other warriors were able to hear, and then he leaned closer. "I thought you'd want to know the prophecy and what it means."

I was going to do everything I could to stop or change the prophecy. "I don't believe in prophecies."

"Even ones involving you?" Svante's smooth question tempted.

Hearing his version of the prophecy might shed light on other ways to stop it, but I'd owe him something. "What do you want in exchange?"

"For you to listen to my proposal."

I snorted. "No way." He was as bad as Charmig who flirted with Lykke while wanting to marry me.

"Not that kind of proposal." Svante's nose curled in disgust.

"My turn to escort Lys Destiny." Charmig pushed the man aside.

Frustration clenched in my belly. I didn't want to talk to either of them.

"Don't bother with him. I'm the one you'll marry." Charmig gave me what he believed was a charming smile.

It didn't work. I wanted to slap him. "You announced that I'd marry you to the warriors in the Proving Sphere. Your father said differently."

He chuckled. "That's not exactly how it works."

I swiveled to face him. "How does the marriage decision work? How does me killing another majik prove anything, especially with the brownies doing all the work?" I didn't want him to know I understood the consequences of my killing a majik.

"The conversation you had with Svante appeared more calm and intimate." Charmig pursed his lips and glared at the man. "Did he stir up trouble?"

"No." I wouldn't take sides between these two. I didn't trust either of them. "Tell me."

By his smile, he believed he'd won the prize and I wanted to slap him again. "My father is Grand Lord Justicar, leader of the Skjult Banshee clan."

Yeah, yeah. I knew that.

Charmig kicked at a rock and it tumbled off the edge of the cliff. If I said too much, maybe he'd shove me down.

"My father chose me and Svante to be your Prospectives. It is between him and I as to who you will wed."

My heart hardened and I fisted my cold hands. Pursing my lips, I clamped my mouth shut. I would not tell him the thoughts blasting through my brain.

"Marrying you guarantees I will become the leader when my father dies." Charmig's explanation made it seem simple.

As if there were no feelings involved.

I didn't understand why I even needed to be part of the equation. "Since he's your father isn't ruling your right anyhow, with or without me?"

"Banshee society doesn't work that way." His superior tone grated on my nerves.

I now understood the banshee ways. Males believed they were superior. Females were treated as chattels and couldn't marry who they wanted or sometimes even marry at all. The brownies were enslaved. Grand Lord Justicar somehow controlled the warriors, and they didn't have decision-making abilities. And he wanted to control me.

I jerked my arm out of Charmig's and hugged myself, rubbing my arms up and down. I didn't want to kill, and I didn't want to marry. I hoped the brownies found a way to help me out of this situation. And if they didn't, I'd figure out something else. Being physically controlled by the sinister leader was worse than all my nightmares combined.

Banshees were callous. Their cruelty to each other presented in a harsh spotlight. "What happens to you or Svante when the other one wins?"

Charmig clasped my hand. "You have to understand being Grand Lord Justicar is a dangerous position. If we don't dispose of the competition, they will dispose of us."

Kill or be killed. The banshee name did mean death.

The harsh realization scraped down my spine and into my soul. I'd always defended banshees, not realizing I didn't know the truth. Now I knew and I hated them for it.

We rounded a corner where the rest of the warriors waited in front of a dark cave.

Wooziness surrounded my head, and I blinked a few times. For some reason, the cave opening looked familiar.

Svante and Charmig conferred in whispers with Teinn. They came to me standing at the back of the pack. The wooziness morphed into a sense of déjà vu.

Charmig smiled and winked. "There's a majik inside."

The same words from my dream except bear had been replaced by majik.

I scrunched my brow. Was this a trick? "Don't smile. A majik is about to meet its demise." The words spewed out without thought.

"Majiks kill." Svante growled.

"So do banshees." In my dream I'd said I didn't want to kill a bear. I didn't want to kill anyone. "Why don't you do it for me?"

Svante was the killing type. I tilted back. I'd thought the same in my dream, although now he seemed less lethal and more determined. Determined to do what?

He frowned and exasperation flashed in his dark pupils. "This trip is for you. It's about you. We've found the appropriate target for you."

He didn't track anything, and still he made me sound spoiled.

"You can do this, Lys Destiny." Charmig's cheering stiffened my resolve not to kill. "Remember this is for your grandfather."

My grandfather was dead. Murdered by Charmig's father. My bruised heart fractured further. I'd had this dream before Grandfather had died. I'd reasoned that the bear pelts would keep banshees warm and the meat would feed them. Had my dream tricked me, or had I been too squeamish to dream about killing a majik in cold blood? I squeezed my eyes tight. In the end, I'd killed Stone. A heavy rasp came out of my throat. No matter who was in there I refused to kill. I didn't know what I was going to do.

They wanted me to believe this is what Grandfather wanted, for me to officially join the clan. But he wouldn't want me to kill an innocent majik. He wouldn't want me manipulated by the leader. He wouldn't want me fulfilling a terrible prophecy.

"Can she handle it?" Svante doubted me. He doubted and questioned everything.

I didn't doubt myself. I knew I wouldn't kill. I just had to figure out how to get away with not committing murder.

"Yes." Teinn leered. "The brownies did most of the work. It's practically dead already."

I wailed on the inside. Stone couldn't be almost dead. If it was Stone. This scenario was a little different from my dream.

"Why don't you come in with me?" I was rarely left alone. Always watched.

"You must be alone." Svante shoved a halberd in my hand and my fingers wrapped around the rod.

My knuckles went white. If I wasn't wearing the anti-magic bracelets, I could heal Stone and conjure a heart.

"It's part of the ceremony. A killing, alone in this cave." Charmig grinned as if this was the entrance to a party.

"This cave?" My eyebrows went up. "Why this cave?"

"This is the Wailing Den." Svante actually answered. "Similar to the Obsidian Precipice, the Wailing Den is enchanted with hereditary magic to fulfill the ceremonial process."

To become an automated monster.

Everything inside me hardened. He was telling me something I already knew. If I killed wearing the warrior tattoo, Grand Lord Justicar would control me and my powers.

"We seal the cave with a magical chant, and you can't come out until you hold a heart." Charmig's voice chilled and shivers ran down my back.

"And what if I refuse to kill and cut out a heart." Problem solved.

"We, the warriors, will break the seal, hold the weapon in your hand, and force you to kill." He'd enjoy forcing me.

"The hereditary magic becomes more erratic and painful." Svante's gaze pierced mine, as if he was trying to send a message that the alternative would be far worse for me. "It would be as painful as performing the ritual killing outside of the cave."

I had to go in the cave.

Blowing out, I tiptoed forward. Nerves danced along my spine. The knot inside me untwisted and tightened again. I edged around the rock to the front of the dark cave.

A dark mound sprawled further back from the entrance. I couldn't tell if it was a bear or a large majik. No blond hair showed. My chest galloped.

The mound moved up and down with its breathing.

Going deeper inside the cave, I heard the warriors chanting. The weapon would be for self-defense only.

The dark fur was matted in places and coated with a thick liquid. Blood.

Stumbling to a halt, adrenaline and fear pumped through me.

The warrior had said the brownies had injured the majik to make killing it easier. My body trembled. Nearly everything about the dream was exact. Could the ending be too?

I raised the halberd high above my head, ready to attack. "Stone?"

Chapter Twenty-Four

"Stone?" There'd be no stabbing before confirming the identity beneath the fur. I'd learned my lesson in the dream-vision. If the mound was an angry and injured bear, I'd face its wrath.

The mound moved and the fur wrap was thrown to the side. The one beneath the mound stood up. Tall, muscular, blond.

My heart clobbered and I dropped the halberd.

Stone.

A magical Norse god. Rough and rugged. Hot and handsome. Protective and passionate. His green eyes pierced straight to the center of my soul. Blond whiskers roughened his strong face with his broad chin and high cheekbones. The ends of his lips lifted.

I yearned to throw myself into his arms, except...

A dark reddish-brown liquid splotched his shirt and pants.

Blood.

Sucking in a sharp breath, I couldn't stop the speed of my pulse. "You're injured. What happened?"

He rushed forward and grabbed me in a hug. His muscular arms squeezed tighter as if he didn't believe it was me. I understood because I couldn't believe it was him. His fingers ran through my hair and his thumb trailed a path across my cheek to the tip of my lip. Everywhere he touched tingled.

"What are you wearing? It doesn't matter." His hard lips brushed mine, teasing and tempting. Magical sparks exploded on my mouth and I responded, kissing him back. He plunged harder and his tongue tickled the seam of my lips. I opened for him, pressing every single emotion into the kiss. How I'd missed him and worried about him and thought he might believe I'd run away. Thought he might be dead.

I broke off the kiss and pushed against his arms. "I didn't run away from the battle. I was kidnapped."

"Yes, I know." He sounded calm as he tugged me against his chest. His heart beat loud, so did mine. "I was worried about you, Prince Zacharye told me to leave and find you. I've been searching for you ever since."

"I heard." I was so glad Cassia had relieved some of my anxiety. "How did you know I was kidnapped?"

"I had a suspicion." Stone nodded at the cave entrance. "Your brownie friends told me to hide in here and they'd bring you to me."

My smile blossomed. I owed the brownies a great debt.

He chuckled deeply. "I wasn't expecting you to greet me with a halberd."

Shaking my head, the sense of déjà vu returned. "I had a dream about this meeting. I killed you with the awful weapon."

He ran his knuckles down my cheek making me realize we were both alive. "You'd never hurt me, not physically anyhow."

I wasn't sure what he meant, and I didn't have time to ask. Nerves jumped in my gut. At any moment, the banshee warriors might come check on me. "I'm here with the banshee warriors."

"The ones who kidnapped you?" His body stiffened.

"Yes. It's complicated." Heaviness filled my center. "They had Grandfather so I stayed."

"They kidnapped your grandfather?"

The heaviness darkened. "He's dead. It doesn't matter now." My eyes stung. It did matter. He mattered. "The head banshee expects me to kill a majik in this cave and bring back the heart."

"That explains this." Stone bent down and picked up an organ. Blood seeped out from it and stained his hands.

"Gross. Now I understand why you have blood on your clothes." My muscles loosened knowing he wasn't hurt. "Where did you get it?"

"It's a pig's heart." He scrunched his nose. "The brownies told me to give it to you. Which I thought was a terrible gift."

"It's a wonderful gift," I gushed, flowing with gratitude.

"And there's a fairly fresh body over there." He held up his hands. "The brownies assured me they didn't kill the troll. They'd heard about a death and while half the brownies pretended to hunt, the other half picked up the body. They'll return the troll's body to his family once this is done."

My lungs heaved. This meant I didn't have to murder a majik and the warriors would think I'd made a kill. They wouldn't have to force me.

The brownies had my back. Iban hadn't let me down. She'd communicated to the other brownies what I needed, and they'd done a superb job. "Pith and Cassia are at the banshee camp."

Stone's brows furrowed and his frown deepened. "I have to get you out of here. And Cassia and Pith." Stone's eyes opened wider. "Unless you want to stay with your kind?"

My disposition softened. It was sweet that he asked. Normally, he was a take charge type of guy. An accuse and ask questions later type of leader. He'd changed. Grown while we were apart. And I'd missed the growth.

"They're not my kind." Murderers, kidnappers, and thieves. I never wanted to be trapped again. I wanted to be free to go where I wanted. I stared into his emerald orbs knowing I wanted to be with him.

"Good." He took hold of my hand. "Trolgar and Lukas are waiting at a small campsite. The brownies found us and brought me here."

Warmth raised my spirits. I missed all of them and my new friends had brought us back together. "Any new information about Violet?"

"Helartha and Gnit should be back soon." Stone tugged me closer. "Let's get out of here."

"We can't leave Pith and Cassia." Anxiety threaded through my bones and pulled tight. The two of us couldn't fight against the warriors and I wouldn't leave my friends behind. Plus, I wanted to help the brownies escape enslavement. And there was also the issue of the female banshees' equality, especially the young girl Reitha.

"I'll come back for them later." Stone projected strength and confidence, and I wanted to believe him. "I need to keep you safe."

Believing him and believing in him were two different things. I did believe he could get me out of here but not without violence or endangering our friends. My pulse ticked. We were running out of time. Charmig or Svante or one of the other warriors would come check on me soon. "There's a dozen banshee warriors standing outside the cave."

Stone narrowed his gaze, calculating odds. "What about the brownies? Will they help us fight against them?"

I shook my head. "They're magically enslaved. They can't rise up against their banshee masters."

"They helped me."

"The banshees didn't know to command the brownies *not* to help you." I gnawed my lower lip. I didn't want the brownies getting in trouble for helping me either. "The banshee warriors didn't know you were here. And they can't know."

Frowning, he twisted his lips. "I hate to say this. You need to go back with the banshees for now."

I relaxed. We weren't prepared to fight, especially with me wearing the anti-magic bracelets. If he knew I was supposed to marry one of them soon, he'd insist on fighting single-handedly. I didn't want or need him jealous. I needed him calm and thinking rationally.

"We can't fight our way out of the cave." Stating the obvious put things in perspective. "And we can't leave without Cassia and Pith. And I want to figure out a way to help the enslaved brownies."

"*And* I'm under the orders of King Zacharye to continue following the regent." Stone gripped my hand tighter. "While tracking you and the banshees, we discovered the regent's small group. When I communicated that information to the king, he requested I follow them inconspicuously and find out what the regent is scheming."

"The regent is in the area? When will he move on?" My mind morphed dark, remembering how the man made me feel at the palace.

"I don't know. The regent keeps a small number of confidants." Stone brought my hand to his lips and kissed my skin. A good shiver went from my fingertips to my toes. "He's been traveling in a similar pattern to the banshees. It's how I've been able to track you both."

Odd. I angled my head.

"Although you're more important." Stone swooped in to press his lips against mine.

The second kiss was passionate and sweet at the same time. It was saying hello and goodbye. It showed he cared.

"Lys Destiny?" Teinn's deep timbre echoed from the front of the cave. "If you don't finish soon, I'm going to break the barrier and come in after you."

I stiffened and pulled away from Stone. The jerk warrior had probably come because Charmig and Svante didn't want to see the blood or be hurt by what they believed was a wounded troll.

"I'm almost done!" I shouted back and pushed Stone further into a corner. "You can't get caught."

"I don't like leaving you." He lowered his voice, although the passion came through loud and clear and weakened me.

"We don't have a choice." I considered the cave entrance. I had to stay strong. "Hide for now and talk to the brownies who come to clean up. Try to set up a meeting."

"Soon." His tone dropped low, and his gaze drilled deep into my soul.

Sadness seeped around the hole. We'd be together again. I had to believe. "Yes, very soon."

That night, the drums pounded extra loud. The music was more restrained, almost thoughtful instead of all out abundance. The female banshees danced with more abandonment and yet were also on their best behavior. The banshee warriors didn't drink. They seemed to be waiting for something. The off-kilter atmosphere left me off balance.

Unsettled, I took my assigned seat between Svante and Charmig.

The two of them wore their finest warrior attire with multiple beads hanging around their necks and decorative daggers at their sides. Grand Lord Justicar wore fur leggings and the short skirt garment. His bare torso revealed old scars and gray hair. His beads hung low on his large belly and a fur cape attached around his neck. His knuckles were white, wrapped tight around the ceremonial halberd.

The bonfire flamed higher. The smoke filled the clear sky making my throat dry.

When Charmig stood and stepped away, I quickly followed him. "Is something happening tonight?"

He took a lustful glance at Lykke and glared at me. He might want to marry me for power, but he wanted Lykke. "I'm not at liberty to say."

Telling me outright wasn't going to happen. If I asked without asking, winding my way to the real question, maybe he'd tell me something. "When are we moving again?"

"Not for a while." He wasn't his usual fake-charming self, ill at ease and in a hurry to slip away.

"Why?" I didn't want to relocate now that Stone knew my location. Plus, relocating made so much extra work for the brownies and the female banshees.

"I'm not at liberty to say." His snootiness raised my hackles and the repetitiveness annoyed.

I kept calm. I needed information, not for him to realize he was my enemy.

"Really? Someone as important as you?" I trailed my fingers down his arm. I hated flirting to get information.

He skimmed the area, stopping his gaze where his father and Svante sat. They both watched us.

Bending closer, Charmig whispered in my ear, "King Theobald's entourage has been spotted by the enemy."

"King?" The man wasn't a king. Stone and Cassia had told me that Prince Zacharye had won the battle, and he was now king. I wasn't supposed to know though.

"Yes, King Theobald. Why would you question it?" Charmig's gaze darted around. Was he nervous about talking to me or talking about Theobald?

I couldn't take the lies any longer. Maybe the regent had lied to Grand Lord Justicar. "Whoever told your father that Theobald won against Prince Zacharye was wrong. Prince Zacharye won and is now King Zacharye."

"Where did you hear that?" Charmig's gasp told me he knew more.

I bit my lip. I couldn't get Cassia in trouble or speak of Stone. Trying to blow it off, I shrugged my shoulders. "Guards gossip."

"King Theobald will be king soon enough and rule Alandaska." Charmig's passionate statement rushed out and tried to pin me down.

My mouth gaped. "Why would you want the regent to rule? You're a majik."

He glanced around again and tilted closer. His stinky breath whistled in my ear. I wanted to scrunch my shoulders and step away, but he wanted to tell me something and wasn't sure he should. Which meant it was important.

Finally, he whispered. "King Theobald is arriving in our camp tonight."

My jaw dropped further, wide enough to catch more than lies. Stone had said the regent's and banshee movements followed a similar pattern. Were the banshees following the regent or was it the other way around?

"Why is he coming here?" Indignation rammed through my body. After every heinous thing the regent did to majiks, why would he meet with the banshees? "We're majiks. His enemy."

"Other majiks might be his enemy. Banshees are not." Charmig's chest puffed out. He was proud of the connection.

"Why? He tried to exterminate majiks and steal their powers." I gripped his arm, wanting to yell to the sky. "Why is your father allowing the evil man here? Why is he trusting him?"

"My father does more than trust the human." Charmig's beautiful smile turned sinister. "My father works for the rightful king."

His words stabbed me in the back. I hated Grand Lord Justicar's ways. But I never expected him to betray majiks. I believed he was greedy and overprotective of the clan to the point he'd do anything to keep them and himself in a superior position. But to side with the villainous regent? Pure madness.

Charmig patted my hand. "We all work for King Theobald. Our warriors, our enslaved brownies, and especially our magical Lys Destiny."

CHAPTER TWENTY-FIVE

M^{e}.

The word pounded in my head.

Me and my magic were supposed to work for the evil regent.

No way. My worst possible nightmare. Using my banshee skills for sinister activities. Using my witch magic for the malicious regent's bidding. Using my power on the powerless.

I'd refuse.

Clamping my mouth shut, I hurried away from Charmig. Protesting now would do nothing. Holding my arms up, I glared at the anti-magic bracelets. If I wasn't wearing these, I'd wait for the regent to arrive and take care of him myself.

"Charmig told you, didn't he?" Svante slouched against the pole outside my tent.

My body tensed. Was this an ambush?

He straightened, becoming more menacing. "The charmer can't keep his mouth shut. What kind of ruler would he make?"

Sensing jealousy, I took a step back.

I didn't care why he thought he'd be a better leader. In my opinion, no male banshee would rule justly for all banshees, and aligning with the regent would get every single banshee killed. "There won't be a banshee ruler if we align ourselves with the evil regent."

"Why do you think he's evil?" Svante's casual tone didn't commit to my statement or deny it either.

Angling my head, I contemplated him. He was more intelligent than his counterpart or the leader. More mysterious and quiet. Maybe I could persuade him that this partnership with the regent was wrong.

"Because the regent captures and tortures majiks." Glancing at the nearby guards, I cleared my throat and tried to keep my voice low even while panic thrust inside of me. "Because under his reign, majiks became second class citizens." No class citizens. No rights and no status. Similar to the female banshees in this group. "Because he had a machine invented that steals majik powers."

Svante waved away my concerns. "For regular majiks. Banshees are different."

I puffed out oxygen. I knew banshees were different. So different from the other majiks I knew.

"We will be assisting the regent in regaining the kingdom." He kept his expression straight, not displaying any emotions. "Our warriors are fiercer than any human guards."

"The SCUM." I spat.

He chuckled. "I've heard that before. The Security Collectors of Unique Magic."

"Not unique. Just powerful."

"Like you." His statement of fact, again with no emotions, bothered me.

Whose side was he on? He did everything Grand Lord Justicar wanted, but something about his flat tone agitated my emotions, swirling thoughts around into a different picture.

I pulled back my shoulders. "I'm not going to work for the regent. I refuse to use my powers to help the heinous man."

"You won't have a choice." He leaned closer, threateningly. "And the scenario plays in perfectly with the prophecy."

My gut clenched. The destroyer of all majiks, destroyer of the kingdom.

Svante placed a gentle hand on my arm. "You already know the prophecy, don't you?"

"So it has my name in it. Doesn't mean the prophecy relates to me." I knew it did.

Part banshee and part witch. I was the only one.

"Oh, it's you." His sneer sounded more hopeful than deceitful. "And it's all playing out according to plan unless—"

"Unless nothing." Jerking away, I let his hand fall and continued to my tent. I had to get away from him and Charmig and Grand Lord Justicar. If I stayed by the campfire for the arrival, would the regent recognize me from staying at the palace? Probably not. I'd been a low level majik being trained.

I remembered the regent though. Remembered the dark aura clinging to him.

A shaky breath escaped. Had Charmig's father told the regent about me and my combined powers? Another shaky breath escaped. Was I part of their deal?

"Are you okay?" Iban stood near the back entrance to the tent waiting for me.

I'd already thanked her and told her to thank the other brownies who'd helped arrange the meet up with Stone, the dead majik's body, and the pig heart. I blew out another shaky breath and trembles traveled through me. I wished I could talk to him now. Tell him about the regent and his scheme with the banshees.

"We have a problem." She said as she tiptoed forward. "Several actually."

"Don't I know it." I sunk onto a chair, overwhelmed. My body sank with the weight of my problems.

"Teinn told Grand Lord Justicar that not a single banshee wailed when you made your kill of the majik in the cave."

I swallowed the pig heart-shaped lump in my throat. Dead body or not, I hadn't made a kill which is why no one wailed. Placing my elbows on my knees, I put my head in my hands. I should've thought of the outcome and consequences. All I could think about was Stone and the bloody heart I'd used as evidence. "What can I do?"

"Nothing." She tugged on her ears. "They're questioning the brownies on the hunt. What type of majik did they capture? How did they injure the troll? What type of slash did your weapon leave?"

My stomach eddied. "What did they say?"

"They coordinated their stories and answered the same."

I sighed. Hopefully, we'd gotten away with the deception.

"Grand Lord Justicar has asked the healer to examine the organ." Iban tugged on her ears again.

My relief evaporated and anxiety rained down on my head. I didn't know what to do. I was going to get caught and I didn't want the brownies to get in trouble. "I'll take the blame. Say I ordered them to help me lie because I didn't want to kill a majik."

"Not necessary yet." She snickered giving the perception of another sneaky plan. "The healer has been indisposed."

"Permanently?" I didn't want anyone committing murder on my behalf.

"No. Only enough where she can't examine anyone or any organ." Iban winked. "Goodnight."

My gaze blurred. I was tired. Everything was happening so fast. I needed time to think events through and put it all together. Standing, I staggered to the bed and collapsed. Maybe a dream would provide an answer. One had helped in the cave.

A scratchy noise brought me to a full upright position.

My body tensed and I scoured the tent. I didn't have the energy to deal with Charmig or Svante sneaking inside my tent. "If it's Charmig or Svante, go away."

"It's Stone." His deep voice came from behind me. "Do you want me to go away?"

His teasing tone had me swiveling around and grinning. He wore a banshee style cloak and I wished for a glimpse of his bare chest. No luck. He wore a regular shirt and pants underneath.

Pure joy ignited inside me. "No. I want you to stay forever."

Reaching out for him, I needed the comfort of his hug. He crawled onto the bed and wrapped me in his arms. His evergreen scent wove around me. If he got caught sneaking in, we'd both be in trouble.

He kissed me on the temple. "Everything okay? You seem upset. And who are Charmig and Svante?"

The jealousy in Stone's voice warmed me further. Although he had nothing to be jealous about. But he did need to know about another of my predicaments.

"They are my Prospectives." I ran a finger through his blond hair, yearning to touch more of him. To be alone with him and not worry about interruptions or complications. "One of them plans to marry me and become the future leader of the banshees."

His arms tightened around me and his face reddened with rage. "Never."

My heart melted. If I let him, he'd run out of the tent and challenge both of them right now. They were the least of my problems.

"I agree, and they are a problem for another day. There's more important news to share." I inhaled and kept my arms wrapped around him, needing his strength. "Regent Theobald is arriving in the banshee camp tonight."

"I'm aware." Stone's nonchalant answer shocked me. I tilted back. "I've already sent word to King Zacharye. But he and his troops won't arrive for a couple of days."

My spirits lifted and I snuggled into Stone's hard chest. Having the new king's help would be much appreciated. He'd be able to free the brownies, too. Or Princess Ellery could using her fairy magic.

Stone took a piece of my hair and twirled the strand around his finger. "I've been informed the regent has convinced the banshees to fight on his side. They want to take King Zacharye's throne."

"It's true." I remembered my conversations with Charmig and Svante.

"I've heard the banshee warriors will be the regent's enforcers." Stone's serious expression belied his soft caress on my skin. "The warriors will do any atrocious deed, including suicide attacks."

I pressed myself closer to him. I'd seen their ruthlessness. They'd been preparing to fight against other majiks. "They are ruthless."

"Ruthless and robotic because they're controlled by their leader through a magical tattoo."

I glanced at my marked wrist. I couldn't keep this secret from Stone even though I knew he'd be furious.

I held up my arm. "This tattoo?"

"*Hvitspyd*." Stone yanked my arm closer to inspect the awful mark. "No." His brows furrowed and his eyes narrowed. "No." His mouth pursed together in a glower. "No."

He couldn't believe what he saw.

"Yes." The tattoo was real. "I—"

"Why did you—"

"I didn't know."

"How could you—"

"I was drugged, unconscious." Remembered anger struck me like lightning. Grand Lord Justicar had marked me for life. He'd marked Cassia too, albeit in a different way.

"Does the banshee leader contr—"

"No. That's the reason the pig heart was needed." The earlier lightning sparked a fire thinking about what would've happened if the brownies hadn't helped. "Since I didn't kill, the leader doesn't control me. Although he doesn't know the truth." I quickly explained that the leader believed I had killed a majik although there were suspicions this wasn't true, that the tattoo had been forced, and that the banshees believed they were the regent's partners, and ended with, "The banshee warriors will be strong as a unit. They're cruel and beat each other up for sport."

Stone jerked to sitting. "We have to leave. Now."

His urgency buzzed into me. I wanted to leave but knew I couldn't. "We can't leave without Cassia and Pith."

"I'll come back for them." Stone swung his legs off the bed and stomped them on the ground in a note of finality. "You're the one in the most danger."

"I'm the one in the best position to spy." I refused to let him have the final word. There were too many things I needed to do here and helping Stone was one of them. "I can spy on Grand Lord Justicar and the regent."

"It's too dangerous. Something could happen. What if you have to defend yourself and you kill..." A plea stretched in Stone's voice. His haggard expression showed more than concern. Worry lines formed around his eyes and his mouth went flat.

I appreciated how much he cared. Still, he couldn't control my life just as the banshee leader couldn't. If Stone cared for me, he couldn't think I was helpless. I wasn't. "Too dangerous for me to stay but not for Cassia and Pith?"

"No. It's just that you—"

"This is a repeat of the same fight we had before the big battle against the regent. I wanted to stay and you insisted I leave." I chopped my hand through the air. "And look what happened."

The lines around his eyes softened. He blew out and ran his fingers through his long blond hair. "Even though I don't like it, I agree with the idea. What can I do to help?"

"Hold me a little longer." I grabbed his hand and tugged him onto the bed. The weight of his frame brought me closer. Not close enough. I threaded my fingers through his long strands. Longer than what they'd been in the dungeon. In the cave, I hadn't had time to notice. Using the palm of my hand, I pushed the back of his head toward me, pulling him in for a kiss.

A demanding kiss.

His lips curved into a smile against my own. He repositioned his body so we were mouth to mouth, chest to chest, and heart to heart. His fingers caressed my cheek, ran down my arm, and across my bare belly.

Shivering, I thrilled in his touch, in his closeness, in him.

I responded by trailing my fingers down his back and his butt, and a tease of my tongue against the seam of his lips. His mouth opened welcoming me inside.

His unique taste acted as an aphrodisiac, slowing my movements, making them more sensual, causing me to forget everything.

"Destiny, are you asleep?" the soft call startled me from the kiss.

"Lykke." I jerked apart from Stone and pushed against him. "You have to hide."

Stone rolled away and landed on the floor on the other side of the bed. He made no noise.

"Sorry to wake you, Destiny." Lykke slipped in between the tent flaps. Her gaze gleamed with excitement. She hadn't even thrown on a cloak to keep warm against the cold night. "Grand Lord Justicar wants you to meet our honored guest."

Nerves crawled against my skin and I jolted out of the sensual haze. Stone couldn't get caught. Rolling over, I leaned up on my elbow trying to block her view of the other side of the bed. "You mean Regent Theobald?"

I should be more worried about the evil man.

She pouted. "How do you know? And it's King Theobald."

Swinging my legs off the side of the bed, I used my foot to push Stone further under. "Maybe to the banshees, but not throughout the kingdom."

"He's the king to you too." She strutted toward the bed.

With shaking hands, I tugged the covers down to cover the opening under the bed and skirted around the end. "Yes, let's go meet the regent." I wondered how much of the truth the regular banshees had been told. Maybe they believed he truly was the king. They'd told me he'd won the battle against the prince and it had been a lie. "Did you know he lost the battle against Prince Zacharye? Now *King* Zacharye."

"I understand that the battle was unfair. Prince Zacharye had majiks on his side." She stepped up to the other side of the bed and pulled the covers toward her, evening them out.

My lungs deflated. I took hold of her arm as bewilderment swirled in my head. Why couldn't she see the truth? "Because majiks believe in him and he believes in equality."

"I don't even know what that means." She waved her hand suggesting the definition wasn't important.

I tugged her toward the table and away from the bed. "You know the meaning of equality." I knew she wasn't stupid. She could be quite cunning. "You've just never experienced it with the unfair roles and places in the banshee clan. Females have the lowest place of all."

Except for the brownies.

Disgust roiled in my midsection. I wouldn't go there now. I needed information from her. Maybe if I shared intelligence, I'd get intelligence. "Charmig tells me the banshee warriors are going to fight alongside the regent."

Her gaze narrowed in on the bed and her expression fell. "Did he tell you when you were in bed together?"

"He didn't sleep with me," I responded louder than necessary.

"Why is there an indentation in the second pillow?" She yanked her arm out of my hold and pointed at the bed.

My stomach went queasy. My pulse fluttered as my body stilled. Stone had made the indentation. I couldn't use him as the excuse. He'd get caught.

"It wasn't Charmig." I kept my tone calm, holding in my abhorrence. "I couldn't fall asleep, I was tossing and turning. I switched pillows thinking the other one might help me sleep better."

She plodded toward the bed. My eyes widened with each step. She picked up the pillow and sniffed. She was an excellent spy. Would she report a second indent in a pillow to Svante, Charmig, or his father?

"You're very observant. I bet you notice all sorts of things." I hurried back to the end of the bed, blocking her way and acting casual about my next, very important question. "Like whether I have the same exact tattoo as the other banshee warriors?"

I'd woken up mid-branding and tried to use my mind to force the leader to stop. My only hope was that maybe if the tattoo wasn't complete, it wouldn't work in case I ever had to fight and kill someone.

She shot me a suspicious glance.

"I mean, because I'm female I wondered if we'd have the same tattoo." My fast mangled speech gave away my nervousness.

She took hold of my wrist and peered at the intricate design. "Charmig and Svante's are a bit different from the regular warriors. When they became Elders another line was added."

"Really?" I held my breath, hoping mine was different too. "Let's sit by the light."

I tugged her toward the table and we both sat down. My shoulders sagged.

She studied my wrist. "I think it's the same." Her fingers brushed at the circle with the pointed knots meeting in the middle. "This one line seems shorter. Of course, you're smaller than the males."

The tightness in my chest loosened. "So it's not the same? Different somehow?" I hoped Stone was listening. I wanted to lessen his worry. I might not have killed anyone yet, but I could in the future. A battle was brewing.

She shrugged and let go of my wrist.

"Can you tell me something else before we go to meet the regent?" I wanted her out of the tent, but I also didn't want to meet the regent or leave Stone.

Her brows arched. "Maybe."

I bit my lower lip thinking about the best way to question something I already knew and dreaded the confirmation of the answer. "I've been told Grand Lord Justicar controls the warriors through the tattoo. I haven't felt anything."

"The connection takes time to bind after you've made your first kill since having the tattoo. You recently made your first kill. The first time he controls your actions, you'll know it."

So it was a combination of the tattoo and the kill that controlled the warrior. I glared at the mark on my wrist.

Lykke sounded so positive, while the entire idea of losing control freaked me out.

Good thing it would never happen. I was free from his manipulation because I'd never killed anyone for him. Iban had saved me from a terrible future by helping me get the pig's heart. Becoming an uncontrollable killer would be the worst thing to happen.

"Are you okay?" Lykke asked.

I forced myself to smile. "Yes. I'm wonderful."

"Good." She picked up my cloak from the chair and handed it to me. "Grand Lord Justicar wants you to meet the soon-to-be-king." She winked, playing a game with the evil regent's title.

Except this was no game.

Chapter Twenty-Six

The darkness hit me before I even entered Grand Lord Justicar's tent. I remembered the darkness from when the regent roamed the corridors of the palace. The pure corruptness of his soul must manifest in black.

I stepped inside and stayed by the decorative doorway. The interior of the tent had changed. The large bed had purple drapes instead of netting. The bureau sported a large oval-shaped mirror. Several new trunks designed with a royal crest had been set throughout the interior.

Had the regent escaped with his clothes and possessions?

"Bow before King Theobald." Grand Lord Justicar sat in one of the smaller chairs usually reserved for Charmig or Svante.

Theobald sat in the leader's heavy gilt chair. He wore the splendid robes of a king and a gaudy crown perched on top of his head. He appeared thinner, gaunter in the face. His balding head had lost more hair. Even though he was human and didn't use a block like the professor, I couldn't read his mind.

"Bow." A blond woman stood next to the regent.

I sucked in. She'd been in a dream-vision.

"Thank you, Bee." The regent didn't peer at the woman as he spoke.

I didn't want to begin the meeting making waves. I bowed.

"This is the banshee I've been telling you about." The banshee leader spoke as if I was an object.

My skin heated and I wanted to take a swing. I couldn't show my hand. Not yet.

"The one in the Wicked End Prophecy?" The pretend king angled forward and examined me. "Look at me, zauber."

I flinched and stood upright to glower. Why would the leader believe he'd treat banshees differently?

Grand Lord Justicar pinched his mouth. "She's a banshee."

I pulled back my shoulders. "Part banshee."

He leaned back in surprise. Then, a dawning expression showed on his face. He realized I knew the truth about my heritage. "The other parts don't matter."

My legs quivered, I hoped he didn't think Cassia had told me. I couldn't stay quiet. "Most of my magic comes from being a wit—"

"Don't speak unless you're asked a question." The regent dropped to his feet from the large chair. He walked around me. "How powerful is she?"

I clenched my hands into fists and clamped my mouth shut. I wanted to say, *more powerful than both of you.* But I'd said enough already, and if he asked the leader the questions, I wouldn't have to talk to them. Plus, the leader controlled the warriors and the regent had a small group of soldiers with hi-tech weaponry posted nearby.

The banshee leader got to his feet and did jazz hands at my face. "You know the prophecy..."

Twisting my lips, I forced myself to stay silent.

"Knowing and seeing are two completely different things." Regent Theobald's petulance was like a small child. "Show me."

I slowly exhaled. I'd love to show him. Let me loose.

The banshee leader strolled around the other side. "Partners should trust each other."

Holding in a guffaw, I couldn't believe his naivete. The regent would double cross his own mother. If the rumors were true, he'd killed his brother to steal the crown.

"Remember, you work for me." The regent's frigid tone scraped down my spine even though he wasn't talking to me. "You will be rewarded when your job is complete, and I'm installed on the throne."

What would the reward be? Enslavement of the banshees? The regent wants to steal powers from majiks and kill them, all majiks. Why would the banshees not have their powers stolen and be killed too?

"Give me a demonstration of what she can do." Regent Theobald glared at the banshee leader. He trusted no one because he knew he couldn't be trusted himself. "What can we do with her talents?"

I held my breath. He referred to the banshee leaders' ability to control the warriors.

"Brownie, unlock her anti-magic bracelets." Grand Lord Justicar ordered and flashed a reassuring smile at the regent. "Thank you for the special bracelets and the other hi-tech items you've supplied. The items have been helpful."

My brow furrowed. I remembered the transport from when I'd been kidnapped and hi-tech weapons I'd seen around the camp. It must be part of the deal with the regent.

The brownie climbed on a trunk and took hold of my wrists. His small hands trembled as he twisted the key and took off the bracelets.

I rubbed my wrists, glad to be free for a little while.

"Choke and kill the brownie." Grand Lord Justicar swiped his index finger across the tattoo on his wrist.

"What?" My belly lurched.

The brownie stood motionless on top of the trunk. His eyes widened and his gaze pleaded with me.

"The bond between me and my warriors gets stronger with time. This one recently made her kill." The banshee leader's superior smirk exhibited a nervous tick.

I wasn't doing as ordered. I couldn't do as ordered. My pulse spiked. I didn't want to kill, but I needed to protect my cover. Yet if I pretended the bond worked and killed this brownie now, then

I'd actually be under his control because I'd killed. If I didn't, he'd know the truth. A sticky, life or death situation.

For me and the brownie.

He swiped his index finger on the tattoo again and scowled at me. "Choke the brownie to death."

I froze with indecision. I needed to pretend the bond was working. Reaching my hands toward the brownie, I clasped around his neck. I tried to message him with an expression saying I'd find a way out of this predicament.

But how? And when?

The brownie didn't resist. He stood and let me wrap each finger around his tiny neck. He wasn't very big and it would easily snap. His rough skin braided against my hands. His eyes got even larger. His tiny mouth dropped open to scream but he didn't say anything. His chest went up and down and the triangular mark glowed. He was being forced to stand still just as I was being forced to kill.

I didn't want to murder him. I wanted to help the brownies. If I killed him, how could I look at Pith, Iban, and the other brownies?

"Kill the zauber, already." The regent sounded bored.

I gritted my teeth. The man hated majiks. How could Grand Lord Justicar be stupid enough to trust him? There'd be no fair deal.

Regripping the brownie's neck, I tried to think of a way out of this situation and fast. I didn't have many options. Listen and kill a brownie and truly be under the leader's control. Or not listen and divulge I wasn't ever under his control. How could I get out of this trap made of my own lies?

My mind whirled and my heart ticked resembling a doomsday clock.

The banshee leader made the same action over his tattoo. "Do it this second! Twist its neck and kill the brownie!"

Chapter Twenty-Seven

My breath strangled in my throat.

It was as if I was choking myself.

My fingers pressed into the brownie's thick skin. I didn't even know his name.

The brownie struggled for air.

I couldn't kill him. I didn't care if Grand Lord Justicar discovered the truth that I had no bond to him.

"Is brute strength really proving to King Theobald," I hated using the title, "my magical prowess?"

The banshee leader pursed his lips and his cheeks reddened and swelled. He hated the fact that I wasn't doing exactly as ordered and killing the brownie immediately.

"She's right." The regent flourished a beringed hand. "Anyone can strangle a brownie to death. I want to see some of the magic the prophecy has professed."

My sigh of relief came out unsteady.

"Let the brownie go." The banshee leader fisted his hands. "I'd hate to lose a servant."

A slave.

I released the brownie and took a step back. My taut muscles loosened.

The brownie clutched his sore neck.

I hoped I wouldn't be asked to do something worse. What was worse than committing murder?

The brownie sagged while staying on the trunk, afraid or unable to move. He knew not to celebrate too soon.

"She's raised a boulder and wounded a dragon." The leader sneered, probably remembering that I'd also set the dragon free. "We can definitely give her a better test, a bigger test. I'll have to think about it overnight and she will perform tomorrow. Something really big."

Tension knotted in my stomach. What would his test consist of?

The brownie scurried off and hid behind the trunk. He didn't want to be part of the next demonstration.

I wished I could do the same.

When Cassia arrived at my tent the following morning, we hugged. I immediately used the sound shield spell.

"I have so much news to share." I quickly told her the regent was in the camp, the banshees were fighting for him, and Stone knew because I saw him last night.

"Wow." She released the hug. "You had a much more exciting night than me."

We practiced magic as we talked.

"Stone wants the three of us to escape." Using a teacup from breakfast, I performed the duplicate spell. Now I had two cups, and more for the female banshees and brownies to pack up and carry when we relocated next. Except I wasn't going with them this time.

Cassia swiped at her forehead, emphasizing the banshee mark. The redness was gone, and the tattoo appeared natural. "Try transporting both cups from the table to the floor."

The cups floated and gently landed on the ground. Cassia's training had boosted my own confidence.

She waved her hand and the cups filled with tea and floated back onto the table. "I found out where they're holding Pith. Thanks to Iban, the brownies know I'm not a banshee and they trust me."

"Good." I needed the two of them to be safe. "If you see a chance to get yourself and Pith out, you should leave."

"What about you?" Cassia snapped her fingers and a candle materialized.

I shook my head. While the fear of being under the leader's control could become an issue, I had other things to accomplish. "I can't leave yet. I need to spy on the regent and help free the brownies."

"How're you going to do both those things?"

"I don't know, but I have an idea." An idea with no actual knowledge behind it. Only hope. "When you get to Stone, ask him to send a message to Princess Ellery. They're friends."

She nodded. "I'll find out what I can while I'm here."

I hugged her. "Thanks Cassia. You're a great friend."

"So are you." She held me a few seconds longer. "Go kick some banshee butt."

⟫⟫⟩ ⟨⟪⟪

Grand Lord Justicar put off the demonstration until evening. My nerves jumped all day, waiting to be told what he wanted me to do. I'd hoped they would tell me in advance so I could figure out a way to handle the demonstration. No such luck. I thought and planned for every possibility.

That night at the campfire the flames leapt high in the clear night sky. Everyone partied—drinking more, dancing wildly, laughing with extra merriment. The warriors displayed their battle skills in the Proving Sphere, putting on exhibition fights for the regent and his soldiers.

Regent Theobald and Grand Lord Justicar sat in their chairs. The regent wore a velvet purple robe, frequently rubbing his chin against the softness. Svante and Charmig stood beside them. The regent kept Bee and several soldiers next to him.

I sat by the leaders and Lykke kneeled at the regent's feet. My blood boiled. I wanted to yank her up.

A banshee in the Proving Sphere attacked a second warrior with his fists. The men were not throwing punches, the fights were real. It didn't matter to Grand Lord Justicar. He knew his warriors would do exactly what they were commanded to do.

A drunken warrior stumbled toward us, tripped, and landed on the ground with his head in Lykke's lap. "Sorry, beautiful. Maybe you should put me to bed. And stay." He tried to wink.

My body tensed watching the exchange.

Lykke's nose curled and she tried to shift him away. The heavy warrior didn't budge.

I got out of my chair, bent down, and pushed the guy. "Get off."

She smiled her thanks. Why hadn't Charmig come to her defense?

The drunk stumbled back into the dancing crowd. Everyone was having a good time except the ones around the two leaders.

"Are we trying to impress the regent with our fighting skills or our drunkenness?" I whispered.

Lykke giggled and covered her mouth.

The fighting stopped and Grand Lord Justicar stood. He used his index finger to swirl across his wrist tattoo and the music and drumming stopped. He gave me a wicked grin.

My stomach flipped and I slipped into my seat, trying to control my trembling legs.

"We welcome King Theobald." The banshee leader boomed.

Everyone clapped and shouted.

"We've displayed our fighting skills, our hospitality, and our beautiful women," Grand Lord Justicar leered at Lykke. "Now, it's time to show him our magic."

My muscles tightened. *My magic.*

"Lys Destiny will demonstrate banshee magic." His announcement had me squeezing my eyes tight.

I stomped to my feet. I wanted everyone to know the truth about me. "It's not banshee magic."

Svante grabbed my arm, tight. I didn't know if he'd done it because he was ordered to or because he wanted me to shut up.

The banshee leader swiped his tattoo again and looked at me expectantly.

Tension threaded through my body. I didn't know if he'd given me a command to be quiet or not. Not wanting him to know that I wasn't bonded to him, I smashed my lips together and didn't say anything more. Otherwise, I would've shouted how my magic came from being part witch and I'd never help the regent steal the throne.

"Take off the anti-magic bracelets," Grand Lord Justicar ordered.

A guard jerked my wrists up, unlocked, and removed the bracelets.

Glaring at the leader, I waited for him to give me an order. Now, I could do anything, destroy everything, kill the regent. But I refused to kill in cold blood. The act would turn me into a controlled warrior. Whatever order Grand Lord Justicar commanded, I'd counter it somehow.

Everyone went quiet. No talking or laughing. Only anticipation for the demonstration.

"I told you she raised a boulder and flung it at a dragon, wounding the beast." Grand Lord Justicar relished the attention. "Tonight, she will demonstrate her strength by..."

I willed it to be something simple. I locked my knees so I wouldn't fall. Would he want me to kill another brownie? Make a banshee or human sacrifice?

"...destroying the cliff." He pointed to a cliff high above the encampment. "Showing her strength. For if she can bring down a mountain, then she and the banshees can help you bring down the kingdom."

I went from relieved I wouldn't have to kill, to crushed because his words matched up with the prophecy.

The cliff was a humongous piece of earth. I'd crushed rocks and shook the earth. But to demolish an entire cliff seemed impossible. And not very imaginative on the leader's part.

Charmig and Svante regarded me. One appeared worried and the other confident.

Is this how the prophecy would come true? Begin with destroying a cliff and then the entire kingdom?

The rest of the banshees stared at me or the cliff. Silence permeated the camp.

My mind ticked. How close was King Zacharye and his army? If I brought the cliff down, would I hinder their arrival or would I block the regent's escape? I glanced around the entire area. The encampment sat between several tall cliffs.

"Just one cliff?" I blustered, a plan forming in my head. "Why not both those cliffs?" I pointed to the one on the right.

If King Zacharye was coming from the palace, he'd take the most direct route which would bring him through the pass behind us. I wouldn't attempt anything in that area. But I'd block any banshee escape routes for when the real king arrived.

Grand Lord Justicar studied me, searching for a scheme.

I held back a slight smile and kept my chin up.

Regent Theobald slapped his knee. "Amazing. Yes, have her do it."

The banshee leader snarled. "Lys Destiny, destroy both those cliffs." He made the same movement over his tattoo.

There was no urge to do as commanded.

I peered at the two cliffs, raised my hands, and spread my fingers wide. An electrical charge sizzled through my veins as I held my emotions inside with the internal heks scream.

I'd crushed rocks before. This was a lot larger.

Gathering my inner strength, I let the electrical charges heat up and snap. Currents sparked from my fingers.

The crowd murmured. I used their tension to increase the force, pulling from the tautness of their bodies and the fraught atmosphere. The ground rumbled beneath my feet.

Grand Lord Justicar grabbed his wine glass before it fell.

I snorted, but quickly returned my focus. I wanted to succeed and prove to him I had major power. Banshee power and witch magic. Power I'd use to help King Zacharye. And at some point, Grand Lord Justicar would realize he didn't control me.

A force grew inside me. A deep, rushing force, a current in a raging river. Magical synapses crackled throughout my body. I'd never experienced this type of strength in my magic.

The ground shook harder. Not like the earthquake I'd produced the other night, more of a trembling beneath earth's core. A large crevice formed on the face of the first cliff.

I stumbled and swung my arms to keep my balance.

The murmuring grew. A couple of shouts added to the mix.

A large crevice formed in the second cliff. The cracks widened and lengthened. It was like watching a building implode. Boulders cracked off and blasted into the ground. Rocks and stones tumbled. The noise deafened. The side of the first cliff tumbled and rumbled to the ground. An echo boomed through the encampment, as if thunder had struck nearby and set off a chain reaction. The second cliff imploded.

The two cliffs were gone, reduced to a pile of rubble.

The rumbling stopped. The booming and crashing ceased. I scanned the banshee encampment. Everyone gaped at the spot where the cliffs had been. Everyone was silent.

My tense shoulders dropped and my body sagged. I'd demonstrated my strength.

Regent Theobald and Grand Lord Justicar grinned with satisfaction and observed me.

I grew hot in the spotlight. I'd proved my powerful magic and now they believed they were going to use me to kill humans and majiks, to steal the crown from King Zacharye, to take over the kingdom.

My lips lifted into a smug smile. The best way to help the new king at this moment was to show him the way.

Even though I was tired, I lifted my hands toward the sky. I let the energy flow through me and electrify my body. Sparks shot from my hands, and I let them grow and grow. I used the sparks in the night sky to draw a picture.

A simple outline of Regent Theobald high in the sky. So high the entire kingdom could see. His sharp nose and moon shaped face. His pointed chin and partially balding head. I even etched the gaudy crown on top.

"What is the meaning of this?" Grand Lord Justicar sounded insulted as if he'd punish me for insubordination, for doing something he didn't tell me to do.

"To honor," I forced my lips to say the name, "King Theobald."

"Oooh," The regent beamed at his likeness in the sky. "What a splendid display of magic and artistry."

The banshee leader's gaze narrowed. He wasn't buying the honor statement. Would he realize he didn't control me?

I shimmied my shoulders. I enjoyed besting both him and the regent. This wasn't the end. But so many things could go wrong before Stone and my friends, and King Zacharye and his troops, arrived.

Grand Lord Justicar started a slow clap.

Charmig and Lykke joined in the appreciation for the magical art. The other banshees clapped too. Svante crossed his arms and watched every move I made. He was suspicious.

I sunk onto a log and Lykke joined me. "Are you allowed to sit here?"

"For a while." She'd been sitting at the regent's feet and normally she tried to take a position by Charmig's side. "Grand Lord Justicar wants me to flirt and keep King Theobald happy."

I'd noticed. Frowning, I decided how to approach the subject of my disapproval. "How does the banshee you love feel about the way you're treated?"

She flattened her lips together and searched for Charmig.

"On to the main event." Grand Lord Justicar signaled the drummer to get everyone's attention. He took out a small drawstring bag and plodded around the Proving Sphere, dumping black ash as he walked. "Ancient ash from our Grand Lord Justicar forefathers. The powerful ash charms the circle ensuring the winner of the match will receive my powers when I pass."

I nudged Lykke. "Did he say spreading ash from earlier leaders?"

"Yes." Her serious expression told me this was no joke. She angled closer to whisper, "The ash is enchanted and contains the hereditary power inside the circle."

"His power?" I couldn't see him giving away his power.

"Yes and no. His power which is hereditary power. This is how the Grand Lord Justicar picks the next ruler."

I was surprised he didn't just bestow the honor on his son. "How did it come down to Charmig and Svante?"

"The warriors battle in the Proving Sphere. The best were chosen and the others killed."

I gasped. Charmig had said something similar. "What? Why?"

"So they don't become a threat to the future leader." Her emotionless tone told me this was standard practice.

It also explained why there were no middle-aged male banshees. They'd all been killed. You either became a bonded warrior or an Elder. No wonder the clan was small. Of course, being small made the clan easier to control.

"Charmig." The leader nodded at his son and then at his son's competitor. "Svante."

There'd been no difference in the leader's tone or even a bigger nod at his son. The leader appeared to consider them both equal. Did he?

Svante and Charmig stepped into the Proving Sphere. Two female banshees removed the fighters' heavy cloaks revealing bare chests and unadorned shulas. They were each handed a sharp halberd.

"The Elders will demonstrate their skills and power." The leader raised the ceremonial halberd. "And fight to the death."

Nausea crawled up my throat. I didn't like either of them, but I wouldn't wish them dead. I'd noted how the warriors fought each other without holding back. Now, I understood why. "If they both want to become the next leader so bad, why didn't they kill each other earlier?"

"It's an honor to fight in the Proving Sphere and receive the blessing from the hereditary ash." Lykke's reverence showed she believed in the patriarchy.

"Why doesn't one of them kill the leader?" That would solve my problems.

She gave a shocked gasp. "It wouldn't be honorable."

I had news for her—banshees had no honor.

"Plus, you'd have to kill the leader in the Proving Sphere for the hereditary ash to transfer power." She monitored the spectacle with a riveted expression.

The regent sat straighter and tilted forward in his seat. The banshees leaned in closer, wanting to see every second of the action.

I didn't want to watch, and yet I couldn't turn away.

"The winner will become the future Grand Lord Justicar and will lead the banshee warriors into the coming battle." The leader's happiness edged with pride. He whipped up excitement and anticipation for the fight by letting everyone know how important the odds were. "The winner will also marry Lys Destiny tonight."

Chapter Twenty-Eight

I clutched Lykke's arm. "What did Grand Lord Justicar say?"

The words were clear, but understanding didn't make it into my foggy brain.

"You shall marry the winner." Her deeply sad tone wasn't sad for me. She was sad for herself.

"Ridiculous." I shook my head trying to clear my mind. "No way." My pulse raced, heating up my core. "I don't even like either of them." Sweat formed on my lower back. "I'll never marry either of them. I'll die before I marry either of them. I'll kill myself before I marry either of them. I'll kill them before I marry either of them."

I thought I'd have more time to escape.

Charmig and Svante circled around the ring, facing off against each other. They each held long-sticked halberds with points sharp enough to puncture a major artery. Sharp enough to kill.

My lungs shrieked and I clutched her arm tighter. "Don't I have a say in this?"

"No."

Charmig used the weapon to stab at Svante. He easily evaded the strike. They both raised the wooden handles and crashed into each other. The *clack, clack, clack* pounded between my ears.

I hated fighting, and yet I wanted this to be the longest fight ever.

I peered around the small arena. The warriors bet on the winner. The females ogled the two men. I cringed. One of them would be dead soon and the women ogled the fighters the same way the males usually ogled them.

My eyes widened. Had Cassia or Pith heard about the fight or the marriage?

Svante swiped the blade across Charmig's bare abs. Blood seeped from the gash.

The crowd *oohed*. Edginess emanated from the banshees watching. Some of them must have favorites.

Charmig stumbled back. He squeezed his fingers around the halberd and his face scrunched in furor. He charged and swiped up, going for Svante's neck. Svante ducked and came in low, hitting Charmig on his bleeding wound.

Charmig howled in pain.

The howl struck my center. I didn't know who I was rooting for. Really, I wasn't rooting for either of them. "Why don't they use magic? Is it against the rules?"

Lykke quirked her head to stare. "They don't have magic."

I gaped. "You mean the ash takes away their magic?"

She angled her head further and her brows arched. "Our clan has no magic. We were cursed by witches about nine years ago."

Tension tightened my muscles like a bow. I knew the females had no magic. I'd discovered most males didn't possess magic either. Charmig had told me that he, his father, and Svante possessed magic. Charmig had lied. Knowing they had none, I understood why they were so desperate for my power, especially considering their association with the regent. The clan would never let me leave.

A chill settled in my bones.

Charmig feinted to the left and stumbled. Svante exhaled and waited for his opponent to stand. Instead, Charmig attacked his opponent's thigh with the sharp point. A trick. He hadn't stumbled. He'd pretended so Svante would relax.

My brow furrowed. "How does Grand Lord Justicar control the warriors through the tattoo if he doesn't have magic?"

"It's from the enchanted ash which can never be drained of power. The ash is a powerful banshee relic passed down through generations. That's how the brownies are enslaved as well. It is the only magic we have left."

Grandfather and my parents had magic because they weren't part of the clan. Plus, Mom was part witch. I furrowed my brow. Or all witch and pretending to be a banshee. I had memories of her without the banshee mark on her forehead.

The enchanted ash ensured the leader controlled the warriors and the brownies. The brownies would never be set free.

Not when Grand Lord Justicar died or the leader after him or the leader after him. A sour taste filled my mouth. The male banshees wanted to become good warriors or they'd be sacrificed. Every warrior had volunteered—except me. When a banshee killed someone while wearing the tattoo, he'd be controlled forever. There was no exit.

Did that mean if I ever killed anyone, even when I left the clan, I'd become beholden and controlled by the leader of the banshees?

Some of the marks on the brownies were hereditary like Iban's. Once someone in a brownie family was marked, everyone else from that point forward would be enslaved. They and their descendants would never be free.

Despair swam through my veins, making my head and heart heavy. At least I wasn't beholden. Yet.

Svante growled and wiped at the dripping blood from his thigh. He bent forward and stomped his foot. He was ready to fully attack. Either him or Charmig would die tonight.

Killing unsuccessful warriors was evil. Enslaving brownies for life, and their offspring too, was sinister. Forcing me to marry someone I didn't love was barbaric.

Itching to get up, I wanted to stop the fight before someone was killed and a winner declared. Adrenaline scratched along my spine. The bystanders were glued to the battle. Their bodies moved with the punches. A couple of *oohs* and *ahs*. Everyone was enraptured, even the children. They were brought up with a lust for blood.

I glanced down not wanting to see their passion for death and spotted my wrists. My empty wrists. I sucked in a breath while trying to stay calm. They'd forgotten to put the bracelets on after my performance. I had access to my witch or banshee or whatever magic.

And none of them could stop me because they didn't have magic. None of them. Just the control of the warriors that the leader exhibited. My skin tightened and I crossed my arms trying to cover my bare wrists. I had to think, to figure out the best way to use my power to end this.

To end all of this.

Svante parried and thrust with his halberd. He hit his opponent on the shoulder and fighting arm. Blood poured from both men now. It seeped into the ground of the Proving Sphere. How much blood had been lost?

My stomach reeled.

Lykke leaned forward. Her gaze followed the fight, but mostly Charmig. Every time he received a punch, she flinched. Every time he fell to the ground, she clutched her chest. Charmig was the banshee she loved, even though she'd known all along that he'd marry me. Or die.

Softening toward her, I remembered how I'd felt not knowing if Stone had survived the battle. For her it was worse because she had to possibly watch Charmig be killed.

Everything inside me hardened. I flattened my lips and glared at the scene. This was neanderthal. I was embarrassed that my kind acted this way. Well, half my kind. I couldn't sit here and watch.

And I had the power to stop it. I had magic.

Regent Theobald perched on his elaborate chair, wearing the gaudy crown and robes. Grand Lord Justicar gripped the ceremonial halberd, the one sign showing that he was affected. It was his son who could die. His beady pupils observed the fight with vigilance.

The banshees taught children to fight and hate. No wonder Grandfather had kept me hidden from them. Pain pulsed. They'd killed him when he'd come for help. Fisting my hands, I let the pulsing flow and grow into fury. The time to avenge him was now.

I jumped to my feet. "Stop."

Charmig and Svante kept fighting. Their weapons clanked and clattered. The crowd kept staring at the two men.

Only Lykke noticed. She peered at me with a fearful expression.

Filling my lungs with oxygen, I raised my arms. They'd notice me now. I leapt into the air and flew into the center of the Proving Sphere, hovering above the fighters' heads.

The crowd stopped talking. Grand Lord Justicar sat up straight. The regent beamed believing he was going to witness the power he'd soon order into war. Svante looked up. He kept Charmig in a choke hold with the handle against his throat but didn't hurt him further.

Letting my power flow inside of me, I focused on the two fighters below and pushed my hands out to the sides. The two of them flew to opposite sides of the circle just like I'd done to Teinn.

"Stand down!" Grand Lord Justicar hopped off his chair and rushed into the ring. He swiped his index finger across his tattoo.

Laughter bubbled inside and I continued to hold the two fighters apart from above. He couldn't control me.

Svante had several bleeding wounds and bruises. Charmig appeared as if he'd been through a torture machine like the auraguillotine. Weak, defenseless, bloody, and bruised. I didn't feel sympathy for either of them.

"I said stand down, Lys Destiny." Grand Lord Justicar swiped his tattoo again. He stomped his foot in the dirt. "Why isn't it working?"

My laughter erupted out loud as satisfaction oozed through me. Although admitting the truth was risky, I didn't care. "I never killed anyone for you, and I never will."

He grabbed the halberd sitting at the edge of the ring.

I wanted to laugh again because I knew his weapon was ceremonial. It wasn't sharp. It couldn't kill.

My energy waned with the effort of holding back the two fighters and my magic slipped. Cassia had told me there were ways to gain magical strength. An advanced class. She'd promised to teach me once I got through the basics.

Charmig struggled to stand so holding him back wasn't difficult. Svante wrestled against the force keeping him in place. He either wanted to attack me or kill off Charmig. I grappled holding him. My body dipped lower. I needed to focus on flying or holding the fighters off, not both.

The leader threw the ceremonial halberd right at me.

I froze and my gaze tracked the weapon.

Grand Lord Justicar's arm had thrown the weapon with accuracy while I wrestled with holding Svante and Charmig back. Even though it wasn't sharp, I didn't want to be hit. I was already losing my magic strength. I had no time to think.

Releasing my hold on Charmig, I flung my arm in the direction of the halberd. Tossing a magical force to block the weapon's path, in more of a protective action, the weapon flipped and rebounded. Straight as an arrow, the ceremonial halberd soared back toward Grand Lord Justicar.

Svante's eyes widened. He couldn't react in any other way with me holding him in place. Charmig stayed on the ground. His lips twisted into a slight smile. He knew the blade was too dull to do any real harm to his father.

The dull point of the tip pierced the banshee leader's bare chest. The halberd clattered to the ground.

Everyone went silent.

The leader's strange reaction should've warned me. He stared at the tiny nick, his expression going from shock to horror. No blood poured out, so I didn't understand his concern. He placed his palm over the wound in dramatic fashion.

The man was a total wuss.

He crumpled to the ground.

My brow furrowed. What just happened? I meant to stop him, not injure him. And how could the tiny nick cause him to collapse?

Lowering myself into the center of the Proving Sphere where the leader lay, I stayed tense and ready to fight. I didn't know who would attack first.

Charmig stumbled to his feet and ran toward his father. He fell to his knees and cradled the man's head. "Father, talk to me. Give me final words of wisdom."

Final words? I squinted at the crowd.

The banshees stayed silent. Their skin pale. They all peered at the sight before them.

Regent Theobald's troops surrounded him. The blond woman clutched his arm. He believed there was danger. From where?

Me?

The regent peeked through his armed guards, watching with interest. He was probably trying to figure out a way to take advantage of the situation. A group was always vulnerable when their leader was ill or injured.

Lykke darted to Charmig's side. She kneeled next to him and placed a hand on his arm proving she cared.

His father lay motionless. His chest didn't move.

A heavy weight crushed my heart. Was he dead? Had I killed him with the tiny nick? Or did he have a heart attack? "Call for the healer!" I didn't care that Ursee was indisposed.

Svante stood gripping his halberd with white knuckles. Neither him nor Charmig had died. If Charmig's father died, who would be the next leader?

My mind whirled like a tornado. Thoughts spun and coiled. If Grand Lord Justicar died, I'd made a kill and would be bonded by the tattoo to the new leader. I swallowed and glanced at Svante and Charmig.

If so, who would control the banshee warriors, and me?

CHAPTER TWENTY-NINE

My head stabbed with each confused question. Horror scraped inside and my belly did somersaults. If Grand Lord Justicar died, I'd have killed while sporting the tattoo. Since it would be the leader I killed, what would happen? Would control of me and the other warriors pass to the next leader? Lykke had said the only power they had left was hereditary.

The leader couldn't be dead. It was a scratch.

The crowd hadn't moved. Not a blink of an eye or the twitch of a finger. Regent Theobald stayed behind his guards wearing a calculated expression. Would he try to rule the banshees?

Anguish and uncertainty knotted inside. Even though he was a terrible leader, I didn't want to murder Grand Lord Justicar. I'd tried to stop the senseless killing. Why was everyone acting as if the injury was a big deal?

Why wasn't he moving?

Charmig lifted his face toward the night sky. He wailed.

His scream hit the center of my chest. Denial choked in my throat.

Lykke put her arm around his shoulders. She wailed too.

A pulse pounded in my neck. Banshee wailing meant death. I felt no need to howl at the sky. No internal gloom or doom.

Svante joined in. So did Teinn and the other warriors. The females joined next, including Reitha and her grandmother, the women I talked to right before the dragon attack.

I cringed. Why wasn't I wailing? A panicked breath rasped out. I'd wailed before when someone had died. In the dungeon and before the transport crashed. Another raspy breath choked through my clogged throat. Was the reason I didn't wail because I'd made the kill? I wished I understood.

Regent Theobald covered his ears. His nervous gaze darted about. I bet he feared for his life even though there was no need.

I dashed to Svante's side. "Why doesn't someone get the healer?"

"There's no need." He bowed his head.

Tension ran through me. They should be doing everything possible to save the man.

"Grand Lord Justicar is dead." Charmig announced in a hard tone. He shoved his father's head off his lap and it bounced on the ground. Grief must be making him angry.

My eyes prickled with unshed tears. Any loss of life was a tragedy. My lungs suffocated and I gasped. I'd killed him. Maybe I was a terrible banshee. As terrible as the banshees surrounding me.

I took a step back and glowered at the angry warriors. What would they do to me?

"Grand Lord Justicar is dead," Charmig repeated and grabbed the ceremonial halberd and stood. He sauntered away from his father.

Truly sorry for his loss, I wished there was something I could do or say. I still didn't understand how a slight cut could kill.

Why didn't Lykke stand by his side and comfort him? She watched Charmig as he strutted further away from his father, closer to me and Svante. Her stiff body told me something was about to happen.

My muscles tightened. Would Charmig attack Svante and finish the fight? Or me because he believed I'd killed his father?

The other banshee wails quieted.

"How could the leader be dead? The halberd barely punctured his skin." I tried to wrap my head around how I'd killed someone.

Svante raised his head and gripped the weapon tighter. "The ceremonial halberd is dipped in a lethal poison."

My chest walloped and dropped into the pit of my stomach. "I didn't know." That's why the leader had been so dramatic. Swiveling to Charmig, I pleaded for understanding. "I wasn't trying to kill your father. I was trying to stop him from attacking me."

"Sorry doesn't matter." He whipped out the anti-magic bracelets and slapped them around my wrists.

Upset about the death, I couldn't react in time. The bracelets circled my wrists resembling a rope around my neck.

His hard expression didn't exhibit grief, just discipline and authority. His glare pierced through my distress and confusion. "From this point forward, I will control your magic."

All my emotions stilled, pinned down by his expression and his words.

Svante's body tensed beside me about to spring into action. To defend me? Why would he? More likely to attack Charmig.

"Warriors of the Skjult Banshee Clan." Charmig took hold of my hand in an iron grip. There was no charm in his touch, only domination. "Arrest Svante until his execution for being a threat to the new clan leadership."

Charmig was taking control. Of me. Of Svante. Of the entire clan.

Warriors surrounded Svante and took hold of him.

"No!" He struggled against them. "Charmig is not the leader. It hasn't been decided. We never finished our fight."

"You said it yourself." Charmig raised our entwined hands. "*My father.* I will inherit his position and I will marry Lys Destiny."

My heart exploded and crumbled into pieces. My knees went slack. I would've fallen down if he wasn't holding up my hand. I dangled physically and emotionally.

Lykke gasped, stood, and pushed her way through the wall of warriors. She loved him and comforted him in his moment of grief. A very brief moment. He should marry her, not me.

But I knew why. He was marrying me for my magic.

And now that I'd killed, he'd be able to control me along with the other warriors. The banshees were doing his bidding even now by locking up Svante.

"Lock her up too." Charmig slid a finger down my cheek. "Until our wedding."

I swiped my skin. "I'll never marry you." I raised my voice so everyone could hear. "Your father planned to use my magic and his control of the banshee warriors to be enforcers for the evil regent." I glared at the regent. "That man isn't the king and never will be. He hates majiks and wants to steal our power."

Just like the banshees were doing to me.

The bracelets tightened. I couldn't do magic. I'd be forced to marry Charmig and he'd control my powers. He'd force me to help the regent and in doing so I'd destroy the kingdom.

Like the Wicked End Prophecy said.

I scanned the crowd. This might be my last opportunity to speak freely. Reitha stood on tiptoes straining to see and hear.

"The banshee way of life is unfair and unequal. Females should not be treated as property and servants. They can fight, too. They can lead." Possibly better than the males. "And the brownies should be freed."

Teinn slapped his hand over my mouth. "Lock her up and make sure she can't be heard."

The banshee clan took away my rights, my ability to control my powers, and now my voice.

*　　*　　*

Frustrated, I banged on the bars of my cell. The anti-magic bracelets clanked against the metal. I kicked at the bars. I was locked in a cage, located in a row of cages behind the tents. I had no access to my magic. Charmig would control me through the tattoo because I'd killed.

I'd killed his father.

Gasping, I sunk to the cold ground. Regent Theobald would exploit the banshees and my power. I didn't want to help him, but I wouldn't be able to refuse.

Plus, I hadn't seen Cassia or Pith all day. I couldn't communicate with Stone. And marriage to Charmig could happen at any second. My heart pounded to escape the cage of my ribs. He wouldn't give me a choice.

Exhausted just thinking about it, I jammed my finger between the bracelet and my wrist and tried to yank it off desperate for any shred of hope.

"These cages are impossible to get out of, even with magic." Svante sat on the ground in the cage next to me. He'd been silent the entire time, watching me pace and kick and struggle. He rubbed his hands across his arms and bare chest, wearing only a shula. "Another gift from the regent."

At least I had a cloak to keep warm. "How do you know magic won't work?"

"I've put plenty of majiks in these cages." His self-derogatory tone rang true.

I didn't believe he had regrets.

"Good speech, by the way. I would've clapped but..." He held up his locked hands.

While my bracelets were individual to stop me from accessing magic, the metal cuffs he wore were attached by a chain.

"Yeah, right." I snarled. "You're part of the patriarchal problem. If Charmig hadn't inherited his father's power, you would've taken control."

"Did he?" Svante raised a single dark brow.

A niggle of doubt wormed into my head. I brushed it aside. "You didn't believe a word I said."

"You're wrong." His truthful tone couldn't be legit. He must be a good liar. "I don't think we should be working for the regent, and I hated how Grand Lord Justicar treated the females."

"Grand Lord Just Crazy." Maybe it was too soon to make fun of the dead.

Svante chortled and got to his feet. "My sister, mother, and grandmother are part of the clan. I hate how they're treated. I worked hard to become an Elder so I could become leader and equal things out."

I shook my head. I didn't believe him.

"Not right away. But as soon as I could. After all, I'd control the warriors." He leaned against the bars closest to me. "My sister told me you saved her life during the dragon attack."

Reitha was his sister? That's why I'd seen them talking so intimately together. "She saved my life too." She'd pushed me out of the way of the dragon. My brow furrowed. If he'd climbed the ranks to change the rules, could he become good? I remembered the conflicting things he'd said. "If what you say is true, why did you plan to ruin my life by marrying me?"

"I wouldn't have forced you into marriage." He waved a hand in front of his face. "I would've convinced you to stay and help your fellow banshees, especially the females."

"Yeah, right." I wasn't buying his sudden turn around. He had no options and was about to be executed, he'd say and do anything to get out. He was pretending to be nice. "You're just saying that because if I get out of this cage and have access to my magic, you just want me to help you."

"I want you to help all the banshees." His seriousness sounded believable. He spoke calmly and with authority. His expression stayed smooth with no telling tick.

I twisted my lips. I didn't believe him. Staring at him, I watched his face as I asked, "What about the brownies? Would you have helped them too?"

His hatred for the brownies would show in a disgusted curl of his nose, a frown, or a shudder. I waited for him to react.

"Destiny." Cassia crawled on the ground to get to the cage. A few guards stood further away, believing Svante and I couldn't escape. "Pith is on his way to get Stone."

The fragments of my heart pieced together. Stone would be here soon.

Svante wrapped a hand around a bar. "Why wait for your giant friend? Rescue yourself."

Tilting back, I studied him. He knew about Stone and that he was half giant.

"He and your other friends," Svante nodded at Cassia, including her in with my friends, "Will be outnumbered."

Worry bunched and tangled inside. My throat burned. Stone would come charging in because he worried about me. Between the warrior banshees, the regent's men, and their advanced weapons, he and my friends would be slaughtered.

I couldn't let that happen. Peering at Cassia's braceleted wrists, I knew her magic was locked up too. At a total loss, I didn't know what to do. "You should leave the encampment now and tell Stone not to come."

"You could get us out right now by using the tattoo control." Svante's suggestion jarred.

I'd told them I could control human minds. I glanced at Cassia and she shrugged. The mind control could work on the regent and his human guards. But I could only control one mind at a time, and it was the banshees who patrolled the cages guarding me.

"What mind control?" I tried to play dumb, all the while thinking about how I could control the regent. He was human. And dark. I quivered.

"You killed Grand Lord Justicar in the Proving Sphere which was ringed with the hereditary ash." Svante's pitch lowered.

My breath caught in my throat.

He gripped the bars with both hands. "*You* control the banshee warriors."

His words punched me, and I gasped. Impossible. I chuckled even though I found nothing about his statement funny. "Then why did the warriors listen to Charmig and arrest us?"

"The warriors have been trained to follow orders, not think for themselves." Svante's disgust edged his voice. "Non-cursed banshees, like your family, pass powers down when someone older dies. When your grandfather died—"

"He was murdered." Everything inside me hardened.

He nodded in agreement taking me by surprise. "When your grandfather was murdered, his powers came to you. It's why they waited to kill him until you'd recovered your other powers and your memories. Now, you have all your family's banshee powers, plus your witch magic."

"You know?" Cassia bit her lip.

"Of course, I know," he boasted. "One of the reasons I fought my way to the Elder position was to be knowledgeable about the clan's past and its future. So I could be a better leader than Grand Lord Justicar."

We both agreed the man was a terrible leader.

I was starting to believe Svante. And even though I didn't completely trust him, I could use him and his knowledge to help. "Can a female banshee even become Grand Lord Justicar?"

"It's never been considered." His lips didn't twitch and he didn't blink. "You...you're special."

"What about Charmig? He took control."

"The banshee warriors assumed Charmig became leader when his father died, especially when he shouted orders." Svante's gaze narrowed. "I know differently. And so do you."

"I do?" My voice trembled and I glanced at a bewildered Cassia. I studied the tattoo on my wrist. "Are you saying I'm the new banshee clan leader?"

Chapter Thirty

"Excuse me," I called to the nearest warrior guarding the cages.

Svante shook his head. He thought I was being too nice. His red cheek was proof that I could demand banshee warriors obey. With our cages next to each other, we'd sat by the bars and he'd taught me how to use my index finger to swipe the tattoo in the patterned way Grand Lord Justicar had. I'd used Svante as a test subject, making him slap himself in the face over and over.

Cassia had laughed at the antics. Now, she hid behind a large boulder waiting to see how I did on an unwilling subject. If I could do it at all. Doubt dug a trench inside of me. What if Svante had pretended to be controlled?

The guard marched to the cage and glared. "What do you want?"

I made the motion on my tattoo. "Let me out of the cage." I waited for the guard to chuckle.

He blinked a few times and took out the key. Sticking it in the lock, he unlocked and opened the door.

I froze, not sure what to do and still not sure this wasn't an elaborate joke, and the joke was on me.

"Destiny." Svante urged, "Tell him to let me out."

I switched my focus to the guard. "Do you have keys for the anti-magic bracelets?"

"Yes." His expression was blank.

"Give them to me." This way I'd have access to my magic if Svante betrayed me. "And uncuff him and let him out of the cage."

The guard handed me the keys and I took off the bracelets. "Cassia."

She emerged with Pith and Iban at her side. Pith had been unable to find Stone and my other friends.

"What are the brownies for?" Svante sounded more wary than disgusted as he stepped out of the cage.

"Pith and Iban are my friends. They will help with our plan." I unlocked Cassia's bracelets, giving me an ally and a powerful witch at my side.

"Now what?" She regarded me for guidance.

I looked at Svante, wary about trusting him. If he didn't do what I wanted, I'd turn him into a frog with my witch magic.

"Now, we secretly take control of the banshee warriors, including Charmig." Was there a touch of revenge in Svante's statement? "And we imprison the regent, his aide, and his soldiers as we discussed while you were forcing me to slap myself."

I hid a slight smile and focused on the task at hand. My shoulders straightened and determination sprang in my step. While training, we'd hatched a multi-step plan.

Iban saluted. "I'll tell the brownies to lead the children away and to get ready."

Anxiety tingled across my skin. I bent down to give her a hug. "Tell them when this is done, I'll figure out a way to set the brownies free."

She hugged me back, then she and Pith took off running.

Svante watched the brownies leave. I couldn't tell if he was pleased or displeased. I didn't care. We were doing things my way.

"I'll locate the regent and figure out a way to constrain him." Cassia flicked her fingers and sparks flew. She snapped and disappeared.

I couldn't wait to learn how to apparate.

"Charmig is mine." Svante's gritty tone sent a chill through me.

"We want him alive, not dead. Do you understand?" I sized him up. "We're not going to lead like his father."

His mouth dropped open. "We?"

"We'll discuss it later." I didn't want to stay with the banshees and be their leader. I wanted to be with Stone. But I also wouldn't abandon them to the old ways or Svante's whims. I was working with him and trusted him to a point. "Let's go."

Through the darkness, Svante and I snuck toward the edge of camp. We crouched down and observed.

The female banshees packed things up. We were relocating again. I stomped my foot. Not if I didn't want to. The warriors prepared their weapons and trained. Their stark expressions showed they didn't know what was going to happen to them. They believed they were going into battle for the regent with Charmig leading them.

Brownies surreptitiously led the children away.

I let out a sigh. Pith and Iban had done part of their job.

Charmig strolled pompously toward his old tent. He surveyed the warriors as if he were their overlord. He was in for a rude awakening. He strutted into his tent and stationed guards outside.

Guards didn't worry me. They didn't know I controlled them.

"He's alone." Loathing dripped off Svante.

I knew there'd been animosity and competition between the two of them. The pure hatred surprised me.

Pith and Iban were waiting for us when we arrived at the back entrance of the tent. She opened the small flap.

"Thanks." Grateful for my new friend, I got to my knees and crawled through the opening.

"Yes, thank you." Svante acknowledged the brownie before getting to his knees and crawling in behind me.

My chest lightened, hopeful he'd work with me on the brownie issue.

Charmig stood in front of a full-length mirror admiring himself. He wore the banshee leader's cloak and crown. It hadn't taken long to raid the dead man's wardrobe. He must've spotted my partner and I through the mirror because he whirled around. "What're you doing here? How'd you get free?"

I wasn't going to answer his questions. "Surrender and you won't be hurt."

Fear flashed in his gaze and his hand reached for something behind the mirror.

Sparking my fingers, I jerked his arms forward, using my magic to stop him.

The ceremonial halberd clattered to the ground. The weapon that had killed his father.

Svante charged forward, wrapping his arms around the pretend leader's waist. Momentum carried them, and they smashed into the mirror. The glass shattered.

The clattering carried through the tent and possibly outside.

I sparked my fingers again and put a sound shield over the tent. No one could hear the noise or Charmig screaming.

The two men fell to the ground and rolled around in the tiny pieces of glass. The scrunching sent a shiver through me. Svante had no shirt, and he must feel the sharp edges of the glass. He kept fighting.

Wringing my hands, I prowled toward them. I wanted to help but was afraid I'd injure Svante in the process. What if I cast a spell and hit him instead? Sighing, I needed more magic training.

They rolled again. Charmig ended up on top.

I snapped my fingers and lifted him.

Svante swung at nothing.

"Ahhh!" Charmig screamed and kicked and punched. Being four feet off the ground, he did no damage.

"Put him in the chair." Svante leapt to his feet and grabbed a bunch of long, beaded necklaces.

Holding Charmig up, I floated him toward the chair and dropped him into it.

Svante tossed me a few necklaces. "Tie him up." He yanked our prisoner's arms back and wrapped the beads around his wrists.

I used more necklaces to tie Charmig's legs to the chair legs. I wasn't sure how to tie him down with magic and trying the warrior control might make Svante do the same action. Another thing I needed to learn how to do.

Using the Grand Lord Justicar's cloak, Svante tied Charmig's arms back. "He won't get loose."

"Screaming won't help." I glared at Charmig. "I've used my witch magic," I emphasized the word witch, "to seal the tent for sound."

"Yeah," Svante leered.

All this time, Svante had tried to act tough and cruel so the leader would pick him to rule, but each step he took with me proved he was on my side.

Charmig stretched for his tattoo. The beads loosened enough for him to stroke his wrist. "I'm going to use the hereditary tattoo to call the warriors. They will kill both of you."

A smug smile bloomed on my face. Placing my elbow against a trunk, I crossed my legs and took a relaxed stance. "Go ahead."

He held his index finger above the tattoo but didn't move.

"Yeah, go ahead." Svante snickered.

"I'm going to do it right now unless you let me go. Maybe I'll show you mercy." Charmig made the maneuver.

I tapped my foot. "How long do you think it will take the warriors to get your command and respond?"

Svante chuckled.

Our prisoner made the maneuver again, faster and more desperate. "They'll be here. Any second now. You should run."

"No. They won't come at your bidding." My amusement lessened and my patience frayed. "And you know it."

"You don't have the leader's hereditary control. You just started issuing commands and the warriors listened." Svante kicked the leg of the chair. "You're not the next Grand Lord Justicar."

"Do you think you are?" Charmig spat.

"No." Svante swung his gaze to me. He wouldn't announce my news.

Straightening my shoulders, I took a deep breath and let it fill my lungs with possibilities. "I am."

Chapter Thirty-One

Svante and I left the tent and headed toward the center of camp. No hiding this time. I'd ordered the guards standing outside to watch Charmig. He struggled with the fact that I had control of the tattoo and was officially Grand Lord Justicar.

Though if things went according to plan, I wouldn't be in the position for long.

Climbing onto the leader's chair by the campfire, I motioned across the tattoo and silently called a meeting.

The banshee warriors went silent and moved toward me.

I let out the breath I didn't know I'd been holding. Even with controlling Svante and the guards, I still doubted my abilities. Both the magic and the controlling of the banshees.

The sky grew darker and the stars weren't visible any longer.

The warriors gathered around. Teinn glared and had a deep frown. "Why aren't you locked up?"

I smirked and made the maneuver on my arm again while thinking about what I wanted them to do to prove what I said was true. "I'm the new Grand Lord Justicar. I have control of the tattoo bond."

Teinn struggled against giving a single clap. The other warriors followed in unison.

Heat rushed my cheeks. I didn't want the warriors to do things because I controlled them. I wanted them to listen and respect me. This was only a simple act to prove what I said was true.

Svante nodded in encouragement.

"We will not be fighting for Regent Theobald." I surveyed the human soldiers nearby watching the banshee spectacle. I did not control the regent's soldiers. "We will be taking them prisoner."

The soldiers reached for their weapons on their backs or at their waists. They skimmed around searching for guidance from the regent, their leader.

The tense atmosphere strung my body tight from my toes to my shoulders to my neck and head.

Bee took a step from behind a soldier holding an advanced weapon. The blond woman seemed to be the regent's subordinate, although I'd seen the way she looked at him. Similar to how Lykke looked at Charmig. "What is this about? Where is Charmig, the new leader?"

"A better question is where is the regent?" I kept my gaze trained on her, even though I wanted to glance at the tent the regent was staying in. "I guess I'll tell you because I'm in charge of the encampment. Regent Theobald is my prisoner, as is Charmig."

I hoped the regent was a prisoner. Cassia hadn't shown up yet.

"Put down your weapons." My tone went hard and authoritative. Inside, I was a quivering mass of nerves. If there was a battle, we'd be slaughtered. I was the only banshee with magic.

Bee raised the weapon. "If your warriors make a move toward us with their archaic halberds, we'll blast them to pieces."

Adrenaline spiked inside of me, raising my tension. My midsection clenched and I waited for some type of action. I raised my hands. "I don't want bloodshed. I just don't want my people involved with the regent."

"Too bad." Her coldness sliced through me, as did her final word. "Fire."

CHAPTER THIRTY-TWO

Bee pointed the big, ugly, modern, deadly weapon straight at me.

My pulse vaulted. Scenes of my life flashed. I didn't even get to tell Stone goodbye or that I loved him. Squeezing my eyes tight, I waited for a bullet or laser to hit me.

Click, click, click.

It never came.

No weapon discharged. No laser light blazing or bullets rocketing.

Opening my eyes, I slapped my torso and stomach and legs. I was fine.

Svante was fine. All the warriors were fine.

Relief poured through my veins, and I stood tall. Pith, Iban, and the brownies had completed their task.

Pith and Iban slapped each other's hands in a high five. Other brownies crawled out from their hiding places, behind a log, a tent, a rock. They hugged and clapped. Pith and the brownies had damaged the human weaponry.

My chest lightened and at the same time filled with hope and satisfaction. Smiling, I gave Pith and Iban a salute. They'd saved us. We'd celebrate later.

Determination snapped my spine straight. First, I cast a spell that Cassia had taught me to immobilize the humans. I made the action across my tattoo with the hope that in the future the banshees would listen and respect me without the control. "Arrest the human soldiers."

Banshee warriors bolted into action. They rounded up the soldiers and took away their weapons. Svante helped organize the roundup. The female banshees joined in, helping them handcuff and restrain the soldiers. Already the women were proving their worth.

Like the brownies did.

I glanced at the tent where the regent should be. Worry tied my stomach into knots. Still no Cassia.

Lykke sauntered toward me and charged into a run. "You will never take Grand Lord Justicar's or Charmig's place." She held the ceremonial halberd. The one tainted with poison. She must've taken it from Charmig's tent.

She lunged at me.

My lungs shrieked and shriveled. I thought we were friends. Lykke didn't have the tattoo so I couldn't order her to leave me alone. I wished I knew how to disappear.

She swung the halberd at me.

I jumped off the chair and hit the ground. My previously injured ankle crumpled and I fell. I inched away on my knees. From my position, I couldn't find Svante or Pith or Iban. I reached to make the movement on the tattoo to signal a warrior for help.

Lykke kicked my arm away and I collapsed, my arms splayed out to my sides. I rolled over. She loomed over me. The dull but poisoned point of the halberd an inch from my chest.

Swallowing, I pressed my body against the dirt. My pulse sped, circling up and down and around like a race car on a track. I'd witnessed the damage of a small cut from its blade. My heart boomed. Would this be my final breath?

A blur flew at Lykke, tackling her to the ground.

My eyes widened taking in the sight.

Reitha struggled against my attacker. She scuffled with her on the ground. The poisoned halberd flopped back and forth with their struggle. A small nick would kill either of them.

Fretting, I stumbled to my feet. If Reitha was cut by the poisonous blade, I'd never forgive myself. I concentrated on my magic. Sparks flew from my fingertips, and I held out my hand. The halberd jerked out of Lykke's hold and toward me.

I grabbed the rod and tucked it in close. The blade would be destroyed.

Reitha gave a final punch, knocking Lykke out.

"Thank you for saving me again." I ran to Reitha's side and hugged her. "You'll be a great banshee warrior."

She beamed, her smile lighting up the night sky.

Looking up, I spotted a large object flying toward us. My shoulders tensed. I couldn't take any more surprise attacks.

"Dragon!" one of the warriors yelled.

I peered closer. It wasn't any dragon, it was Drago. And there seemed to be someone riding the beast.

"Should we shoot it down?" Svante held a bow and flaming arrow.

"No. The dragon is carrying a friend." More than a friend. My chest swelled.

The dragon flew lower.

Stone sat on top of Drago. His long blond hair whipped in the wind. His intense face peered down and zeroed in on me.

I wanted to fly as high as him.

The dragon swooped lower, right by me, and Stone jumped from the wings.

A conquering Viking with his long blond hair, chiseled chin, muscled arms, and defensive stance. Stone had arrived. He wore a short, black leather tunic with his muscled arms on display. His leather breeches clung to his thick thighs. Dark boots completed the outfit.

"I'm here to save you." He wielded a sword. "And everyone."

I didn't wait to explain. I launched myself into his arms and kissed him.

"Everyone is already saved," Svante drawled. Amusement tinted his tone. "By Lys Destiny."

Breaking off the quick kiss, I couldn't take all the credit. "Thanks to you, Svante. And Cassia, Reitha, Pith, and Iban, and the other brownies. Where is Cassia?"

"I'll go search for her while you have your reunion." Svante wiggled his eyebrows.

Holding back a giggle, I wrapped my arms around Stone again. "There's something important I have to tell you."

"You didn't marry the guy?"

"No." Forced marriage had been too close. My blood charged in my veins. What if Stone didn't appreciate the fact that I was part witch? I'd forgotten to tell him in our last two rushed meetings. It wasn't something that could be spit out. "I'm a banshee. But I'm also...part witch."

"You've put a spell on me." His lips twisted into a joking grin.

"I'm serious." I hit his arm. "And since I'm only just learning magic, I couldn't have put a spell on you."

His expression went serious. He took hold of my hand. "I don't care what you are, only that you're with me."

He pressed his hard lips to mine and I immediately responded. Tingles of light and love cascaded down my spine and across my skin. I wrapped my arms around his broad shoulders and tangled my hands in his silky hair.

His rough thumb caressed my cheek and thrills shot from his touch. Our own personal fireworks. My mouth opened welcoming him, welcoming us. At the press of his lips, my worries and fears evaporated into mist.

Heavy pounding brought me out of my daze.

Stone let me break off the kiss, keeping his arm around me.

King Zacharye marched in leading an army. His crown glinted in the moonlight and he carried a weapon pointed straight at the banshees. "We saw the firework drawing of the regent in the sky and got here as fast as we could. Some of the paths were blocked."

A few hours had passed and yet it seemed like a year.

Stone tucked me closer. "Destiny has everything under control."

My body heated from his proclamation and affectionate gesture. As soon as we got a second alone, we needed to talk about our relationship. I wasn't worried. Being wrapped in his arm gave me comfort and told me the discussion wouldn't last long.

Marching behind the king were Lukas, Trolgar, Helartha, and Gnit.

My friends. My happiness burst. I ducked from under Stone's arm and ran toward them. Hugs went all around. Helartha and Gnit had returned from their task helping Violet.

Princess Ellery swooped in on her wings and dropped beside King Zacharye.

Now that the king and princess were here, they'd handle the regent's imprisoned allies.

When Princess Ellery joined us, I started to bow to both her and the new king. We were interrupted.

Regent Theobald stumbled out of the tent naked. "All my clothes are gone."

My muscles tensed and I stilled. Everyone went quiet.

Princess Ellery giggled. King Zacharye joined her with a deeper chuckle. Stone and I laughed too. Soon all my friends, the king's men, and the banshees joined in our glee.

The regent snatched the gaudy crown off his head and used it to cover his private parts.

Cassia materialized behind him in a puff of smoke, holding a bunch of his clothes. "This is how we expose false kings."

Everyone laughed again.

Her arrival and the laughter filled my soul with joy. Stone was at my side. My friends had arrived. Everyone except Violet was here.

"Arrest the regent," King Zacharye commanded. "Make sure everyone who worked with him is secured. We'll transport him to the dungeon where he will await trial."

My banshee warriors assisted them. We could work in concert.

I bowed to him and Princess Ellery again. "Welcome to the Skjult Banshee Clan."

King Zacharye took my hand and brought me to a standing position. "Thank you for capturing my traitorous uncle."

A tremulous smile raised on my lips. Happy tears stung. He treated me as an equal. "Thank everyone. The clan and my friends here." I brought Svante forward. "This is Svante. He will become the new leader of the clan and I know he will work with you for the equality of all majiks." I peered at him. "Including freeing the enslaved brownies and making the female banshees equal."

Svante paled and tilted toward me to whisper. "You're the leader."

I shook my head and regarded Stone. I had other priorities. Some he didn't even know about.

Stone smirked and his teasing touched my heart. "We need to celebrate!" He raised his fist. "The regent has been captured. Destiny has been found. And peace reigns in the kingdom."

"Long live King Zacharye!" I shouted in exultation.

Stone grinned. "Long live King Zacharye!"

"Long live King Zacharye!" My friends, the king's men, and the brownies joined in.

The banshees froze. Their blank expressions stated their confusion over who the true king was in the Kingdom of Alandaska. They'd believed they'd be fighting against Zacharye.

"Long live King Zacharye!" Svante shouted and raised his hands, indicating the banshees should join him.

"Long live King Zacharye!"

The banshees, my banshees, joined in the chorus without me forcing them to do it. Joy overflowed inside of me.

"Long live Lys Destiny!" Svante added to the praise.

The banshees cheered again. It seemed more muted.

My joy and my lungs deflated. They didn't accept me. Which was okay.

Using my magic, I floated into the sky and broadcasted my voice. "I am Lys Destiny and I'm the one who killed Grand Lord Justicar in the Proving Sphere circled with the hereditary ash." My eyes stung. I hated the fact that I'd killed someone even by accident, even if he'd been a terrible leader. "I'm also the one who received the tattoo controlling powers and forced the banshee warriors to capture the regent's soldiers." My chest ached. They never would've listened to my orders without it. "I apologize. I will never use any of you by force again."

Murmuring from the warrior banshees. They realized when their actions were controlled.

"The previous Grand Lord Justicar wanted you to fight for Regent Theobald." My voice hardened. "He is not and never will be king."

Stone stood at attention below me. He'd protect me if anyone made a move against me. I hoped it wouldn't happen. I needed the banshees to listen and understand their practices were wrong.

"I'm loyal to the true king, King Zacharye. He will lead the entire Kingdom of Alandaska justly and fairly. Majiks will be equal with humans. It might take time to rebuild trust but with his engagement to Ellery, Princess of the Fairies, everyone will soon see the light."

The king and princess waved.

Swallowing the lump in my throat, I knew it was time to say goodbye to my new family. It was going to be harder than I expected. I also wanted to let them know they were in good hands.

Sparks shot from my fingers. I waved my hand and raised Svante from the crowd.

The crowd *oohed.*

"Whoa." He circled his arms, trying to balance himself.

I set his feet on the elaborate chair meant for the leader. With him standing on the chair, I continued, "I am a banshee, but not a full banshee. I'm part witch." I glanced at Cassia standing by our other friends. I had so many questions for her. "I was not brought up in the clan. And although I believe female banshees can rule, and *can* be warriors," I peered at Svante's sister. "I will not become the next Grand Lord Justicar."

Reitha's face fell. Some of the other female banshees were upset. The male warriors appeared stoic. Were they relieved or did they just not care?

"Svante was one of the Elders, one of the finalists to lead you." I pointed at him standing on the chair. "He believes male and female banshees should be treated equally. He has agreed to work with me to set the enslaved brownies free."

The brownies let up a cheer.

The banshee expressions didn't change.

Knowing I was doing the right thing, I switched the broadcast spell to Svante and lowered myself into the crowd. Stone hugged me tight and kissed me on the cheek. "Great job."

"Lys Destiny has helped us greatly. She will continue to guide us." Svante spoke with authority and thanks, and I appreciated the sentiment. "I will lead us into the next era of our clan. I will forgo the controlling tattoo and the Proving Sphere. We will have law and order and a real tribunal to settle differences. Those of you who are not happy with my leadership, can leave the clan. Once the new king has settled things down, I'm sure you'll be accepted."

I doubted that. Prejudices took a long time to pass. But the fact that he made the offer demonstrated Svante would be a great leader.

"I will promote Teinn to be my second in command. My sister, Reitha, will be the first female banshee to train as a warrior."

The women's cheers rose.

Smiling, I knew the females would kick some butt.

"And Charmig and Lykke will be together as they both wanted, in jail."

"Do you have a second?" Stone whispered in my ear sending tingles down my spine.

"I have a million seconds for you." I wrapped my arm around his waist and never wanted to let go.

He tugged me out of the crowd and off to the side. Hidden behind a tent, he took me into his arms. Our lips met again. Softer and less rushed. Knowing we'd have more time together, knowing the second our lips parted we'd acknowledge our love.

A bird landed on my shoulder, and I broke apart from Stone.

"Shoo. Shoo." I stayed in his arms. We were magnets pulled apart by circumstances. Never again.

The black bird flew a little higher and landed on my shoulder again.

"Shoo!" I wanted to be alone with Stone, to kiss him and stay in his arms.

"The crow has a message in its beak." He unwrapped his arms from around me and held out his palm.

The bird dropped the message in his hand. "It has your name on it." I nodded and he quickly unrolled the small scroll. "It's blank."

"Let me see." Annoyed we'd been interrupted for a blank message, I snatched the scroll from him.

The moment I clutched the paper, the bird flew away.

"It's not blank anymore." My eyes widened as I read. "The message is from a coven." A shudder went through my body. "How did they find me?"

"They're witches."

And they might be able to help me control my magic.

Each word appeared as I read, "If you want to lift the curse of the Wicked End Prophecy, you must discover your heritage by returning to the Inferis Coven."

I hope you enjoyed Snow Warrior White! If so, I'd love if you left a review at your favorite retailer.
The conclusion to Destiny's story...

SNOW WITCHING WHITE

Snow Witching White
A Glass Slipper Adventure Book 6

She must learn to control her unusual magic or risk destroying the kingdom, and her friends.

Destiny Snow hates blackmail, especially when she's the victim. Yet, the threat leads her to what she's always wanted—family. With family though, come demands. A requirement to attend the witch academy, where she's immediately an outcast. A call for her sacrifice. A claim on her heart.

The loyal friends that followed her are outsiders who can't handle the toxic atmosphere adjacent to the underworld. Now, Destiny is caught in the middle of a power struggle between witches and warlocks. Both sides fight over the greater force controlling the devilish double-dealing. A force so powerful the entire coven could be ruined. A force that works against her and will take Destiny away from everyone she loves. A force that prophesized she'd destroy the kingdom.

Can a powerful mixed majik stop the prophecy written about her before it comes to a Wicked End?

Snow Witching White is the sixth book in the twisted fairytale series A Glass Slipper Adventure. If you like magical heroines, split family loyalties, and ill-fated lovers, then you'll love Allie Burton's new installment in this spellbinding series.

Buy Snow Witching White and magically fly into jeopardy!

Excerpt:

The portal shimmered about to fade.

"Why won't the portal last longer?" I wasn't ready to leave. "I thought the witch leader was all powerful?"

"If you leave a portal open too long someone unwanted might sneak through." Cassia held out her hand in front of the shimmering image. "We should hold hands when we walk through so we don't get lost."

My jitters jangled. It was a portal to a specific place. How could we get lost?

"Lost?" Stone asked the question I'd thought.

Cassia shook her hand, urging someone to take hold. "The portal is mostly a straight line, but there are refractions and magical telekinetic waves."

Stone gripped my hand. "I'm definitely going now."

Disappointment seeped into my veins. His statement meant he wasn't positive about going with me before. I hated that he felt the need to watch me like a child.

"If you don't want to come, then don't come." I couldn't stop my peevishness.

"Coming." He nodded at Cassia.

"Okay everyone," She took Lukas' hand and Stone's other hand.

Lukas held Helartha's hand, who held Pith's, who held Gnit's, who held Trolgar's.

My chest filled and overwhelmed with emotion. My friends were coming with me, they wanted to stay by my side and help me on my journey. I squeezed Stone's hand. He returned the squeeze understanding my thoughts.

With Cassia leading the way, we stepped into the shimmering substance of the portal as one. The sucking sensation intensified. My skin puckered and tugged, wanting to pull away from my bones. It didn't hurt, yet the power of the portal made its presence known.

A scream shattered the strange silence.

Stone's distorted face showed pain. His mouth was sealed shut. His body appeared misshapen. Fear shot up my spine, paralyzing my thoughts. Had this been some type of trick? Cassia had seemed so sure.

Peering down the line at her, I noted she was relaxed and normal. No stress or strain in her expression. Lukas resembled a werewolf more than usual. His fangs flashed and his brown hair had gone shaggy. Helartha's red hair streamed behind her as if the strands were being yanked. Her head bobbed back and forth. Pith and Gnit shrunk to half their normal size. Trolgar opened his mouth to a gigantic shape and screamed.

"Ahhhhhhhhh!"

I wanted to cover my ears, but my hand was gripped by Stone. Cassia leaned forward and pulled the line of us with her. I'm glad she knew what she was doing. The sucking sensation tugged me back. She angled forward again and the rest of us whipped through with a final high-pitched sucking noise.

Stepping out of the portal, I was surprised to find nothing stuck to my skin. My entire body relaxed, glad to be free.

Stone's grip loosened and he fell to the ground. My other friends fell, too. Their mouths gaped open. Only Cassia stood beside me.

Panic bulleted through me and I dropped to my knees. "What's wrong, Stone?"

"Can't...breathe..." He gasped and his eyes rounded with the loss of oxygen. He knelt on his knees and clutched his chest.

My own chest constricted as if I couldn't breathe. I surveyed around, helpless. I didn't know what to do or how to help him or anyone else. My friends lay on the ground gasping. "Cassia. What's happening to them?"

"I thought since you were invited and they were our friends it would be okay." Her gaze darted around and she dropped to her knees between Lukas and Pith. "I'm guessing it's a protection curse. In non-witches it manifests in suffocation."

My pulse skyrocketed. They weren't intruders. They were my friends. And because of me they were going to die.

To learn about release dates and what's next in the exciting A Glass Slipper Adventure, sign up for my newsletter at www.allieburton.com

A NOTE

A Note from Allie Burton

I hope you continue to enjoy Destiny's adventure. The fun and excitement keep coming in Snow Witching White and beyond. To get information about the rest of the series, A Glass Slipper Adventure, join my newsletter and receive a free book. You can join at www.allieburton.com/contact.html.

If you enjoyed SNOW WARRIOR WHITE, please leave a rating or review at your place of purchase. Reviews help other readers find books they may love, and help authors gain traction and be able to write more books.

I love to hear from my readers! If you have any questions or comments, or just want to say "hi," please feel free to email me at allie@allieburton.com or connect with me on www.twitter.com /@allie_burton and www.facebook.com/AllieBurtonAuthor and www.instagram.com/allieburtonauthor .

If you're interested in my other young adult series, below is additional information. Thanks for reading SNOW WARRIOR WHITE!

Allie

CINDERELLA ASSASSIN

Did you miss the first book in the series, Cinderella Assassin?

Cinderella Assassin
A Glass Slipper Adventure Book 1
She wishes she could fit in. But if humans discover her secret, her life will be no fairytale.

Ellery "Elle" Milford needs to keep her fairy heritage under-cover. But after her wicked stepmother refuses to let her go to the royal ball with the fully human kids, the sixteen-year-old half-breed defiantly parties with her smoke sprite bestie... who promptly gets arrested. And the only way to rescue her is for Elle to cut a deal with her fairy godmother: All the magic necessary to infiltrate the palace in exchange for assassinating the prince.

Determined not to harm a hair on the heir's noble head, the reluctant hitwoman's mission goes sideways when she falls for the very guy she's supposed to kill. And after uncovering a plot to destroy every single supernatural creature, Elle is torn between the desires of her heart and the needs of her magical friends.

Can the headstrong half-fairy juggle a budding romance with a daring prison break before it all vanishes in a puff of smoke?

Cinderella Assassin is the first book in the charming Glass Slipper Adventure YA fantasy series. If you like spirited heroines, clever takes on classics, and unique blends of tech and wizardry, then you'll love Allie Burton's spellbinding story.

Buy Cinderella Assassin to dance into danger today!

"What a great story - super unique retelling! Characters were so dynamic and interesting. I loved it!" – Reviewer

Excerpt:

My stomach jiggled. "How will I ever get past the detectors at the palace with these magical items?"

The clutch, the dress, and my very own fairy blood would betray me.

"That's what the shoes are for." Gardenia, my fairy godmother, held out her hands and two glass-heeled shoes appeared.

The clear shoes sparkled in the light. Two-inch heels led to a slender sloping arch. A decorative green jewel topped off near the toes.

"I enjoy shoes as much as the next girl but how are high heels going to help?" I'd decided on the dress based on practicality. I couldn't run in high heels.

"These shoes are made with Elfin glass and they aren't only high heels." She pinched the gemstone and the heels lowered. The shoes became flats. "The shoes will be acceptable at the ball, and when you go to find Arbor you can make them more comfortable."

I'd known this would be a dangerous quest. Getting past the sensors at the palace, searching for Arbor. If I got caught, I'd be arrested or worse. I might need to run, but Arbor was worth it. "Clever."

Gardenia's arched eyebrows asked what else would be expected. Wearing no make-up from what I could tell, she had a natural beauty. Rosy cheeks, pink lips, white-flawless skin smelling of flowers and cut grass. "The shoes also have deflection technology. Magic and majik."

"So, the SCUM won't detect I'm half-majik." Nodding, I let confidence seep into my skin. This deal was definitely in my favor.

"Or the magical items in your possession." She snapped her fingers and another item appeared in the palm of her hand.

A knife.

I flinched and my skin prickled.

"This is the Dagger of Justice. It weighs the guilt of the intended target." She reached up toward my head. "You will wear it as a hair ornament."

The sharp steel point glinted. The ruby-encrusted handle reminded me of blood. Blood I might make flow.

"W-what do I need a dagger for?"

"To complete your end of the *Binding Promise*." Her pupils flashed with a winning gleam, yet her expression stayed deadly serious.

The words *Binding Promise* sizzled between us having a life of its own.

My muscles tensed and the hairs at the back of my neck stuck up. This wasn't like the bet we'd made earlier today. How bad could my end of the promise be if it didn't include fairy academy? But if it wasn't bad, why would I need a dagger? I should've asked before I'd agreed, except I hadn't been thinking because of my guilt about Arbor.

My throat tightened. "What do you want me to do with the dagger?"

Gardenia's lips lifted in a slight smile. "Assassinate Prince Zacharye."

ATLANTIS RIPTIDE

Atlantis Riptide
Lost Daughters of Atlantis Book 1

When a girl runs away from the circus...

For all her sixteen years, Pearl Poseidon has been a fish out of water. A freak on display for her adoptive parents' profit. Running away from her horrible life, she craves one thing—anonymity. But when she saves a small boy from drowning, she exposes herself and her mutant abilities to Chase, a budding investigative reporter.

Now, he has questions. And so do the police.

Once Pearl discovers her secret identity, she learns she's part of a larger war between battling Atlanteans. A battle that will decide who rules the oceans. A battle raging between evil and her true family. Will she find a way to use her powers in time to save a kingdom she never knew existed?

This is the start of a young adult fantasy action-adventure novel series. "Sweet summer young adult paranormal with death-defying underwater rescues." Reviewer

Other books in the Atlantis series: Atlantis Red Tide, Atlantis Rising Tide, Atlantis Tide Breaker, Atlantis Dark Tides, Atlantis Twisting Tides, Atlantis Glacial Tides.

ALSO BY

<u>A Glass Slipper Adventure-Young Adult</u>

Cinderella Assassin

Cinderella Soldier

Cinderella Spy

Snow Wicked White

Snow Warrior White

Snow Witching White

<u>Lost Daughters of Atlantis Series-Young Adult</u>

Atlantis Riptide

Atlantis Red Tide

Atlantis Rising Tide

Atlantis Tide Breaker

Atlantis Dark Tides

Atlantis Twisting Tides

Atlantis Glacial Tides

<u>Warrior Academy Series-Young Adult</u>

Warrior's Destiny

Warrior's Chaos

Warrior's Prophecy

Warrior's Curse

Warrior's Rising

<u>Castle Ridge Series-Contemporary Romance</u>

The Romance Dance

The Christmas Match
The Flirtation Game
The Playboy Switch
The Billionaire's Ploy
The Heartbreak Contract

Find all of Allie's books at https://www.allieburton.com

ABOUT AUTHOR

Allie Burton has always been a reader and writer. Receiving her first romance from her grandmother, she fell in love with the genre. And as an adult, she read young adult books with her own teens and was excited to find something fresh and new. Now, she writes both.

Having lived on three continents and in four states, Allie has studied art, fashion design, and marine biology. She's been everything from a bike police officer to a mascot escort to an advertising executive. Having so many jobs became great research material for the stories she writes.

A member of several writing organizations, Allie currently lives in Colorado with her husband and two children.